CW00554865

EVERYBODY LIES IN HELL

DAVE ZELTSERMAN

ERASERHEAD PRESS
PORTLAND, OREGON

ERASERHEAD PRESS
P.O. BOX 10065
PORTLAND, OR 97296

www.eraserheadpress.com
facebook/eraserheadpress

ISBN: 978-1-62105-286-9
Copyright © 2019 by Dave Zeltserman
Cover art copyright © 2019 Matthew Revert

All rights reserved. No part of this book may be reproduced or transmitted in any form or by any means, electronic or mechanical, including photocopying, recording, or by any information storage and retrieval system, without the written consent of the publisher, except where permitted by law.

Printed in the USA.

EVERYBODY LIES IN HELL

Chapter 1

Definition of REALITY SHIFT
(noun) A phenomenon that occurs in hell when a soul is absorbed into a more aware reality.

Vera looked up from her romance magazine to tell me that I had some freaky-looking dude waiting for me.

"Did you get a name?" I asked.

She gave me a put-upon squinty look. "He wouldn't tell me it," she said. "I never saw the guy before. He's this real slick fellow, about fifty, bony-thin, and dressed like a mortician, especially how he's got his hair greased back so it looks like it's painted on. I think he's a carny. Or maybe an ambulance chaser." Her lips pushed into the same sort of small, tight circle she might've shown if she had bit into something sour. "He made me nervous sitting out here so I had him wait in your office."

With that Vera once again disappeared behind her magazine. I didn't bother asking her anything further and continued on to my private office.

The man waiting for me was sitting in the chair reserved for clients, and on hearing me, twisted his neck around to get a look. He was pretty much how Vera described him, although what struck me as his most prominent features were how overly red his lips were, especially in contrast to his milk-white coloring, and how tightly wrapped his skin appeared to be around his face. If he opened his eyes too wide or sneezed too violently there was a chance his skin would rip open.

For several seconds those overly red lips tried hard to twitch themselves into a smile before finally succeeding.

"Mike Stone?" he asked in a nervous, twitchy voice. "I'm assuming that's your name since that's what's stenciled on your outer door."

"That's right."

"And you really do private investigations?"

"I guess I have to since that's also stenciled on the door."

My answer made his lips start twitching again, but this time they didn't quite manage themselves into a smile. I made my way to my desk and sat down behind it.

"You got a name also?" I asked

"Certainly, but I don't care to share it presently."

He was an odd duck, that was for sure, with his funeral-home black suit that matched the color of his greased slicked hair. That same suit was also two sizes too small and his ankles and wrists stuck out from the cuffs and sleeves looking like broomsticks carved out of ivory. As odd looking as he was, there was something else about him that made my skin crawl. The mortuary man. That was what I thought as I stared at him.

"Suit yourself," I said. "What can I do for you?"

More of his lip twitching. Then, "I came here partly to satisfy my curiosity. I've been hearing rumors about a private investigation office operating here of all places, and I needed to see if it was true." He paused to glance around my office. There wasn't much to it. A cheap wooden coatrack, three beat-up file cabinets against one wall, an even more beat-up oak desk complete with ink blotter, Underwood typewriter and rotary phone, a wooden swivel chair for myself, and the leather-cushioned one that he was sitting on. "Mr. Stone, if you don't mind my asking, what do your clients usually hire you for?"

"Any number of things," I lied. Because it was almost always one of three things. Most of my clients were murdered when they were alive, and now that they're in hell they want to know who killed them. Some of the less aware ones only want to know how they died. The ones who were deep in denial more times than not want me to tell them what they did to end up here, as if they weren't only kidding themselves. We all know what we did to end up here, even if we want to pretend we don't.

"Interesting." The mortuary man steepled his fingers so that his manicured fingernails touched his still quivering blood-saturated lips. "Mr. Stone, I've heard rumors about the fees you charge. That they can be quite steep."

I shrugged. "If I'm going to do a job, I'm going to damn well get paid for it."

"Of course. Nobody can say that you shouldn't. This is hell, after all. We're all opportunists, are we not? Otherwise we wouldn't be here. And it's not as if your clients have much choice on who they hire since you appear to hold a unique position. If the rumors I hear are true, you demand that your more attractive lady clients bare all and engage in *flagante delicto*—"

"That's only if I deliver the goods."

A brief moment of lip twitching, then, "Yes, how utterly chivalrous of you. Besides, what else should they be expecting? It's not as if there are any white knights here in hell to come to their rescue. But it does beg the question of what you would charge me."

"I'm sure we could come to an arrangement. So are you going to keep wasting my time, or are you going to tell me what you want to hire me for?"

That seemed to amuse him to no end as his lips began quivering like crazy before finally settling into an impish smile. "I believe we will be doing business in the future," he said. "But not now. My coming here today was merely exploratory."

With that he unfolded himself from the chair. He was much taller than I'd realized from him sitting down. Close to seven feet. It must've been his beanpole thinness that fooled me. He also appeared unnaturally stiff as he made his way to the door. Once he was out of my office and the door was closed behind him, I took a bottle of Canadian whiskey and a glass from my bottom desk drawer. My hand shook slightly as I poured a shot. Here in hell I've dealt with more dangerous characters than this mortuary man, but for some reason he crept me out. I had to bite my tongue to keep from telling him not to bother coming back. It would've been a mistake doing so. I'd learned long ago it was never a good idea to turn down clients here in hell—that it can cause unforeseen consequences.

I took the whiskey in one gulp. In my hell, the whiskey tastes and smells like I remembered it from when I was alive. It doesn't get you drunk—hell's not about to be that kind—but something about its burn on your lips and throat can be comforting. I poured myself another shot, and tried to put the mortuary man out of my mind.

Chapter 2

The split second after I died I found myself standing on Montague Street in Brooklyn Heights, but I knew I wasn't really in Brooklyn. First off, I was murdered in Newark, New Jersey, and I remembered my death vividly, but even without that I would've known I wasn't really in Brooklyn given how unnaturally quiet it was without another single person in sight. And while Montague Street looked pretty much as I remembered it, some of the buildings were wrong, and some of the stores lining the street were from my childhood instead of the present day. I probably couldn't have articulated at that precise moment that I was in a version of hell of my own making, but at some level I knew that was what had happened.

I started walking west on Montague Street so I could see whether the Manhattan skyline was still there, and it was, at least mostly as I remembered it. I'm sure some of the buildings were wrong, but it still seemed very real to me even though I knew it wasn't. After I stood gaping at the skyline for what seemed like an eternity but was probably only minutes, I headed south toward Coney Island. I don't know why exactly but I guess I wanted to see how much of my version of Brooklyn existed. I knew many of the street signs I passed weren't right—they were from other neighborhoods, and some of them from other boroughs. And then there were other street signs that were too blurry to make out. But none of that mattered, because by then I knew where I really was. Still, though, I kept walking. At one point, I stopped to look at my reflection in a storefront window and realized that I was wearing a cheap suit and a fedora. When I was alive I never wore a hat, and almost never wore suits, and certainly never the fifty-nine dollar variety that I had on. At the time I was murdered I was wearing jeans, tennis sneakers, a polo shirt, and a leather jacket, which was what I usually wore when I worked my job as an investigator. Still, on seeing my reflection in that window, the suit, scuffed up shoes, and hat seemed right

I was somewhere in Bay Ridge when this man who looked like he'd been dropped in from the eighteenth century wandered into view. I was never much of a history buff, but that was the way he looked given his blue satin waistcoat, frilly silk shirt, and knee-length breeches, as well as his overall shaggy appearance. As he shuffled toward me, he looked almost like he could've been an extra from a zombie movie, although one set several hundred years in the past. His expression was a rictus of fear, and there was only deadness in his eyes. I gave him a wide berth as he ambled past me, and watched as he staggered to the front of an eight-story brick building. He stood transfixed for a long moment, and then all at once started clawing at the brick wall and violently smashing his face against it, and he did this quietly without ever uttering a sound.

I picked up my pace after that trying to put some distance between us, and it was only seconds later that I left Brooklyn and found myself someplace entirely different. Instead of the Brooklyn streets where I'd been walking for hours, behind me now were meadows and a mountain range that was of such lush greenness that it seemed more like a painting than anything real. The sky that had been a grayish white in my version of Brooklyn was now a deep blue, and the sun that had earlier been missing behind New York smog and clouds was shining brightly overhead. Off in the distance were groves of a tall and thin variety of pine tree that I'd never seen before, as well as other types of trees, shrubs, and plants that were foreign to me, and up ahead past rolling meadows was a sparkling ocean made up of different shades of blues and aquamarines that were very different from anything I'd ever seen of the Atlantic Ocean from Coney Island.

I trekked across the meadows toward the ocean, and as I got closer I could see palm and coconut trees along a crescent-shaped beach, and in the middle of this a person lying on a lounge chair.

I had to climb down a steep incline of rocks to get to the beach, and as I did this, I could see that the person was a woman wearing a floral-patterned beach cover-up, her hair a perfect silver. There was an empty lounge chair next to her, and between her chair and the other was a small drink stand on which sat a glass containing a brownish-orange drink with a hibiscus flower floating in it.

She heard me approaching and turned her head toward me. She was wearing sunglasses so I couldn't see her eyes, but her expression at first was one of disinterest. That changed as she smiled thinly at me, and with a wave of her hand, invited me to sit next to her. She looked ageless yet not young with perfect, unwrinkled skin and a slender, attractive body. If it wasn't for her well-coifed silver hair, she could've passed for being in her thirties. After I settled into the lounge chair next to her she held out a manicured slender hand and introduced herself as Olivia Danville, her accent sounding as if she came from England and was from money.

"Mike Stone," I said.

When I took her hand I expected to feel something cold and clammy. After all, we were both dead. I was surprised to find how warm and dry her skin felt.

"Where am I?" I asked.

That caused a wan smile to form over her lips. "Where do you think you are, Mike?"

"I'm guessing I wandered from my version of hell into yours. Yours isn't bad. We're on a tropical island in the Pacific?"

"Very good, Mike. Yes, my reality, or hell, ended up being Kapalua, Maui. We're on probably the nicest beach on the island. Not the biggest by any stretch, but the prettiest."

As I looked out at the ocean I realized it wasn't just the two of us out there. There were others in the water. I could make out several bodies that were floating face down before they sank, and only a minute later an elderly woman's face popped up out of a wave before she disappeared for good. Olivia must've noticed me staring at these drowning people, but she didn't comment about them. Instead she asked me if I knew how I died.

"Yeah," I said. "It would be hard to forget this soon. It only just happened."

"What do you mean by that?"

DAVE ZELTSERMAN

"It was only a few hours ago that I was fatally shot, and then the next thing I knew I was in Brooklyn wearing different clothes than what I had on when I died and without my chest ripped open by a .45 slug. Except it wasn't really Brooklyn, only a version of it that I somehow created. And now I'm in your version of hell, which lucky for you happens to be Hawaii."

She shifted in her chair to get a better look at me. I couldn't see her eyes because of her sunglasses but I knew she was staring at me intently. She shifted again in her chair so that she was back to gazing out at the ocean.

"Do you know what you did to end up in hell?" she asked.

"Yeah, I know exactly why I'm here."

We sat quietly after that for several minutes. When she spoke next it was to ask me why I thought I ended up in her version of hell. I told her it was probably because her version was stronger than mine. "Somehow I got sucked into yours, although I'm guessing if I walked back to where I came from I'd find myself again in Brooklyn."

She picked up her drink and brushed the flower away from her mouth so she could take a sip. She carefully placed the glass back on the stand. "Your level of awareness is quite remarkable," she said. "Out of the billions of souls here in hell only a tiny percentage have any sense of awareness, and very few of those would know what you already do this quickly after dying. Do you feel sick yet?"

"I feel fine."

"Incredible. You should've been feeling quite ill by now."

"Why is that?"

"It's what happens when you're pulled into a stronger reality, at least for the first few times in that same reality."

A larger wave than any of the others crashed onto the beach, and it washed a man's crumpled body onto the shore. The suit he wore was badly torn and he was covered in seaweed, and from what I could tell it looked like the type of suit someone would've worn in the early nineteen hundreds. His face was hidden from me, but from how unnaturally bloated and white his hands and exposed skin looked I would've guessed he'd been in the water for months, if not much longer. It probably shouldn't have surprised me as much as it did when he pushed himself to his knees and crawled back into the ocean, and he soon disappeared under another wave.

"Those souls out there drowning," I said. "What is it with them?"

"You should be able to explain that as well as I can."

She was right. I knew what the story had to be with them, just as I knew why that eighteenth-century man who stumbled into my Brooklyn bashed his face in right in front of me. "They get confused when they get sucked into your world. I guess their own realities must be pretty bleak, so they try to create something equally hellish by drowning themselves. Do they do that for all eternity?"

"I couldn't say," Olivia mused. "I haven't been here for all eternity. Only since 1952. But I suppose that is probably the case."

As I lay there I realized two things: how hot I was feeling wearing my suit and fedora while Olivia's Hawaiian sun beat down on me, and how badly I wanted a drink. I removed my hat and sat up so I could take off my suit jacket and tie, as well as also unbutton the top four buttons of my shirt. After I lowered myself back down, I asked Olivia who I had to sleep with to get a scotch on the rocks.

That caused another wan smile to form on her lips. She picked up a silver bell lying next to her and rang it several times. Seconds later a man dressed in black emerged from behind a rolling hill to the left of us, and I watched as he moved swiftly toward us. Olivia explained that there was a resort over the hill, and that was where this man came from and where she resided. As he got closer I could see he was wearing a black tuxedo with white gloves and perfectly polished black shoes. He must've been hot as hell dressed like that, but when he stopped and bowed slightly to Olivia there wasn't a drop of perspiration on his face.

"Yes, madam," he said.

"Henry, another mai tai for me and a scotch on the rocks for my friend."

Something about being in the hot sun made scotch less appealing than it had been only minutes earlier, and I told Henry that I'd have what the lady was having. I'd never had a mai tai or any fruity drink before, always figuring I wouldn't be caught dead drinking something like that, but now it seemed like the right time to try one. Henry repeated that he'd be bringing two mai tais. He waited while Olivia drank a final sip of the one she'd been working on, then took her empty glass and headed back from where he came. I watched as he disappeared behind the hill, and then asked Olivia whether he was real or someone she had created.

"He's very real," she said. "The realities we create, at least those of us with awareness, consist only of places and objects. When someone with awareness stumbles into our realities, like you stumbled into mine, they'll always return back to their own realities if they're able. It's very different when the unaware stumble in, though, as you've witnessed with those souls drowning out there." She nodded toward the ocean, her lips thinning as a pensive look came over her features. "Most of the unaware are too confused and too deep in their pain to fully comprehend that they have left their own hells, but then you have others, like Henry, who are different. Let's say they're in limbo. They're not quite aware, but they're not so utterly confused that they're doomed to eternal torment. When those souls wander in, they grasp onto our realities as if it were a lifesaver tossed to a drowning man, and soon they adopt our realities as their own."

"So Henry's not the only one squatting in your reality?"

"Heavens, no. I've got a whole staff at the resort. And dozens of others who've checked in as guests. And many others besides them."

I chewed on all that for a while, and picked up on a nuance of something she had said. "Are the unaware able to create people for their hells?" I asked.

"I'm not sure. I know that they often populate their private hells with monsters and demons to torment them, but I don't know if they're able to create human torturers as well. I haven't seen any yet that have done that."

"You're able to look into their hells?"

"Certainly, and I'm sure you'll be able to also very soon. Although, I must warn you, it's never pleasant."

"Let's see if I got this straight," I said. "Here in hell we've got souls like you and me who are aware, we've got clueless souls like those zombies drowning out there who find ways to suffer for all eternity, and finally we've got squatters like Henry who are somewhere in between. Am I missing anything?"

A weariness momentarily aged Olivia, giving me a glimpse of what she must've looked like when she died.

"There are only a handful of ancient souls who are aware, but they're another kind entirely," she said. "The countless eons they've spent in hell have altered them where they've taken on more demonic properties, at least in their own realities. So far none of them have been able to absorb my reality into theirs, but they're a pernicious bunch. There's one in particular you need to be careful of. A brute by the name of Al Zaoud. He's from some long forgotten realm that I believe would've existed in Afghanistan five thousand years ago. He's someone who if you ever see, you need to run and run fast."

"What does he look like?"

Olivia shuddered. "You'll know him if you see him."

I spotted Henry reemerging over the hill with our drinks, and it wasn't long before both of us were served mai tais. I was surprised how real the drink tasted. As I had mentioned earlier, I had never had one before and when I'd ordered it I had no idea what was in it, but I could easily taste the rum, lime juice, and an orange syrupy flavor. And it sure as hell felt real going down my throat.

"Thanks for the drink," I said. "And for clueing me in on how things work around here."

"You're quite welcome regarding the mai tai, but Mike, while I've been frank and honest with you, you should never take what anyone tells you here at face value."

"Why is that?"

"As you'll be discovering soon enough, everyone lies in hell."

She said this with such nonchalance that I couldn't tell whether she was joking, being honest or playing some sort of mind game with me. Later I would learn that Olivia was indeed one of the few people in hell I could trust, at least usually.

I finished my mai tai before telling her that I was beginning to feel sick like she had warned me I would. The truth was I had started feeling that vertigo-like sickness while I was waiting for Henry to return with the drinks. It would end up getting much worse where I would feel as if I was disintegrating, and later I would be left barely able to crawl out of her reality, but at that moment it was more like a bad migraine mixed with some dizziness. "I guess I should be heading off for my own hell," I said.

"Yes, that would be best. Feel free to visit again."

As I steadied myself getting off the lounge chair, I commented how at least our hells weren't that bad. "You've got this nice beach on Maui, I've got Brooklyn. It could be worse. At least we're not one of those poor souls out there drowning for eternity. All in all, hell doesn't seem as bad I would've imagined."

She smiled thinly at that. "Give it time," she said.

DAVE ZELTSERMAN

Chapter 3

It didn't take long after the mortuary man left before Vera popped in, asking, "You didn't let that creepazoid hire us, did you?"

"What? No, he didn't come here for that."

"That's good," she said, some anger flushing her cheeks. "I'm glad we're not working for him." She shied her eyes from mine and in a lower voice added, "He was forward with me when he was leaving. I won't repeat what he said, but it was very inappropriate."

"Jesus, Vera. He might be a creepazoid, but he's still a guy. What guy with a pulse isn't going to want to hit on you?"

She blushed at that as if she were the innocent, wholesome small-town Midwestern girl now in the big city that she presented herself as. She wasn't that girl. Maybe in my reality she had become that type of girl, and maybe that was the type of girl she needed to believe she was, but after she showed up in my office one day acting as my secretary as if she'd always been there I decided to look into who she really was and what she had done to be sent to hell. Even though squatters took on whole new identities, they always kept one link to their past, and with experience I've gotten pretty good at identifying that link. In Vera's case, the name of the high school she created for her made up identity was the name of her flesh and blood mother. That one opening allowed me to learn all about her real life, and what I found was ugly.

"What did he come here for?" she asked, more to change the

subject than that she had any genuine interest.

I could've told Vera anything and she'd believe me, even something along the lines that she had only hallucinated the mortuary man entering and leaving my office. That's the thing with squatters: they need so badly to latch onto your reality that they'll believe anything you tell them. The times that I lie to Vera I try to keep the lies believable. Whenever I tell her something too outrageous, I always feel like I've just pulled the wings off an insect.

"You remember the Al Diamanté case, right?" I said.

She nodded as if she knew what I was talking about. She didn't know about any of my cases, and especially not what any of them were about. I don't know how long ago it was that Vera first showed up. Time has no meaning in hell. I know I died on October eighth, 1998, and I know one of my clients died in 2013, so it's possible I've been dead for only fifteen years, but it seems as if I'd been coming to this office for thousands of years already. However long it's been since Vera first appeared, it's always been the same with her; she's here when I show up and she's here when I leave, and she's always wearing the same blouse and knee-length skirt, and with that same red sweater tied around her neck. And she's always chewing a wad of gum while she's either filing her nails or reading a romance magazine. Sometimes we shoot the breeze and sometimes we flirt a bit. I have to admit I like having her here. She's nice on the eyes, and she's a fun kid to trade a little banter with. You might even say I've grown fond of her.

"He's got information that's going to help me blow the Diamanté case wide open," I said making it up as I went along since there never was any Diamanté case. "This is going to be a big win for us. Should really get us on the map."

"Really? Wow!"

"Wow is right. There might even be a bonus for you, Sweetheart."

She blushed whenever I called her sweetheart, and this time I also succeeded in coaxing a smile out of her. Vera was a brunette in her mid-twenties, and she had a nice shapely body and a sweet face that showed dimples whenever she smiled. It was kind of funny that she blushed so easily with me. From what I was able to find out there was probably little that would've ever made her blush when she was alive. But I guess she was able to reimagine herself the way she is now

DAVE ZELTSERMAN

when she escaped her private hell for mine. I was glad that my reality provided her the refuge that it did.

"I better get back to work," Vera said, still blushing nicely.

She left the door to my office open so I could watch the exaggerated sway of her hips as she made her way back to her desk. It was her way of letting me know that she was there for me if I'd only make more of an effort.

Sam Vogel has been one of my oldest unsolved cases. Like most of my clients he had hired me to find out who murdered him. When he was alive, Vogel had been a criminal defense lawyer working in Los Angeles. He was fifty-seven when he was shot dead behind an East Hollywood apartment building. He probably saw his killer since he was shot in the chest at close range, but he insists he didn't see anything. He also claims that his being sent to hell was a mistake—some sort of clerical error—and he's deluded himself into believing that if I can figure out who killed him this clerical mistake can be fixed and that he can then be sent somewhere else. It doesn't work that way, but that's what's stuck in his head. Up until recently I'd been hitting nothing but dead ends, but I had learned that a key witness I'd been needing to talk to has died and is now here in hell, so I'm hoping to finally get this damn case resolved.

After I left my office I stopped off at a nearby diner to get a bite to eat and a cup of coffee while I reviewed my notes on the Vogel case. Charlie, a barrel-chested, thick-armed guy in his forties worked the grill, and Doris handled the counter. At first glance Doris appeared to be a wrinkled grandmotherly-type with her bluish-grayish hair always done up in an old-fashioned beehive, even though she had thicker forearms than Charlie. The thing was, though, there are no grandmotherly types in hell, and Doris was no exception. During one of my few slow stretches I dug into her background. She died in 1983 and when she was alive her real name was Lois McComber, and she spent decades as part of a gang that smuggled teenage girls out of Juarez and sold them to brothels throughout the southwest. As much as she has tried to resurrect herself as a kindly grandmotherly waitress, it was a thin façade at best.

Both Charlie and Doris were squatters who showed up in the

diner years ago acting as if they'd always been there. I now have quite a few squatters in my reality, and I seem to be getting more all the time. But that is nothing compared to the number of confused zombie-like types I get. Most of the zombie ones end up making their way to the Brooklyn Bridge where they jump off into the East River. Some days there are so many of them jumping into the river that I worry they might clog it up, but there's really no chance of that ever happening. While their heads might bob up and down in the water for a while they eventually sink to the bottom where a current washes them out into the Atlantic so that they can spend all of eternity drowning.

I sat down at the counter, and Doris carried a coffee pot with her as she made her way over to me, hobbling in an arthritic manner. "What will it be, hon?" she asked as she filled up my cup.

"A grilled ham and cheese on rye."

Doris yelled my order back to Charlie, and he grumbled that he heard it the first time when I said it. There was the sizzling sound of ham being dropped on the grill, and I could swear I could smell the butter and the meat cooking. When I first died my reality was little more than buildings and other structures. It was too sketchy for things like food and booze to have existed within it, but over time my reality has strengthened and now I can go into a diner and order a ham and cheese or a burger or anything else on the menu, and I can go into a liquor store and always find it well stocked with Canadian whiskey. I have no idea why that is or how it works, but it does. Every time I come into this diner, Doris has a freshly brewed pot of coffee waiting for me that tastes like the real thing, at least from my memory of it, and Charlie has the ingredients to cook up whatever diner food I ask for.

Doris used a rag to mop up the counter space in front of me, then leaned one of her thick forearms against it. "Mike, you working on anything juicy?" she asked. She was attempting to be casual about it, but I caught a hopeful gleam in her eye that I'd be spilling some gossip. In case I hadn't spelled it out earlier, existence can be pretty damn tedious in hell, especially for squatters.

"A murder case," I told her.

That got her leaning closer, greedy for details. A slight pink flushed her cheeks and her tongue slowly wetted her lips. "Murder?" she said. "No kidding? What happened?"

DAVE ZELTSERMAN

"A lawyer was shot to death behind a building where he kept an apartment for rendezvousing with his girlfriend."

"His girlfriend, huh? Rendezvousing? So the bum was married?"

"Yep."

"Did the wife find out he was a no good cheater?"

"Nope, she never knew about the affair. But the girlfriend happened to be married to one of his clients. A mob enforcer who was serving a six to ten year sentence at a max. security prison thanks to a shoddy performance by this lawyer."

She laughed at that—one of those closed mouth types of laughs that sounded like she was giving somebody the raspberry, and the pink in her cheeks turned beet red. "What a genius that lawyer was, huh?" she said when she could talk. "It takes all kinds, don't it?"

"That it does."

"I guess it don't take a genius to figure out what happened, huh? That mob enforcer found out why his lawyer screwed up his case, and he sent someone to pay this jerk lawyer back?"

"That's what I'm hoping to find out later today."

A deafening crashing noise exploded behind me, and it sounded as if lightning had struck within feet of me. The whole diner seemed to shake from it. I twisted my neck around and looked out the plate glass front window, and sure enough the sky had turned an ominous bluish-purple with jagged streaks of lightning bursting through the air. That didn't make any sense. In my reality the sky was always a grayish white, and there was never any change in weather. As my gaze shifted toward the horizon, I could see that my Brooklyn was melting away and was being replaced by a harsh mountainous landscape.

An icy fear froze me. Without any conscious thought, I murmured "Oh shit" under my breath, and then I was running as fast as I could to get out the door.

Chapter 4

One of my squatters who acted as a cabdriver and went by the name of Edwin usually kept his yellow cab at the corner of Pierrepont and Hicks. All I could do was hope he was there now. As I ran thunder exploded beside me as if bombs were being tossed at me, but what was coming my way was a hell of a lot deadlier and scarier than any bomb.

I didn't look back as I ran. I knew I'd see more of Brooklyn melting away and being replaced by a desolate mountain terrain, and in the middle of all this Al Zaoud and his horde of murderous cutthroats would be riding their demon stallions at full gallop. In my mind's eye I could imagine those horses' eyes shining blood red and froth pouring from their mouths and steam blowing out of their flaring nostrils. I knew they still had to be a half mile or more away, but I couldn't shake this sensation of them being directly behind me. I could almost feel on the back of my neck the pungent steam that they'd be exhaling; a steam that would smell no different than burning sulfur.

I wanted to kiss Edwin full on the lips when I saw him sitting in his cab where I hoped it would be, and given that he resembled a bloated bullfrog with a really bad complexion, that was saying something. I jumped in the back of his cab and told him to start driving. "Go over the Brooklyn Bridge into Manhattan and head uptown towards the Bronx," I ordered him breathlessly. "And there's an extra fifty for you if you ignore the speed limits."

"Unusual weather we're having," he stammered out dumbly, his reflection in the rearview mirror showing a dead fish paleness to his face, his eyes wide open but with little life in them. Squatters have a defense mechanism where they go catatonic whenever they're confronted with the fact that the reality they've adopted isn't real. He was close to shutting down, but I didn't have time to pull him out of the driver's seat and take his place. I looked behind me and could see that the Brooklyn landscape was erasing quickly. Al Zaoud and his horde were close enough now that I could make out the severed heads tied to their horses manes.

"If you don't start driving now I'll put a bullet in the back of your skull," I yelled at Edwin. "I swear to God I will!"

"Jesus, what's the rush?" he muttered half under his breath. Even if he looked directly at Al Zaoud and his murderous horde he wouldn't acknowledge their existence. But he pulled away from the curb and headed toward the bridge and away from Al Zaoud. He wasn't going nearly fast enough but at least he was moving. I reached over the back of his seat and pinched the top of his right ear and gave it a hard twist.

"Ow!" he cried.

"Give it more gas or I'll bloody rip your ear off!"

He gave it more gas and the tires squealed. Al Zaoud was still gaining on us as more of my Brooklyn faded from sight, but at least we were moving now at a more reasonable speed. At least we had a chance. If Al Zaoud's reality causes a ravine or mountain to materialize in his path, that would slow the bastard down enough where I might be able to escape him. Still, though, the buffer between us was disappearing quickly, and if something didn't change it would only be a matter of seconds before I'd be pulled into his godforsaken reality.

"You better damn well floor it! And if you as much as touch the brakes I'll fucking kill you!"

"Jesus, Mike, what's gotten into you?" Edwin cried, but the taxi leapt forward as he pushed down on the gas pedal. The car did a little side-to-side jig as he almost crashed up, but he got it back under control and had it speeding over the bridge. We were maybe three quarters over it when the other end of the bridge faded away, replaced by Al Zaoud's hellish world. I watched as one of the zombies jumped from the middle of the bridge but never made it into the East River as he disappeared beneath the rocky terrain that replaced my reality. I guess given a choice of being drowned in the river or crushed under tons of rock and soil there wouldn't be much of a difference as far as that zombie was concerned

Edwin had the cab shaking again as he almost lost control for a second time. "I'm gonna crash up with the way you're making me drive," he cried out.

"Don't you dare slow down!"

He didn't slow down, but he started blubbering. "The cops are going to throw me in jail and take away my hack license. I don't know what I'll do without my hack license. Jesus, Mike, you're killing me here."

I laughed at that. A nervous, excitable, near hysterical laugh. It wasn't me that was going to be killing him. If Al Zaoud caught up to us, it would be that crazy medieval warlord killing him for all eternity. And besides, my reality didn't have any squatters acting like cops, at least none that I'd ever seen, so he had nothing to worry about on that front.

"Let me deal with any cops, you concentrate on getting us the hell out of here."

"What's the rush? For Chrissakes, what's the rush?"

I didn't bother answering him as he continued to blubber away, but I did let out my breath when I saw that we caught a break. A ravine appeared between us and Al Zaoud. It wasn't steep enough to stop him for long, but it would slow him down, maybe enough for me to escape him.

I let go of Edwin's ear and patted him on the shoulder. I also nearly collapsed back into the passenger seat. Damn, that was close. "You can ease up a little on the gas if you want," I said. "Not too much, but a little."

Edwin was sobbing noisily, his arms shaking as he gripped the wheel. He slowed the cab down to something closer to the speed limit and let go of the wheel with his left hand so he could wipe a sleeve under his nose. "You had me scared to death, Mike," he forced out between sobs. "Why'd you act crazy like that?"

"You didn't see that black sedan on our tail?"

He shook his head, now sniffling instead of sobbing. "I didn't see it."

"The Mahoney gang was after me. They would've killed me if

DAVE ZELTSERMAN

they caught up to us. You also for helping me. But we lost them."

"The Mahoney gang? Oh, Jesus, Mike. That explains it. I don't know how I missed seeing that sedan, but Jesus, that was close." He crossed himself and wiped a hand across his forehead. "Where to now? The police?"

Of course, the Mahoney gang shouldn't have meant anything to him since I made the name up, but now the Mahoney threat was as real to him as the rest of my reality. Without Al Zaoud breathing down my neck I had a chance to think more clearly, and if I could circle back to Bay Ridge I could take refuge in Olivia's reality. I wouldn't be able to stay there forever—if you're aware you can only stay in another aware's reality for a few days or so before you start losing yourself and risk becoming one of the zombies—but I should be able to stay there long enough for that madman to lose interest in me. With some luck it would be another few years or longer before he came after me again.

We wouldn't be able to double back the way we came. The Brooklyn Bridge was gone, as was Brooklyn Heights and most likely a large swath of the borough. But we could go through New Jersey to Staten Island, and from there take the Verrazano Bridge, and that would take me right to Bay Ridge and Olivia's reality of Maui. I just had to hope that she still had a stronger level of awareness than Al Zaoud, otherwise I'd be dooming her as well.

I had to direct Edwin to the Holland Tunnel since he didn't know Manhattan. He barely knew the neighborhood of Brooklyn where he kept his cab. I couldn't hold that against him. This was my reality, not his.

We were only a half a mile from the entrance to the tunnel when all of lower Manhattan to the right of me disappeared, and my blood chilled as I realized that Al Zaoud must have found a way around that ravine. I heard the pounding of the horses as if they were right on top of me and then I saw him and his cutthroats out of the corner of my eye. Everything changed then as I was absorbed into his reality. I still had on my cheap suit, but the cab and the rest of my reality was gone.

I went hurtling through the air the same as if Edwin had slammed his cab into a brick wall and I had crashed through the windshield. It made sense since we'd been traveling at forty miles an hour before our abrupt stop. After a hundred feet or so, I landed shoulder first against the rocky terrain and flipped over half a dozen times before my body came to a stop. I knew I didn't really have any bones and tendons and internal organs. That it was all part of the illusion. But as I lay there in a heap, I felt as if the shoulder I landed on had been torn apart, that my hip had been shattered into a dozen pieces, and that my insides had been put through a Cuisinart. I tried to lift my head, and as I shifted weight onto my right arm I clenched my mouth shut to stifle a scream as I realized the bones in the arm had all been snapped.

I collapsed fully on the ground then, and as I moaned in my misery I heard the snorting and hoof beats from dozens of Al Zaoud's demon horses and could sense that I was surrounded by them. A powerful hand the size of a large ham hock grabbed me by the scruff of my neck and lifted me off the ground, and I found myself staring directly into Al Zaoud's eyes and all the ancient insanity that they held.

"I should gut you and wear your intestines as a necklace," he growled. This wasn't any idle threat but something he was seriously considering. He also didn't say this in English, but in some long ago dead language. Since I was now absorbed into his reality I understood him the same as if he had spoken in English.

Al Zaoud was still on his horse and he held me in the air with one hand so that my face was less than a foot from his. I was six feet and a hundred and ninety pounds, and he showed no strain as he held me as if I were weightless. In case I hadn't mentioned it yet, Al Zaoud was a giant of a man. Close to eight feet in size and over four hundred and fifty pounds of hardened muscle. His arms were thicker than most men's thighs, and his neck wider across than my waist. His skin was a dark bronze, and while his large round skull was as bald as an egg, his face was covered with a thick coarse black beard that could slice you up like razor wire. The squatters who made up his marauding band were all big enough to have been NFL linemen, but Al Zaoud dwarfed them.

I wanted to scream out in pain from my ruined body, but somehow I swallowed it back and forced out in that same dead language he had used that I didn't know why he was so upset with me. "I've been working like a dog for you and I'm close to solving your problem."

DAVE ZELTSERMAN

He sniffed in the air as if he were trying to smell out my lie. "Why did you flee me?"

I didn't mention the threats he had made the last time he sought me out. If I did he'd follow through on them so he wouldn't lose face with his men. "You are a fearsome sight that would frighten any man into flight," I said.

His eyes were blazing, but otherwise he wore an inscrutable mask as he studied me. "You claim you are close to finding me a solution?"

"Yes. I swear I am."

"How?"

"There's a wizard who holds a key to your problem. I need to trick him into revealing the answer to me."

His lips curved down enough to show that he found what I was saying dubious at best. "Why haven't you done this yet?" he demanded.

"This is a powerful wizard. He can pull your heart from your chest without ever touching you. I can't enter his world. I have to wait until I'm strong enough to make him enter mine. Then I will have him."

Uncertainty flickered in his eyes, as if he considered for the first time that I might be telling him the truth. "What is this wizard's name?"

"Beelzebub," I said.

I was taking a big chance. Al Zaoud had been in hell for untold centuries, and I had to hope during that time he had visited enough private hells to have heard tales about Beelzebub, and more than that, to have been frightened by them. Regardless of how strong his awareness was, he was still a superstitious sonofabitch.

He studied me for what seemed like an eternity before tossing me to the ground. I didn't know whether he fully believed me but at least he had enough doubt to give me more time.

"Do you know what will happen to you if you fail me again?" he said.

I nodded. I had little doubt about what he would do to me.

Al Zaoud barked an order to one of his marauders who was holding Edwin upside down by his ankle. The cabdriver was now fully catatonic, and the marauder handed him over to Al Zaoud as if he was handing over a sack of flour. Al Zaoud carried on his person a broadsword, an axe and a large dagger with a curved blade. He could've used any of these to separate Edwin's head from his body, but instead he chose to rip it off with his bare hands, and he did this with no more effort than I would've needed to pull a leg off a roasted chicken. Al Zaoud tossed the head to the marauder who had been holding Edwin, and threw the body to the ground. The marauder drove a spike through Edwin's skull and attached the severed head to his horse's mane so that it joined dozens of others. A group of demon horses surrounded Edwin's headless body and began ripping the flesh from it, their muzzles quickly turning as red as their eyes. While this went on, the horses that weren't able to squeeze their way into this feeding frenzy snorted out angrily.

You never fully die in hell. You might feel as if you're dying for all eternity, but your existence never ends. I forced myself to look at the severed heads decorating Al Zaoud's stallion, and I could see their eyes locked on me. Some of their mouths were moving as they silently pleaded with me to help them. Or maybe they were damning me. I was never any good at lip-reading so I couldn't tell which it was. I looked away from them.

"I will give you three cycles of the moon to do as you have promised," Al Zaoud said. The fire that had been raging in his eyes had burnt out leaving them little more than black holes. "If you do not have an answer for me when I return for you, what I do to you will be far worse."

He gestured with his hand toward the severed heads to make sure I had no confusion over what he was referring to. The gesture wasn't needed. I had fully understood him.

He reared his demon horse up onto its hind quarters and turned the beast around. As he rode off, his men followed. It didn't take more than a few minutes after that before the rumbling of thunder abruptly stopped and a familiar grayish-white sky replaced Al Zaoud's violent bluish-purple one. The next thing I knew lower Manhattan had reappeared, and I found myself lying on pavement in the middle of the street. I couldn't get to my feet—my body, or at least my imagined body—was too broken up for that. As I lay in my agony I remembered Olivia's words to me when I first arrived in hell. This was when I had commented about how being in hell didn't seem so bad for those of us with enough awareness so that we could spend our eternities in places like Maui and Brooklyn, and she told me to give it time. As I thought about Al Zaoud coming back for me in three months, I understood fully what she meant.

DAVE ZELTSERMAN

Chapter 5

At an intellectual level I knew that everything I believed I experienced physically was only an illusion. It had to be. As much as it seemed as if I still had a heart beating inside my chest and blood coursing through my veins, it couldn't possibly be the case. The same with the whiskey I drank and the food I ate. It might seem like I was tasting what I thought I was drinking and eating, but it was all because I believed it to be real, even though I knew none of it was.

So as I lay face down in the street in more pain than I would've ever believed possible, I understood logically that it wasn't real but it didn't help me any. Worse, as my New York reality solidified around me, the pain became far more intense. If when I was in Al Zaoud's reality it had been a ten on a scale from one to ten, it was now a hundred in mine. As much as I knew I didn't have a hip that could be shattered or a radius bone that could be snapped in half or tendons and joints in a shoulder that could be torn to pieces, I couldn't move without screaming in agony.

A terror filled me as I realized that my injuries would keep me stranded where I was for the next three months helpless to do anything to save myself from Al Zaoud. Even though I knew I didn't really have any of these injuries, it all just seemed too real for me to ignore.

After the terror came utter despair, and I might've broken out sobbing over my fate except that the slightest movement brought the pain to a level that sucked the breath out of me. I had given up all hope when a miracle happened, and it really was a miracle because I had no idea that I had squatters acting as EMT workers, but off in the distance an ambulance siren screamed and every second it seemed to grow louder as it approached. No more than a minute later the vehicle screeched to a stop within feet of me. Car doors opened and slammed, and two men were soon kneeling by me. One of them said to the other that it looked like they were going to have to make a trip to the morgue.

"Get me some morphine," I forced out in a ragged voice.

The fact that I was alive and conscious seemed to surprise these two clowns. Even though they had reinvented themselves as EMT workers in my reality they clearly didn't have a clue what to do since neither of them made any attempt to assess my injuries--or even bother taking a pulse--before assuming that I was dead.

"We don't carry narcotics," one of the clowns said.

"Yeah, you do. They're in a lock box in the back compartment of the ambulance. Right behind where you keep the stretchers. The key's in your pocket."

"This guy's delusional," the same clown said.

"Harry, why don't you humor him?" the other one suggested.

I could hear Harry grumbling as he left me for the ambulance. Soon after that he shouted out several expletives. "Ed," he yelled out from the back of the ambulance. "The guy's right. I had the key in my pocket like he said I would, and the lock box is back here like he claimed. And it's stocked with morphine."

"What are you talking about?" Ed yelled back. "I thought you were kidding about not knowing we had morphine back there!"

Ed was only lying now, as any squatter would to protect his sense of the reality he had adopted, and when Harry came out from the back of the ambulance, he did likewise, insisting that he was only joking around. "You think I don't know what's in the back of my own ambulance?" he asked as if he were deeply insulted.

The two of them let it drop. They had to. Harry might've had no clue about how to be an EMT worker, but he must've been a drug user in his previous life because he had no trouble filling the hypodermic from the vial of morphine and injecting it into a vein in my left arm.

DAVE ZELTSERMAN

I'm guessing morphine didn't work as fast in the physical world as it did right then in my reality. All at once I was overcome by a warm fuzziness spreading throughout my body, and the pain lessened to where it was something closer to what I had felt in Al Zaoud's world.

Neither Harry or Ed knew what to do next, and I had to talk them through rolling me onto a stiff board, and then lifting that onto a stretcher so they could roll me into the back of the ambulance, and I had to do it in a way that didn't threaten the reality they were grasping onto—I couldn't afford for them to go catatonic on me. Once I was secured in the back of the ambulance, Ed said they were going to take me to New York Presbyterian, which was just south of Greenwich Village.

"You got to take me to Bay Ridge instead."

"Why? What's in Bay Ridge?"

"They've got a special facility there for the type of trauma I've suffered. I'll give you directions."

He didn't argue with me. It was really a case of self-preservation. His illusion of being an EMT worker in Manhattan would've shattered if they brought me to New York Presbyterian and there weren't any other squatters there acting as doctors and staff. I made up the name of a trauma facility in Bay Ridge and gave him directions that would send him back over the Brooklyn Bridge. I told him that when he got to the intersection of Colonial and Eighty-first he would have to come to a complete stop. "The stop sign there is hidden by tree branches, and the cops are always staking it out. They'll nail you if you don't come to a complete stop. Even if you got your siren on they'll nail you."

"Alright. Thanks for the head's up."

The two of them left me alone to go back to the cab area of the ambulance, and shortly after that the siren turned on and we were moving. Since they didn't strap my forehead to the stretcher I was able to lift my head enough to look out the back window. At first all I could see was the whitish-grayish sky, but when we went over the Brooklyn Bridge, I could make out the suspension wires that stretched over the structure. It probably wasn't much longer after that—no more twenty minutes—that the ambulance lurched to a stop, which I was guessing was due to my warning about the police trap. When the vehicle started up again, it rolled about twenty yards and we were then absorbed into Olivia Danville's reality. In less than a blink of an eye the ambulance vanished, as did the board and stretcher I was strapped to. This time when I fell to the ground it was far less violent than when Edwin's cab had disappeared inside of Al Zaoud's world. It was also far less painful than I was expecting it to be. Something had changed when I entered Olivia's reality. I still hurt like hell, and I wouldn't have been able to get to my feet even if it meant saving myself from an eternity of being tortured by Al Zaoud, but the pain had been cut back enough so I could now crawl along the ground. Not without a great deal of difficulty, but at least I could make my way toward Olivia's beach.

Ed and Harry were both lying on the ground, fully catatonic. There was a chance they'd adopt Olivia's reality and become squatters here, but the odds were far greater that they'd end up as zombies instead. If I was capable of doing so later, I would drag them back to my reality. I set off toward the beach Olivia liked to spend her days at.

It was brutal crawling over those fields, and I won't bother with all the gory details, but eventually I reached the drop-off point to where I could see Olivia and a companion lying on lounge chairs as they looked out over the ocean. I tried yelling out to them, but they couldn't hear me over the wind blowing with how weak my voice was. All I could do was try to crawl down that steep path to the beach, and I ended up falling down it and hitting rocks below. I must've screamed like bloody hell when that happened. In any case I got their attention then.

DAVE ZELTSERMAN

Chapter 6

Olivia had her companion and one of the waiters put me on a surfboard and carry me down to her. Her companion, a good-looking blond, blue-eyed surfer type of about twenty-five, didn't look too happy when she asked him to give her some privacy while she tended to me, but he joined the waiter in leaving the beach after they placed me onto one of the lounge chairs.

Olivia waited until we were alone before asking what had happened to me.

"Al Zaoud's what happened."

I told her the whole story; of how I tried to flee Al Zaoud in a cab, what happened when he caught up to me, and how I tricked two of my squatters into driving me to her reality.

"You're such a clever liar," she said, a wisp of a smile showing briefly on her lips. "That's one of the reasons I'm so fond of you. But I don't understand what you think I can do for you."

"I need you to heal me."

"How am I supposed to do that? By putting my hands on you like a faith healer in a tent revival show? I'm sorry, Mike, but it doesn't work that way."

"Then explain how it works."

She grew quiet for a long moment, her gaze fixed upon the horizon. Finally she shook her head. "I can't. It would be like trying to tell a living person how to breathe in air, or how to swallow food.

This is either something that comes natural, or it can't be done. I'm surprised with your level of awareness that you're struggling with this."

"I know full well this pain isn't real. That it's only something I'm imagining—"

"No, darling, it's not something you're imagining. The pain you're feeling is very real right now, because it's something you're manifesting."

"Okay, so I'm manifesting it. But I know logically that I haven't suffered any of the injuries that I believe I have. I know that it's not possible for me to have suffered any of those injuries. But knowing that isn't helping me any."

She grew quiet again, her features drawn. When she spoke next it was to ask if I knew what would happen if I stayed in her reality for too long.

"Yeah. I'd either end up a squatter or a zombie."

"I do like the terms you use to explain those two phenomenon. They're very vivid. And yes, you'd eventually become confused about your own identity, and you'd either adopt my reality or lose yourself completely in some nightmarish hell. And if either of those happened, you'd be able to get up out of that chair and walk, and you'd do so without any awareness of the injuries that you believe are incapacitating you right now. Perhaps if you reflect deeply enough on that it will help you with your present situation."

"What are you trying to say? That I need to be more aware of being less aware?"

"Something like that."

I tried to make sense of what she was suggesting, but I couldn't quite wrap my mind around it. "This is all too metaphysical for me right now," I said. "I know you think there's nothing you can do to help me, but that's not true. The instant I entered your reality, the pain became much less. Maybe as much as half of it went away. And I swear when I look at your hands now, I can see them glowing—"

"I assure you, my hands are not glowing with healing energy or anything else for that matter."

"I know they're not, but that's how I see them. And I can't shake this feeling that if you were to touch me you'd heal me."

Olivia had shifted in her chair so she could study me. Her soft hazel eyes had turned translucent and her ageless face had the dispassionate look of a coroner looking at a body that needed to be autopsied. Finally she came to a decision.

"Perhaps you're using me as a crutch," she said. "Let us see what happens."

She raised herself from her chair and moved over to me so she could crouch by my feet, and then she proceeded to remove my shoes and my socks. After that my suit pants, suit jacket, tie and shirt were taken off, leaving me in only my boxers. She then moved back to the front of the lounge chair and slowly glided her hands over my feet and up my legs before gently touching my hips.

It was all very sensual the way she did this, especially with how her beach cover-up lightly draped over me as she worked her way up my body, her knees touching me as she shimmied herself along the length of the chair. She finished with her palms holding my face.

"Are you healed?" she asked, her eyes searching deep into mine.

"Hallelujah," I said. "It's a miracle. Praise the lord."

"Really? Are you joking?"

"I'm serious as all hell. You fixed me."

She gave me an uncertain look as she moved aside to see if I could really get off the chair, which I did without any pain. First thing I did after I got to my feet was drop to the ground and pound out twenty quick pushups.

"You appear quite vigorous."

"I feel like a million," I grunted out as I did an additional ten pushups. After that I got back up on my feet and gathered up my clothing so I could put it back on. My suit might've been in tatters, but my body seemed perfectly fine.

Chapter 7

Olivia had gone back to her lounge chair. She studied me while I dressed but once I finished she moved her gaze back out to the ocean. I squinted to make out what she was looking at. Off in the distance several zombies were bobbing up and down in the water. After several minutes they sank completely.

"You do realize I didn't do anything," Olivia said.

"That's what you keep telling me."

"And it's true. But no matter." She picked up her service bell and rang it several times. "I would say drinks are in order."

I wasn't about to argue with her. I wasn't going to have any of her fruity mai tai-type drinks after what I'd gone through with Al Zaoud—my nerves were more jangled than a million Christmas bells, and I needed right then a double bourbon to help settle me down. I joined her on the other lounge chair, and we waited in silence while Henry in his black tuxedo and white gloves came hustling down from a hidden path to take our order. Tagging along with him was the blond surfer dude wearing the silk seashell patterned Hawaiian shirt and blue swimming trunks that he would always be wearing in his adopted reality. The surfer dude tried to give the impression of being a good-natured goofball, but I caught him a few times glaring at me in a hostile, predatory manner, as if he thought I must've been faking my earlier injuries so I could horn in on his action. I couldn't help laughing seeing that. Olivia noticed it also and a thin smile crept over her lips even though she scolded me. "Please be gentle with Clark. He's a sensitive young man." Then more seriously, "And don't say anything to make him doubt my reality."

"Don't worry. I'll be good. I owe you plenty as it is. And if you want I'll look into your gigolo's background. No charge, of course."

"That won't be necessary."

It didn't take long for Henry and Clark to reach us. While Henry took our drink orders, Clark moved behind Olivia and began massaging her shoulders. "Isn't it about time for your friend to leave?" he asked, attempting and failing badly to keep his manner casual.

"Clark, darling, I need to discuss a private matter with Mr. Stone. Please follow Henry back to the resort. And don't be jealous. Mr. Stone is simply a dear friend. Nothing more."

Clark removed his hands from Olivia's shoulders. He swallowed back whatever outburst was stewing inside of him, and in a snippy tone remarked, "Very well." Without another word he stormed off sulking while Henry had to nearly run to keep up with him. I once again broke out laughing watching this gigolo's act. "Your Clark seems to be quite the jealous fellow," I said. "He has no idea how lucky he is. Imagine what would've happened to him if he had ended up squatting in Al Zaoud's world."

"Never mind that. You should instead be focusing on what it is that you've been repressing."

"I haven't been repressing anything."

"Of course you have. Otherwise you wouldn't have needed me to overcome those imagined injuries. The one thing that seems to hold most aware souls back is their refusal to accept what they did to send them to hell."

"That's not the case with me. I know damn well what I did to end up here."

"Why don't you tell me anyway?"

"It's not necessary."

"Mike, darling, my plans were to spend the day making love on this beach," Olivia said, her voice dripping with ice. "You do realize that I have altered my plans, and not for my benefit, but for yours?"

"Okay, okay, Jesus, don't bite my head off."

I didn't want to tell her or anyone else about what had happened, but I didn't see how I had any choice, at least not if I ever wanted to seek out her help again. My voice sounded hollow in my ears as I mentioned how I'd already told her long ago that I'd been a private investigator when I was alive, which I was sure she remembered since it was her idea that I set up practice here in hell. A lump formed in my throat as I told her about how my last case was finding a missing twenty-year-old girl for her distraught parents. My voice trailed off as I spotted Henry off in the distance hurrying toward us as he balanced his drink tray on one hand. I was grateful for the double bourbon he was bringing me. I badly needed that drink to lubricate my throat.

I fell silent as I waited for Henry to deliver us our drinks, and when he handed me mine I drank down half my bourbon in a single gulp. I then waited until Henry headed back toward the resort and was out of earshot before I continued telling Olivia my story.

"This girl's parents were from a small farming community in Iowa. Real decent folks. Just nice people who were at their wit's end. Their daughter, Sarah, had come to New York two years earlier to make it as an actress. She was only eighteen when she left, and was a cute kid with kind of a healthy farm girl look about her. Blonde, blue eyes, freckles, shapely, but with this innocent awkwardness to her. Her parents hadn't heard from her in over ten months. They had filed a missing persons report with the police, didn't get anywhere with that, and were besides themselves with worry. I pretty much knew how it was going to turn out with Sarah, but I accepted the case anyway. I figured as far as the parents went, the not knowing would be worse than anything I ended up finding."

My voice caught in my throat and I finished off my bourbon. I found myself staring absently at my empty glass, then shook myself out of the funk I'd drifted into. Smiling weakly, I told her how Sarah's story, up to a point, was pretty much what you'd expect.

"She shared a crap apartment in the Bronx with three other hopeful actresses, and for the first nine months tried to support herself waiting tables at a nearby dive, although from what I heard from her roommates she was barely scraping by, and most times not even that. After those nine months she got a job getting naked at a strip club in Queens, and she started making enough money then to pay her share of the rent on time and eat a little more regularly. And here's where the story veers off from the norm, or maybe not so much. Two months after taking that job she got involved with a

DAVE ZELTSERMAN

really bad guy. Yuri Tretiak, a hitman for the Russian mob. Three months later she vanishes."

I stopped to rub a hand across my eyes. It wasn't at all cathartic to retell this story. If anything, it only made me feel deader inside. I continued anyway, telling Olivia why I was convinced Tretiak had murdered Sarah. The problem was that I never found any solid evidence that I could take to the police, so there wasn't anything I could do about it, at least legally.

"I'm guessing either Tretiak or one of his associates let something slip in front of Sarah, and Tretiak decided he had to get rid of her. Or maybe he was just a sick, twisted psycho who got off on killing young, pretty girls, because I was sure he also killed at least three other girlfriends before Sarah, making sure their bodies disappeared as well. But whatever his reason for killing her, I was stuck and was only hitting dead ends in proving any of this, and I certainly didn't want to dump what I knew on the parents. What I decided to do was abduct Tretiak and do whatever I had to to make him tell me what he did to Sarah and where I could find her body, and afterwards I was going to put him down like any other mad dog. But my plan went all to hell. Instead of abducting the sonofabitch killer cleanly, bullets started flying and an innocent thirteen-year-old boy died because of me."

"This was how you also died?"

"Yes and no. Tretiak ended up killing me, but not that day. I should've been bright enough to realize that he would've figured out who was gunning for him. After all, it would've been easy enough for him to find out that I'd been looking into Sarah's disappearance, and it wouldn't have been a big leap from there. But I was dense and thought that I'd have another shot at him. And two weeks later I walked into a setup and took several bullets to the chest. Right before I died I knew I'd be going straight to hell."

"Because of that thirteen-year-old boy?"

"Yeah."

"My God, Mike, from what you've told me you're a saint, at least compared to any of the rest of us here. Even if you were the one to have fired the shot that ended that boy's life—"

"I was."

"But it was still an accident!"

"You don't understand. It wasn't that I accidentally killed that boy that doomed me to hell. Or that I decided to take the law into my own hands regarding Yuri Tretiak. He was a piece of human slime who would've deserved whatever I could've done to him. What sealed my fate as far as hell was concerned was that I had convinced myself that I would wait until I dealt with Tretiak before I took responsibility for what I did to that boy, but I was only lying to myself. The very instant before Tretiak's first bullet hit me I knew in my heart that I never would've told anyone that I was responsible for that boy's death. That I would've lied and cheated and done whatever I had to to hide that fact, and I would've done that out of shame and cowardice. And that's why I'm here now."

"There has to be something else then that's holding you back." Olivia's normally flawless brow wrinkled as she chewed on the problem. "That girl, Sarah, did she end up in hell?"

"Thankfully, no."

"And that hitman, Yuri Tretiak, is he here yet?"

"Not yet."

"Maybe it's unfinished business that's holding you back," Olivia said. "You never were able to find out what happened to that girl, and that could be what's blocking you. Or maybe it's guilt that you've been holding on to that's kept you from progressing."

Neither of those struck any sort of chord with me, but I told her it was possible.

Olivia sipped her drink and offered me a bleak smile. "You'll need to figure it out, of course," she said. "I am curious. What is it that Al Zaoud wants from you?"

"The crazy bastard wants me to find him a way to escape from hell. I guess nobody ever said hell would be fair, but it's infuriating that that superstitious barbarian has greater awareness than me and can suck me into his reality. How many times have you had the pleasure of encountering that madman?"

Olivia shuddered slightly, her eyes dimming as she maintained her stare out into the ocean. "Just the one time when he and his horde and hundreds of severed heads tumbled onto my beach. It was an utterly dreadful experience. I'll tell you about it sometime, but not now."

"Did his demon horses come onto the beach also?"

"Thankfully no."

DAVE ZELTSERMAN

"How massive was Al Zaoud?" I asked. "Eight feet? Four hundred and fifty pounds?"

"He was a large man, but nothing like that. I'd say around six feet and several inches tall, and about two hundred and fifty pounds."

"Well, you did warn me about him when I first met you, but it's not just him who's taken on demonic properties. Those demon horses couldn't possibly have ever existed on Earth." My voice dropped to a whisper as I asked, "Seriously, how does someone like him have greater awareness than me?"

"He doesn't have any guilt or doubt blocking him. He fully accepts and embraces what he really is, and so he has flourished here. And he has had eons to do so."

She had told me only what I already knew. "Olivia, I'm worried," I said. "He told me he'd be coming back for me in three months."

"Mike, you know that time has no meaning here? Three months for Al Zaoud could be three thousand years for you. Perhaps in that time you'll be able to progress with your awareness so that you can bring him into your world. Or perhaps you can find a solution to his problem."

"Find a way out of hell?" I asked incredulously. "Do you seriously think that's possible?"

She shrugged. "I've sometimes wondered about it myself. And Mike, darling, remember, Al Zaoud might be a bloodthirsty savage, but he has greater awareness than you, so you shouldn't dismiss him out of hand. But in any case, I do hope you find a solution to your problem. I've grown quite fond of you and do so enjoy your visits, and it would sadden me greatly to think of you spending eternity as one of Al Zaoud's severed heads."

Chapter 8

I hung around for a couple of more drinks with Olivia. When Clark showed up looking like he was on the verge of throwing a tizzy I decided to leave. On the way out of Olivia's reality, I found the ambulance drivers Harry and Ed still lying catatonic on the ground, and I dragged them both to my Brooklyn reality and stayed with them until they came out of their catatonic states. It was a slow process where they at first sat up and stared at me blindly, and after twenty minutes of that, Harry began rubbing the back of his head. Shortly after that Ed started groaning and squeezing his eyes as if he were recovering from a bad hangover. Once they were both aware of me I told them a whopper about how we were attacked by the Russian mob who shot knockout gas into their cab and stole the ambulance after dumping all of us onto the street.

Ed's hangdog face scrunched up into a look of total bewilderment. He wanted to ask me how I went from having a shattered body to now appearing uninjured, but at some level he knew the answer would be dangerous to him. As I mentioned before, squatters have a keen sense of self-preservation and they do what's necessary to keep themselves blissfully ignorant regarding their adopted realities. Instead of asking me what he wanted to, he scratched the side of his jaw and commented in an aggrieved voice how I was looking well.

"Yeah, it seems that way. I'm still banged up, but not as bad as I first thought. I'll be okay."

"That's good," Harry cut in, quickly accepting what I told them. He made a sour face to show his disgust. "What's this city coming to? Hijacking an ambulance?" He grimaced as he gave the back of his head another long rub. Somewhat hesitantly he added, "If you still need a ride to the hospital I guess we could call up for another ambulance."

"I don't think I need one. Why don't you two go on ahead without me. I don't know how familiar you are with Brooklyn, but all you have to do is walk down Eighty-first to Ridge Boulevard, and then go north six blocks and you'll hit the sixty-seventh police precinct."

That wasn't true but I wanted them out of my hair. They walked away toward the direction I'd given them, all the while grumbling to each other about what had happened.

I set off on foot to get back to my office in Brooklyn Heights, and the more I walked the more nervous I became. My nervousness wasn't over Al Zaoud. Olivia was right. Time in hell had no real meaning. Three months in his world could work out to three hundred years in mine. Or three days. At some point he'd be charging back into my world like a force of nature. I was going to have to come up with some sort of plan to deal with him, but it wasn't going to get me anywhere worrying about it. What had me nervous was wondering what I'd find when I got back to Brooklyn Heights.

Whenever I got sucked into another reality, it was always a risk to the squatters and zombies in my own reality. Usually the squatters would survive it okay, but sometimes when my New York cityscape popped back into existence it would do so in a way that left a squatter or two embedded within a building or some other object. Over a dozen times in the past I've found squatters left impaled by things like signposts and fences, and at least a hundred other squatters I've known were crushed within building walls. With zombies it was much worse. At least ten percent of my zombie population would usually go missing after a reality shift, but then again, zombies acted at an instinctive level to search out ways to suffer hellishly so it made sense for this to happen with them. This time I had two reality shifts in a short time frame. One when Al Zaoud sucked me into his world, the other when I entered Olivia's. So as I made my way back, I found myself worrying about certain squatters I'd grown fond of, with Vera being at the top of the list. It would be a real kick in the groin if I were to walk past a building and see Vera's head sticking out of the stonework.

It was a quiet walk back to Brooklyn Heights. Almost eerie in a way as I didn't see a single squatter. Usually I would've passed a few dozen. I didn't see any zombies either, but that was more normal. When zombies entered my reality they'd gravitate toward a bridge or the water or a skyscraper or some other way for them to gruesomely kill themselves, even though they never die completely.

When I got within three blocks of my office, I stopped off at a bar I frequented, and most of the usual contingent of squatters were there. Jim was working the bar, Eve the tables, and a half a dozen squatters who had taken on the identity of degenerate alkies sat at the bar. The only one missing was Candy, a working girl who had long ago set up shop there. I sat at the bar and Jim brought over a double shot of my favorite brand of Canadian whiskey without my needing to ask for it.

"That was quite an earthquake we had earlier, huh?" Jim said. "You could feel the walls shaking."

Usually once the squatters came out of their catatonic trances they went right back to their roles within their adopted realities as if nothing had happened. The thing with those two ambulance drivers was a special case since unless I fed them that story it would've been hard for them to reconcile that they'd been driving an ambulance one moment and the next the ambulance had vanished, but under normal circumstances they bounce right back without batting an eye. This earthquake story surprised me. I guess Jim, and maybe some of the others, were aware of the disturbance the two reality shifts caused and came up with the earthquake as an explanation for it.

I sipped at the whiskey and told Jim how I'd read that New York was on a fault line. "Still, a hell of a surprise when it hit."

Relief showed in his eyes that I had gone along with his earthquake story, and a brief smile crinkled his face. If I hadn't backed him up it might've forced him to question whether things were really as he believed they were. He didn't comment about my suit being all torn up. Maybe he thought my clothing got damaged during his imagined earthquake.

One of the alky squatters signaled Jim for another drink. Before he left to refill the alky's glass, he apologized for the jukebox still being broken. This was something he apologized for every time I came in. Music didn't exist in my reality, and I was guessing it didn't exist anywhere in hell. Still a busted jukebox sat against the wall, and since it was my reality it must've been my sense of humor that populated it with songs like *Highway to Hell* by AC/DC, *Sympathy For The Devil* by the Rolling Stones and *Friend Of The Devil* by the Grateful Dead. The last time I'd checked every single song had *hell* or *devil* in the song's name, and I brought my whiskey with me as I checked the jukebox for whether any new songs had been added. I found one that took me aback. *Stairway to Heaven* by Led Zeppelin. I was still puzzling over the meaning of this—whether it was some sort of sarcastic joke or a clue that Al Zaoud might be right about there being a way out of hell—when the men's room door opened and a squatter I didn't recognize walked out, followed by Candy adjusting the way her skintight jeans sat along her hips.

For a reason I couldn't quite explain I felt a little better knowing that she hadn't been crushed by Brooklyn. It wasn't as if I ever used her services, or planned to, but still, I found it a bit comforting knowing that her hell hadn't gotten any worse than it already was. I brought my drink back to the bar, finished it, and had another before leaving.

As I made my way back to my office, I stopped off at other businesses where I knew the squatters, and they were all accounted for until I came to the Busted Grill Diner. This was the place I'd eaten earlier that day. Doris was still working the counter, but Charlie was gone.

"The lazy bum's been goofing off all afternoon," Doris said, a worried look weakening her eyes. She wasn't worried that something might've happened to Charlie, but that his disappearance might force her to face uncomfortable truths about her adopted reality, which might in turn make her question whether any of this was real. She fretted for a few moments as she used her rag to wipe around the counter space in front of me. "I could try making you something if you'd like," she said. "But I gotta warn you, I don't have much experience as a grill chef." She offered a brittle smile and added, "Which would put me on par with Charlie."

"That's alright. Just a cup of coffee to go will be fine."

She seemed relieved about that, and after she handed me the coffee, I left through the front door, but I cut through an alley so I could check out the back of the diner, and it didn't take me long to find Charlie, or at least part of him, as his legs from the knees down stuck out at a forty-five degree angle from the building's foundation. Maybe I recognized him from his shoes, or maybe I knew it was him from some other way. There wasn't a lot of him showing, but I still knew it was him. He must've rolled down toward the back of the building during one of the reality shifts, and when the building popped back up, it did so with most of him stuck in the foundation.

There was nothing to be done for him. I had no idea whether it was possible to knock down buildings in my reality, but even if it were, I'd have to find squatters who could operate heavy construction equipment, assuming that that type of equipment existed here. And even if we were somehow able to dig him out of the foundation, he'd come out of this a zombie, if he wasn't one already. A half dozen garbage cans sat a little ways down the alley, and I moved three of them so that they covered Charlie's legs. After that I broke into a sprint to get back to my office.

While I raced to my building, and then up four flights of stairs to my office, I had this image stuck in my head of Vera embedded in the floor or coming halfway out of the wall. It turned out that Vera was just fine. I startled the hell out of her the way I stumbled like a maniac into the office, all out of breath, but she was her usual self as she sat behind her reception desk reading a romance magazine and chewing a mouthful of gum. Her jaw dropped open, and as she stared at me her eyes widened in a surprised look.

"Jeeze, Mike, you look like you've been fed through a paper shredder," she said. "What happened?"

Right then I could've kissed that sloppy, gum-snapping mouth. "You don't want to know," I told her.

Her eyes widened a little more. "Does it involve the Al Diamanté case?"

I was surprised she'd remembered that. "No, a different matter." I couldn't keep from grinning as I looked at Vera. "One of these days I should marry you," I said.

"That's what I keep telling you."

She picked up her magazine and quickly became engrossed by it, as if I weren't there. Ever since she first showed up, there had been the same pile of romance magazines stacked on her desk. One of these days I was going to have to look through them and see if there were actually stories in them or just blank pages.

Chapter 9

Definition of PRIVATE HELL
(noun) A special type of hell reserved for the truly damned. Usually
(but not absolutely) a private hell consists of a dungeon cell where a soul
suffers in extreme torment typically (but again, not always) at the hands
of demons.

Just as the physical world has natural laws like Newton's law of
gravity to help explain how things works, the same is true of hell.
When you're here long enough you notice certain stuff, and there's
phenomena that occurs here that's every bit as consistent as gravity
is in the real world.

One of these that I've talked about already is what happens when
two realities bump into each other, and when that happens the result
is reasonably consistent: the lesser aware reality is absorbed into the
stronger one. But not always. There's one exception to this I'll be
explaining soon.

A phenomenon that I haven't mentioned yet is how you find
someone in hell. One way is to stumble along until you're absorbed
into a more aware reality. This is what happened that first time I
entered Olivia's world, and of course, it's also what happens with
every squatter and zombie who ends up in my world. But you can't
count on finding someone you're looking for this way. As far as I

can tell hell is infinite, so if that were the only method available, my clients would've had to spend nearly an infinite amount of time popping in and out of different realities before they would've ever found me. And I can tell you firsthand that none of them have ever had a problem tracking me down, just like I've never had a problem finding them or anyone else.

While I'm sure this works a little differently in every reality, the general procedure has to be the same. In my world, the basement of my office building is filled with directories that look like telephone books, except that for each name in the directory there's only an address, and no phone number. I don't know how many thousands of these directories fill up the basement, but there are a lot of them, and they're sorted alphabetically listing every soul in hell. Not just the awares, but every squatter and zombie from every aware's reality, and the billions of unawares that haven't yet been absorbed into another reality. And as you can guess, some of the more common names might have pages of entries within a directory, and a few names, like Bob Smith, can have a whole directory dedicated to them, but whenever that happens I never have a problem recognizing which of them is the soul I'm looking for.

I'd mentioned before that there's an exception to a stronger reality always absorbing a weaker one, and here it is: when I have an address for a soul I'm searching for, I can choose to enter that soul's world instead of absorbing him into mine. Now if the address is for a more aware soul, I've got no choice on the matter—I'm always going to be sucked into that soul's reality when I walk through the portal. But for a less aware, or one that has no awareness, I can step into their world, and in my line of work, I frequently need to do that. First off, I can't absorb souls from private hells into my own reality—once a soul reaches that level their only way out is to sink into an even worse hell. And it would be pointless for me to ever bring squatters or zombies existing inside of another soul's hell into my reality—if I did that I'd get nothing out of them since they've already lost their identity.

Trying to explain how I slip into a lesser aware's reality would be like explaining how to breathe—it's just not something you can put into words, but whenever I need to do it it comes as naturally as opening my eyes. I'm also pretty sure that whenever I step into a lesser aware's reality my own reality continues to exist. I haven't been able to figure out a way to prove this yet, but the squatters in my world seem okay when I return back to my hell, and that's not the case after a reality shift where I'd been absorbed into a more aware's reality. When that happens, the squatters in my world are fully catatonic when I come back, and they always seem to need at least twenty minutes before they wake up.

When I got back behind my desk, I put my feet up and leaned back with my hands clasped behind my neck, and tried to catch a breather after the day I'd had. I didn't get a chance to close the Sam Vogel case like I had hoped. The mob enforcer I'd been wanting to talk to had finally died, and I had an address for him in the Bronx. This was the same mob enforcer who Vogel had screwed in court and whose wife Vogel had been screwing in that lover's apartment. He pretty much had to be the one behind Vogel's murder, and as long as he was an unaware I'd only need a few minutes to get the truth out of him. If he had any awareness it would be trickier, but I'd still get it out of him.

Something I haven't mentioned yet about hell is that sleep isn't possible here. I guess that's pretty much what I should've expected since you can't really expect the damned to get any sort of breaks, and that means you're not about to get the type of reprieve from your suffering that sleep can offer. For those of us who are aware, it would mean a break from the tedium of our existence. And I guess the same would also be true for squatters since the tedium they suffer is far worse. And for all the other unawares, if sleep was possible it would provide an escape from the constant torment that they suffer in their private hells. So without sleep to break up our days and, at least in my reality, with the sky always being the same, the concept of time here gets fuzzy. It's hard to say exactly when one day ends and a new one begins. It's more like you're on a constant treadmill where you trick yourself into thinking a new day has started. Maybe in Al Zaoud's reality different cycles of the moon actually show up in his sky, although I doubt it. Probably like the rest of us, he tricks himself into believing that days, months and years have passed.

Since I never sleep, I had never bothered to stake out an apartment in my reality. It wouldn't make sense to do that. When I'm not working on a case or hanging out in my office, I try to kill time by having a few drinks at a bar or eating at one of the dive places I frequent. And then at some point I'll find myself heading back to my office feeling as if a new day has started. Vera is always there when I come in, and she's always there when I leave. I suspect that she hasn't left the office since the day she first showed up as a squatter, but if I ever ask her how a hot date went, or something along those lines, I'll get a story, and I'm pretty sure she believes what she's telling me. The same is true with every other squatter in my reality. Whenever I go to the Busted Grill Diner, Doris is there behind the counter, and until Charlie got himself swallowed up into the building's foundation, he would always be working the grill. And whenever I go to the Gotham Lounge, the dive where Jim bartended, the same collection of souls are always present.

I sat back with my eyes closed and stayed like that until I was able to trick myself into believing a new day had started.

DAVE ZELTSERMAN

Chapter 10

The next morning it was business as usual at the Busted Grill Diner with another squatter taking over Charlie's role as short order cook and Doris acting as if the guy had always been there. The new cook, whom Doris called Max, was a tall and skeleton-thin sort, with a scrawny neck and the bony, ravaged arms of a drug addict, but what was most prominent about him was his face, which must've been either been set on fire at one point or doused in acid. It wasn't just the grotesque scarring, but that almost all of the skin had been burnt or melted off, and his lips were nearly completely gone. What especially gave me the willies was how large and liquid his eyes seemed as they floated within that mostly skull-like face. Whatever was done to cause the damage must've been what killed him, which made it unusual that he appeared this way. Whether you're an aware or unaware, when you're in hell you're projected the way you envisioned yourself in life, and it's seldom the way you looked at the time of your death. This guy must've had to live long enough with those injuries where he grew to think of himself that way, and it was his bad luck he had to bring his nightmare face to hell.

Whatever his issues were he did a third-rate job cooking up my breakfast as my scrambled eggs came out runny and my bacon burnt. Charlie had spoiled me. But I guess runny eggs and burnt bacon cooked by a cadaverous-looking squatter was about what I should've expected for hell.

After picking at my subpar breakfast I walked to the corner of Pierrepont and Hicks and found a cab waiting there as a new squatter had taken over Edwin's role as cabbie. This new driver was a small feral-looking sort with a dark, closed face. I got in the back seat and gave him an address in the Bronx that would take me to the mob enforcer who I was hoping to pin for Sam Vogel's murder. He pulled away from the curb and started driving aimlessly since he had no idea how to navigate through the city. I gave him directions that would send him over the Triboro Bridge so we would bypass Manhattan, not that there would be any traffic there to worry about. The one way that hell was like paradise was that there was never any traffic. Sometimes you might have to slow down to let a zombie or two pass by, but that was as bad as it got.

Once I had my new cabbie going in the right direction, I asked him what I should call him. He blinked nervously as he tried to remember what name he had assumed, then relief showed in his eyes and he croaked out, "Paulie" in a voice that could've come from an asthmatic bullfrog. It was probably the first time he had spoken since he had squatted in my reality so I couldn't blame him for how thick with rust his voice sounded.

Once we crossed over the Triboro Bridge I continued to give him directions while we made our way through the Bronx. I didn't know the Bronx well, but it didn't matter. It was my reality and at some subconscious level I knew how to get to the address even though the street names were probably all wrong and didn't exist in the real Bronx. The address I needed turned out to be a red brick tenement building in a slummy neighborhood, and I told Paulie to wait for me and we'd settle up later. He agreed without any argument, which never would've happened in the real New York.

I made my way into the tenement building, up four flights over a crumbling and garbage-ridden staircase, and to the apartment where I'd find a portal that would take me to Vincent Borelli, the mob enforcer who had to be behind Vogel's murder. As I'd already mentioned, I can't quite explain how it is that I slip into a lesser reality. It's sort of like taking a deep breath and letting my body relax completely, although it's subtly different than that. But being able to do it has become second nature to me, and as I opened the apartment door I felt the presence of a portal, and I slipped through it into Borelli's reality.

DAVE ZELTSERMAN

The mob enforcer's world was similar to hundreds of other hells I've seen the unaware create for themselves. Or really the hells they envision for themselves. In this case Borelli's hell was a stuffy, claustrophobic dungeon cell complete with flames bursting through cracks in the floor and the smell of burning brimstone filling the air. Borelli was shackled by his wrists and ankles to the stone dungeon wall while a bevy of demons tormented him. The demons in his hell were blood red skinny hairless creatures about three feet in height, and from what I could see, had glistening razor-sharp claws. Not much of Borelli showed with the way they swarmed over him as they bit into his exposed flesh and dug their claws into his body. Borelli was trying to scream, but the noise was muffled as one of these demons had wrapped himself around Borelli's face. I had to hope none of the demons had bitten off his tongue. It was harder getting information from someone once their tongue was bitten off. It amounted to having to play a form of twenty questions.

Several of the demons had become aware of my intrusion and were twisting their heads around to leer at me. They were ugly little bastards with yellow eyes and gaping jaws filled with jagged needle-like teeth. Four of them jumped off Borelli and started toward me, all the while making these insane hyena-type laughs. All I could do was smile inside watching them. I have far more power and control whenever I'm in a lesser aware reality, and even far more when I'm in an unaware one. I'm not sure why that is, but it's the way it works here. And at that moment I was very much in the mood to kick some demon ass.

The closest demon sprang at me like a pit-bull, and in the blink of an eye I had a nightstick in my right hand. In my own world I would never have been able to conjure up a nightstick, or anything else for that matter. In case you're wondering, I didn't conjure up the morphine that had been in that ambulance. Somehow, though, I just knew it was there. But in this reality popping the nightstick into existence was easy. I could've conjured up an AK-47 instead and used it to blow all these demons into some other hell, but it was so much more satisfying to dispatch them the way I was going to.

The split second after I had the nightstick in my hand, I smashed it across the attacking demon's skull, and the impact sent the creature flying across the dungeon cell and into a pit of fire. It would've screamed if the blow hadn't knocked it either dead or unconscious. Three more demons flew at me in a mad fury, and I handled them with the same ease, the nightstick making a satisfying crunching noise as it shattered their skulls. It was over so fast, and I wished the rest of the demons would attack me too, but after witnessing what happened to their brethren they skulked off into the darkness.

With the demons gone I focused my attention on Vincent Borelli, or at least the bloody mess of what the demons had left of him. He was naked, his nose and ears had been bitten off, and ribbons of flesh hung from his body exposing muscles, tendons and bones. It was pretty ghastly but that was true whenever I visited an unaware in their private hell. They might not all get torn to shreds like Borelli, but whether it was being boiled in oil or having snakes or other critters burrowing through them or otherwise tortured, their suffering was never pretty.

The demons had shredded most of Borelli's face, but they hadn't ripped out his eyes and he was using them to watch me. With the damage done to him, including the loss of his nose and ears, his round face looked like a harvest moon, albeit one dipped in gore. All at once that face creased as he puckered his mouth into a wide gaping hole, and I realized from the broken-down garbage disposal noises he was making that he was sobbing.

"Please help me," he pleaded.

"I'll do what I can. But I've got questions for you first."

He started flat-out bawling then, and it was a pretty miserable sight. Through his crying, he begged me to tell him how I'd be able to help him.

"I can banish those demons." I was lying, of course. There was nothing I could do to help him. But he didn't need to know that. "Tell me about Sam Vogel."

My question confused him enough to bring his crying to a stuttering stop. He sniffed several times, then said, "He was my lawyer. Why?"

"Because you had him killed."

"Me? Why'd I do something like that?"

I gave him a hard look. You can't take what anyone says in hell at face value as souls lie all the time here for a myriad of reasons. Guilt, denial, confusion, fear, anger, or just plain wanting to be difficult.

DAVE ZELTSERMAN

I had gotten pretty good at telling when I was being lied to, and if Borelli was lying to me at that moment he had me fooled. The confusion clouding up his eyes seemed genuine and I was beginning to feel more than a trickle of doubt about whether he was the one who'd put a hit on Vogel. Still, though, I persisted, telling him how he must've been unhappy with the job Vogel did for him.

"What are you talking about? That bastard DA had me dead to rights. No matter what I was going to do some time, but Sam did a hell of a job for me." He shook his head, a determined glint in his eyes. "Some of the sleight of hand he pulled to exclude evidence against me was fucking masterful. If it wasn't for him I would've been sentenced to thirty hard years. I have nothing but gratitude for Sam."

The heavy trickle of doubt was now an outright flood. But I wasn't completely sold. "How'd you feel when you found out he was sleeping with your wife?" I asked.

"He was screwing Nina?" There was more head shaking, and his mouth screwed into an angry scowl. "That fucking bitch. I had no idea. If I did she would've been the one I had hit. Maybe I would've had Sam worked over, but I owed him too much to do more than break a few fingers, or maybe a leg."

He was telling me the truth. There was no doubt about it. I couldn't help feeling dejected, which really made no sense. What difference did it make whether I ever solved Vogel's case? But I knew I was lying to myself. It made a difference. Solving these cases was the one thing that made hell tolerable for me. And this one had been nagging at me for close to my whole existence here. No matter how much I might try to tell myself otherwise, I needed to solve this damn case.

"That's it, huh? You don't know who killed Vogel?"

"I might've heard something while in stir."

The way he pursed his lips and lowered his eyelids showed he was getting cagey on me, thinking that he could make some sort of deal. I couldn't help sighing. It was always this way with the unawares. "What did you hear?" I asked.

"Get me down from here first."

I shrugged halfheartedly. I could've gotten the information out of him a number of ways, assuming that he had something real to tell me and wasn't just lying out of his ass. But the easiest and quickest way was to just play along. I looked over at a spot on the floor where I expected to see the keys to his manacles, and sure enough they were lying there. As I said, I have pretty much full control when I enter an unaware's private hell. I retrieved the keys and used them to free Borelli, first unlocking his ankle manacles, then the ones for his wrists. When I unlocked those, he collapsed into a lump of bloody flesh onto the stone floor. Given the severity of his wounds and the way he moaned, it must've hurt like hell when he hit the floor.

"Okay, your turn. What did you hear?"

Borelli had little strength to do anything other than curl up in a ball while feebly rubbing his wrists. "You have to get me out of here first," he gasped out, his face grossly contorted by the pain he was suffering.

Of course, that wasn't possible. It doesn't give me any pleasure to kick the unawares when they're down, but I didn't have any choice with how I handled Borelli. Besides, I was sick of him, sick of his private hell, and I don't much care for the smell of burning brimstone. I wanted out of there.

"Uh huh," I said. "Let me explain to you how this is going to work. You're going to tell me what I want to know right now, and if you do I'll leave the door unlocked on my way out. Otherwise I'll chain you right back to that wall, and I'll take the key with me when I leave. Your choice. But you got to zero."

I started counting down from ten and when I reached two he blurted out that he had heard Vogel was bumped off because of one of his clients. A guy named Tommy Hilliard.

"Why'd that cause Vogel to be killed?"

"I don't know."

He was lying, and probably for no other reason than to be cute about it. I grabbed him by his right wrist so I could pull him up and put him back in manacles. In a panic, he screamed out that he heard some guy was pissed about Vogel getting Hilliard off on a jewelry store robbery that turned sour. "I don't know who ordered the hit! I swear! All I heard was it had something to do with a lady being killed in the robbery!"

His eyes were bulging wide with panic. He was telling the truth. I lowered him back to the floor, and headed out the way I came. From out of the corner of my eye I could see demons skulking out

DAVE ZELTSERMAN

from under the shadows where they'd been hiding. They were pissed, and they were going to take it out on Borelli for centuries to come. He saw them too, and started screaming about how I had promised that I would banish them.

I slipped out of his reality, and in the blink of an eye I was back in the Bronx.

Chapter 11

There were forty-seven Thomas Hilliards listed in the Hell directories. As I mentioned before, when I come across duplicate listings for the same name, I can always pick out the one I want. I don't know why that is, but it's the way it works. This time when I looked over those forty-seven Hilliards listed, I didn't get a sense for any of them being the Hilliard I wanted. Normally I would've accepted that my Tommy Hilliard wasn't in hell yet, but I decided to show due diligence and visit each of them. I'm not exactly sure why I did that. Maybe I needed to keep myself busy so I wouldn't dwell too much on my problem with Al Zaoud, or it could've been I had some other reason lurking in my mind that I hadn't fully realized yet. Whatever the reason was I spent four days visiting these Hilliards in their private hells, and of course none of them was the guy I was looking for. All but three of them had died long before Sam Vogel was murdered. Of those three, none of them were ever in Los Angeles or had heard of Vogel. When I was done checking them all off I decided I was going to have to visit Vogel, and that was something I wasn't looking forward to.

I had the address for Sam Vogel's portal memorized, which was in Red Hook, a neighborhood not too far from Brooklyn Heights. The new cabbie on the job, Paulie, was waiting at his usual corner. If this was actually New York instead of my version of it, and if Paulie had been an honest-to-goodness cabbie who knew the city, I never would've been able to get him to drive me to the tenement building holding Vogel's portal. I don't know what Red Hook is like now, but at the time of my death it was a hellhole known as the 'crack capital of America', and that tenement building was located within probably the worst part of Red Hook.

As we approached the building and the squatters hanging around it, Paulie began squirming in his seat and blinking nervously. There had to be at least fifty of them; some acting as crack dealers, others as addicts, a half dozen street hookers in the mix, as well as some pure degenerate lowlifes. There were a lot more of them than I had bargained for, and at least twice as many as the last time I visited Vogel. All of them stopped whatever they were doing to follow the progression of the cab with predatory stares.

Paulie craned his neck to look at more of the squatters. His normally thick, raspy voice wasn't much more than a squeak as he asked, "You sure this is where you want to go?"

"I'm sure."

It was crazy. This was my reality, and it was because of me that these squatters had this Red Hook refuge instead of having to suffer in their own private hells. I wasn't going to let them scare me off. But at that moment I wished I had a gun. The problem was I didn't know anywhere in my version of New York where I could get one. "Wait for me, okay?" I asked.

"I don't know—"

"There'll be an extra fifty for you."

His blinking sped up to indicate how much he didn't like the idea of hanging around this dump of a neighborhood, but reluctantly he pulled over to the curb. As soon as I got out of the cab the squatters started drifting toward me like a slow moving stain. Their eyes were vacant as they stared at me, their expressions sullen and angry. Just as water will seek its own level, the same is true with squatters as they'll tend to take on identities that fit their true nature. The most vile of my squatters end up congregating in neighborhoods like this one. I had no choice; I was going to have to run a gauntlet through them to get to Vogel. One of the squatters—a skinny man of about thirty-five with a gaunt, haggard face—broke free from the rest of the mob and led the way toward me. He wore a stained wife beater undershirt that showed off thin, heavily veined arms pockmarked with scars as if they'd been bitten by rats. As he got closer, his eyes remained empty.

He smiled at me, showing off brownish teeth that had been rotted down to stumps.

"Hey pal, you want to help a guy out?" he asked, his smile turning more into a hardened smirk.

I didn't say anything. He was holding something in his right hand that he was trying to keep hidden from me, and I knew what it was before I saw the flash of the blade. When he lunged at me I was ready for him, and I grabbed hold of his wrist with one hand and grasped onto his throat with my other, then I swung both of us down to the concrete pavement with me landing on top of him.

"I'm gonna cut you bad," he grunted as he struggled to push the knife toward my face while at the same time working to weaken my grip on his throat. As he did this, I fought back, but I knew I was going to lose this fight. Even if I was able to choke him into unconsciousness, it would take too long, and the other squatters would be on me soon. I had to end this fast. With my voice strained badly from my effort, I asked him why he hadn't realized yet that he was dead and in hell.

That triggered a violent spasm from him. He spat at me, his lips twisted into the type of snarl you'd see on a rabid dog. "Muthafucka. I'm gonna hurt you so bad," he swore through his ragged breathing. "I'm going cut off your head and piss down the open hole in your neck."

"Yeah? When was the last time you pissed? Or emptied your bowels? You can't remember, huh? It's because nobody pisses or shits in hell."

His whole body was shaken by another violent spasm, kind of like I had jolted him with two hundred volts. I pressed on, saying, "Think about it. Why isn't it ever night here?"

"Shut your face!"

"Do you remember ever seeing the police here? Or anyone other than your fellow deluded souls?"

"Shut up! Just shut up!"

"Jesus, you squatters are so deep in denial. Don't you know hell when you see it? If this is Brooklyn, how come there's never any traffic here? Come on, buddy, why don't you try thinking back to the day you died."

I could sense the mob edging closer. Without looking, I knew

DAVE ZELTSERMAN

they had us surrounded, but the danger was over. What I said had clicked fully in the squatter's brain, and a full-blown panic flooded his eyes. He dropped the knife and, while still on his back, tried crab-crawling away from me. I let go of his throat and backed off of him. He made it a few yards before he collapsed, fully catatonic. The other squatters started backing away then as their own sense of self-preservation kicked in.

I got to my feet and picked up the switchblade that the squatter had dropped. The other squatters moved further away, a wariness reflected in their faces. I had taken a big chance and got away with it. Squatters desperately need to hold onto their illusion that their adopted hells are real, and when someone like me tries to enlighten them otherwise, they react in one of two ways: they either go catatonic like knife-boy did, or they fly into a frenzied panic and fight like hell to shut up the truth. I was lucky it ended up the way it did.

My short struggle with knife-boy left my shoulder and leg muscles sore. I made a show of studying the switchblade to give myself a chance to rest before making my way to Vogel's portal. Once I caught my breath and felt more steady, I pushed the blade back into place and dropped the knife into a jacket pocket. The rest of the squatters gave me a wide berth as I made my way to the building. They knew I was dangerous to them—that whatever I did to cause knife-boy to go catatonic I could do to them. But there were going to be more squatters inside Vogel's building, so that meant there were risks of more confrontations once I made my way in there. Fuck, I hated this neighborhood. I wished I could just blow up the damn building. Maybe once I had Vogel's case solved and no longer needed a portal to visit him, I'd see if I could figure out a way to do that.

As I made my way to the building's front entrance, the squatters in my way scurried like cockroaches to keep their distance from me. Inside the vestibule there were half dozen predatory-types standing around, but they quickly disappeared deeper into the building. They must've seen what had happened outside. Good. Hopefully they would spread the word.

The apartment acting as Vogel's portal was on the sixth floor. I made it up three flights of stairs before encountering another squatter. This one was trouble. I could tell immediately from the way he watched me and the harsh way he was breathing as if he were some kind of alpha dog expecting to make me his bitch. He held something behind his back—I was guessing either a lead pipe or a brick. Whatever it was I knew he was planning to brain me with it. Maybe I could've dealt with him another way, but after my wrestling match with knife-boy I'd had enough. I continued to walk up the stairs as if I was clueless to what this predator was planning, and when I got within three steps of him I had the knife out, and without any hesitation, jumped forward and slashed his Achilles tendon. He went down hard, landing on his back. A sack of bricks couldn't have gone down any harder. As he clutched at his injured leg, he dropped what he had been planning to clobber me with, which turned out to be a lead pipe.

I had to pull him down to the third floor landing so I could get past him, but with a sliced Achilles tendon he was no longer a threat. Better yet, with him howling in agony, he'd scare off other squatters, so I left him as he was, and I didn't spot another squatter as I made my way to the apartment that acted as Vogel's portal.

Assuming I still had greater awareness than Vogel I could've absorbed him into my world, but I really didn't want to spend any more time in this slum area of Red Hook than I had to. Besides, it only seemed fair for me to enter his reality since I was the one still kicking around with his case. I opened the door to the apartment and stepped in, letting myself slip into Vogel's world.

Chapter 12

When I stepped into Sam Vogel's hell, I ended up walking in on him in his office as he plowed a young twenty-something blonde girl from behind. Both of them were facing me, but Vogel was too busy in what he was doing to notice I was there. The girl wasn't as preoccupied as Vogel and her eyes opened wide when she saw me.

"I ain't doing nothin' kinky," she said while staring at me.

"Sure thing, baby," Vogel murmured. He continued driving himself into her, oblivious to the fact that I was standing less than ten feet from him.

"I mean it. I ain't letting you two team up on me." She glared angrily at me and added, "Not unless you guarantee me the part already."

"What the hell are you talking about—"

I spoke up then. "Sorry, Vogel," I said, "I would've knocked if I'd had the opportunity."

Vogel realized for the first time that there was someone else in his office, and it scared the crap out of him; at least it would've if crapping was possible in hell. As it was, he jumped back and clasped his chest as if he was having a heart attack. I doubt he recognized who I was at first. He was in that fight or flight mode, and all he knew was someone with awareness had slipped into his reality, and that someone could be very dangerous to him. Pretty quickly a smile tightened his lips as he realized who I was.

The blonde was bent over the armrest of a gold-colored satin sofa, and she was looking more peeved by the second. "Are you two a couple of perverts or what?" she demanded in a high-pitched, squeaky voice. She craned her neck back so she could turn her glare to Vogel. "You screw me while your pervert buddy hides and watches?"

"That's Mike Stone, an executive producer for the movie. He's got final say on all casting decisions." Vogel winked at me. "What do you say, Stone? Want to see if Gloria's right for the part?"

"We've got to talk," I said. "In private."

"Sure." He gave the blonde a slap on her naked ass, then reached for his pants. "Sweetheart," he told the blonde, "why don't you get lost for an hour or so? Take a walk to Marty's on Vine and get yourself something to eat. Have them put it on my tab, okay?"

The blonde blinked several times as she tried to sort out what she was being told, then bit her lip and gave me a worried look. "I'm sorry for what I called you," she said. "I was startled, that's all." She forced a smile. "You look swell to me. Really."

"Don't worry about it, sweetheart," Vogel said, cheerfully. "Stone's got skin thicker than a rhino's. I'm sure he'll trust any casting choice I want to make, unless he decides he needs a session with you to make sure. Isn't that true, Stone?"

"Sure, whatever."

The blonde didn't look too convinced of that as she pushed herself off the sofa and wiggled into her dress, then slipped on a pair of high heels. When she reached the door, she stopped to offer me a forced smile and tell me it was a pleasure to meet me, and that she hoped we could do business later. I stayed silent as she closed the office door behind her.

Sam Vogel's world was circa 1979 Hollywood, and that was reflected in the décor of his office and in the canary yellow polyester suit he always wore. Of course, you can't always tell when someone lived by the way they dressed. I was a good example of that. Anyone looking at my clothing or the way my PI office was furnished would think I had lived in the forties, which wasn't true. I was born in 1960 and murdered in 1998. But in Vogel's cases, it was accurate.

I sat in a matching gold satin easy chair that was cattycornered to the sofa and waited while Vogel finished dressing. With his thick body and a belly that hung over his waist once he zipped up his pants, he had the look of someone who had once been good-looking but was in deep denial that he had gone to pot once he hit forty. He wore his sideburns long and a good part of the thick, curly hair on his head had to be a rug, which made him the only person I've met so far in hell who wore a hairpiece. I could tell he was nervous as he buttoned up his shirt. He probably thought I finally had an answer for him about who killed him and why, but he didn't want to come out and ask me directly. Instead he commented how it had been a long time since he'd seen me last. "I wasn't sure I was ever going to see you again," he said.

"I don't give up on cases," I said. "No matter how long it takes to sort things out."

Vogel shrugged, his face darkening. "That might be true, but things change here." He walked to one of the windows and looked out over his version of Hollywood. "I don't know about you, but my hell has really been going to hell lately."

"Yeah? What do you mean?"

He stood silently for a long moment, the muscles along his jaw hardening, then turned from the window and gave me a pained look. "What are those terms you have again for the souls who wander into our hells and take up residence?"

"Zombies and squatters."

"That's right. Zombies and squatters." He chuckled mirthlessly at that, and the same pained look from before pinched his face. "Very apropos. My squatters these days are either hopeful starlets, like Gloria, or the worst parade of human scum imaginable. We're talking rapists, serial killers, and murderous gangbangers. I've even got a gang of cannibals roaming the Hollywood hills." As he stood trying to smile at me, his shoulders collapsed and his whole body seemed to deflate. "Even if Gloria tries coming back here later to finish our business, there's probably a one in ten chance she doesn't make it past all those demented souls I've got squatting here. So Stone, I'm really hoping you've finally got good news for me."

"How is me finding out who killed you good news?"

He shifted his gaze from me, said, "A mistake had to've been made. I shouldn't be in hell. If you find out who killed me I'm sure I can clear up whatever misunderstanding placed me here." Grimacing, he brought a hand to his face and squeezed his eyes tight, and in a lower voice added, "Stone, I can't stand it here. I really can't. I've got to get out of hell."

Chapter 13

Vogel was delusional. I could've pointed out the obvious, just like I did the last time I visited him. His tricking squatters who had taken on the identities of wannabe actresses into having sex with him proved he deserved to be in hell. But if I tried that he'd give me the same tired argument that he gave me the last time I visited him—that all he was doing was giving these squatters some hope while making his own hell barely tolerable for himself. Still, all that self-denial annoyed me, and I couldn't keep myself from telling him that no mistake was made and that he was where he deserved to be. At first he looked startled by what I had said, then he gave me a condescending smile.

"Very funny, Stone."

"It's no joke. Do you remember Vincent Borelli?"

"What are you talking about?"

"Borelli was one of your clients when you were alive. I know you were banging his wife at that East Hollywood apartment building where you were murdered. And I know you sold him out so you could keep banging his wife after he was sent away to prison."

"That's not true, Stone. None of it."

"Chrissakes, Vogel, how do you expect me to solve your case if you keep lying to me? I know you were sleeping with Nina Borelli. I know you went to that East Hollywood address to see her. And I know you intentionally messed up Borelli's case. So either Nina was the one who shot you dead or Vincent Borelli figured out what you were up to and he sent someone there to pay you back."

What I told Vogel stunned him. His eyes glazed and he stumbled to the sofa and plopped down onto it as if he were sleepwalking.

"It wasn't that way with me and Nina," Vogel said in a dull monotone, his stare fixed on his hands as he clasped his fingers together. "It wasn't something cheap and tawdry. After Vincent went to prison, I was counseling Nina on several legal matters, and it was only then things started between us."

His voice drifted off. For a good minute or so he stared blindly at his hands, then he continued, saying, "What Nina and I had was real. It wasn't just sex. We cared greatly for each other. Nina had nothing to do with my murder. And I did everything I could to keep Vincent out of prison. I pulled off a near miracle getting him a six-year sentence. If I hadn't fought like hell to get key evidence excluded he would've gotten thirty years at the minimum." Vogel shifted his gaze back to me. "Vincent's dead?" he asked. "You must've visited him. He knew about me and Nina? And he thought I purposely let down on his defense so he'd go to prison?"

I had been bluffing Vogel. It wasn't because I thought Borelli was lying to me, but just because Borelli believed what he told me didn't make it true, and I wanted to know Vogel's take on it. If he really did screw up Borelli's defense so he could keep banging the wife then there was still a chance his murder was because of Borelli even if Borelli wasn't responsible for arranging it. I was pretty much convinced, though, that Vogel was telling me the truth and I let it drop.

"Yeah, he's in hell and I spoke with him," I said. "He claims he didn't know about you and his wife, but I wasn't sure whether he was lying to me, and I wanted to see your reaction. I also wanted you to finally come clean about why you went to that East Hollywood address instead of the bullshit story you've been giving me."

Vogel goggled at me, too incensed at first to speak. "You sonofabitch," he sputtered out when he could.

"Can the outrage, okay? I've wasted years on this case because you had to lie to me about why you went to that apartment building that day."

"I didn't tell you about Vincent and my affair with Nina because it had nothing to do with my murder!"

"Maybe that's so. But it still would've helped me. According to what Borelli heard through the prison grapevine, a hit man was put on you because you got a guy named Tommy Hilliard off on robbing a jewelry store."

The hitch that showed along the side of Vogel's mouth gave him away, but he still tried pretending that he didn't know what I was talking about. "Tommy was a client of mine," he admitted. "The police were trying to turn him as an informant. Those bastards framed him for that robbery as leverage. But he wasn't anywhere near the store when it got hit, and I was able to prove that and I got him off. There was no reason anyone would've wanted to kill me over that."

"A woman was shot dead during the robbery."

He lowered his head and shook it. "I don't think so," he said.

He was lying to me, and not very convincingly. But it didn't matter. I wasn't about to drop a client because they lie to me. They all lie to me.

"What was her name?" I asked.

"I don't remember."

That was another lie. "Fine. Whatever. Whether you tell me it or not, I'll get her name eventually," I said. "I've got all of eternity to look for her."

"I swear, Stone, I don't remember her name. And I did nothing wrong with the case. My client was innocent. I proved it in court, and the girl's father knew I proved it. He wouldn't have gone after me because of that. You're heading down the wrong path here."

The girl's father. That slipped either intentionally or unintentionally from Vogel. You just never know with souls in hell. But it did mean Vogel suspected this might've been what was behind him getting killed. The girl who died might not be in hell, but if her dad hired a hit man he'd get here eventually if he wasn't in hell already.

I gave Vogel a hard look. I wasn't going to get anything further from him. As badly as he might want his case solved, he was in too much denial to help me track down this girl's father. I pushed myself off the easy chair I had sunk in to and told him I'd see him again when I had something more to tell him. He seemed surprised that I was letting him off as easy as I was. He forced a weak smile and invited me to party with him first.

"Stone, I've got a bevy of hopeful starlets I could bring up here, all of whom are eager to please. You could consider it a partial down payment for the work you've been doing for me. What do you say?"

I shook my head no thanks, and left his hell.

Chapter 14

I spent the next three days downing shots of bourbon at the Gotham Lounge. There was really no point in me doing that since it's impossible to get drunk in hell. The bourbon Jim poured might taste like the real stuff, or, maybe, I only trick myself into believing that it does, but as far as getting me drunk, forget it. I could guzzle gallons of booze in hell without any effect, or without ever even needing to piss. But even though drinking the bourbon had little purpose, it was comforting in a way sitting in that dive bar with its usual contingency of degenerate alkies. Maybe the comfort was caused by some sort of muscle memory due to the familiarity of it. Or maybe I just need to periodically degrade myself by sitting among the damned. Whichever it was, after three days I'd had enough, and the next morning I found myself back in my office without realizing I'd gone there.

Vera, as usual, was sitting behind the reception desk with her nose buried in one of her romance magazines. If she was curious about where I'd been for the last several weeks, she didn't bother asking me. I stood quietly and watched her as she snapped her gum and acted as if I wasn't there. It wasn't until I turned away from her and reached the door to my private office that she acknowledged my presence and informed me that the "redheaded dame" had shown up again a few days earlier looking for me.

"She seemed desperate to see you," Vera added coolly. While she didn't bother lowering her magazine, I still detected more than a hint of jealousy in her voice. I knew who the "redheaded dame" had to be. Ruby Jane. A young and very pretty client who had hired me recently hired. And it wasn't hard to figure out why Vera would be jealous given the way Ruby's clingy black party dress had hugged her slender body and how her six-inch black velvet stiletto pumps accentuated her stunning calves. Like most of my client's, Ruby had hired me to find out who had killed her.

I thanked Vera for the message and continued on to my office, closing the door behind me. For a long time I sat behind my desk with my feet up wondering why I'd been putting off Ruby's investigation, because that was what I'd really been doing chasing down all the dead ends in Vogel's case. I didn't have a good answer, but decided it was probably so I could avoid seeing the hell Ruby constructed for herself. I knew it wasn't going to be pretty. That was something I'd sensed from the very start. What I couldn't figure out was why that would matter to me.

I made a decision and swung my feet down from the desk. It was about time I visited Ruby Jane.

The portal to Ruby's reality left me in a squalid and unfamiliar-looking city block. I couldn't tell where in the real world her hell was modeled after—it could've been any dirty, rundown street in any large late twentieth-century city, but it was an ugly place. The sky was far grayer and oppressive than my own world, the street and sidewalks were crumbling and strewn with garbage, the storefront windows were broken, and the buildings were covered with a thick layer of soot and filth. As I adjusted to my surroundings, I immediately spotted over a dozen nearby squatters. These were all lowlife predators; the type who would've been alpha males in my version of Red Hook. I could sense them looking at me with their thousand-yard stares, but they hung back and none of them tried approaching me. As I mentioned before, while I have no special control in my own hell, or any hell with greater awareness than mine, that isn't true when I'm in a reality with a weaker awareness. In those cases, my sense of power—both physically and my ability to conjure up what I imagine—tends to be inversely proportional to that hell's level of awareness. I knew given how weak Ruby Jane's awareness appeared to be, I'd have little problem dealing with these squatters if needed. As with most squatters, these seemed to sense the danger I represented and wisely kept their distance. If they thought I was vulnerable, they would've been on me like a pack of rabid dogs.

Most times when I slip through a portal, it leaves me inside the room or dungeon cell or wherever my target is. Sometimes, like now, it drops me off in the general area of my target's location. When it works out like that, I can always sense how to find my target, and this time was no different. I was standing across the street from a nightclub with a marquee sign announcing its name as Diablos. The club had its front secured by a metal roll down security door, and I knew Ruby was inside. As I made my way across the street, half a dozen of the squatters moved along with me. These predators wanted to get inside the nightclub. They wanted Ruby. I imagined that I had a .40 caliber pistol holding a seventeen-round clip, and I couldn't help smiling as I felt the heft of the gun in my suit jacket pocket. Whatever self-survival instinct that drove squatters kicked in instantly, and they drifted back away from me.

There was no intercom or doorbell so I banged on the security door and yelled out to Ruby who I was, and I kept this up until I heard someone from inside approaching the door. Ruby Jane, her voice muffled by the metal barrier, asked me to say again who I was.

"Mike Stone."

"Will any of them get in if I open the door?"

"No. You're safe."

There was a click of a lock being turned followed by a creaking noise as the door was raised. Ruby looked scared as she first glanced at me and then searched past me to make sure that none of the squatters were close enough to be able to force their way in. I slipped past her. In a panicked, jittery motion she forced the security door back down and locked it. By the time she turned back to me she was close to hyperventilating.

"I didn't think you'd be coming here," she said, her words tumbling out in a breathless rush.

"Why not?"

"It's been over a year since I hired you."

Since the only clothes you ever have are what you come into

DAVE ZELTSERMAN

hell with she was wearing the same slinky black dress and stiletto heels that she had on when I first saw her, but instead of looking sexy in it like before, she only looked vulnerable and frail. Ruby's lips pulled down into a bitter pout, and her eyes averted mine. "I thought maybe you dropped my case." Her voice lowered into a whisper as she added, "I thought maybe you decided you didn't care about receiving payment from me."

Receiving payment. That was quite a euphemism, and it made me feel a twinge of guilt hearing it. As I tell my clients, I'm no saint, and if I'm going to do a job I'm going to get paid. Still, as pretty as Ruby was that first day when she came to my office, I wasn't looking forward to *receiving payment* from her. I couldn't say why that was, and I wondered if that was the real reason I'd been putting off her case.

"That's not what happened," I said. "I had a few things come up that I had to deal with, but you need to remember that time works differently for each person in hell. What seemed like a year to you was only a couple of weeks for me. I'm not dropping you. Let's find a place to sit down so we can talk."

She led the way down a narrow hallway and into the nightclub. She had grown timid since I'd seen her, like a small dog that's been kicked too many times. I had a good idea what changed her. It must've been shortly after she hired me that those squatters came into her hell trapping her inside this building. That would do a number on anyone's psyche. Even if it had been nice inside the club, it would've broken her spirit knowing that a gang of vicious predators were waiting for their chance to break in so they could brutalize her. But it wasn't nice in there. Far from it. The nightclub was dank and dreary with dim lighting and cheap, tacky furniture, and it smelled like a mix of stale beer and urine.

I followed Ruby to the bar area, and joined her at a small table. She offered me a fragile smile, which showed how much she'd been beaten down staying holed up in this dump. She told me that the bar was fully stocked. "I'd offer you a drink, but unlike your Brooklyn reality where the booze tastes real, or so you claim, here it's all worse than horse piss. Or at least what I would imagine horse piss to taste like."

"That's okay. Where is your hell supposed to be?"

Her smile turned more into one of a sad variety. "South Bronx," she said. "Third avenue around East Thirteenth street."

I shook my head as I tried to remember if I'd ever been in that part of the Bronx. "I don't know the Bronx well, and didn't recognize the area when I was outside. What neighborhood are we in?"

"Mott Haven."

That was a rough one. Even in my reality, it would be rough, although I doubt it would be anywhere near as bad as what I saw in her world.

"It's a shame I can't move into your version of New York," Ruby said with a tragic sigh. "Your neighborhood seemed much more livable."

"You lived in the Bronx before your death?"

"My whole life," she said.

"This nightclub we're in, Diablos, was this a real place when you were alive? Or is this something you imagined?"

"It was real. The name's just a funny coincidence, I guess."

"Why do you think you're pinned here? Was this where you worked?"

"God no. I came here maybe a few times when I was alive. I have no idea why I'm stuck here now."

"You were killed here, right?"

Her eyes grew wide again as she stared at me. A flicker showed in them as she considered lying to me, but in the end she told me that I was right. "I didn't realize that happened until you just asked me about it. How'd you know?"

"A lucky guess," I told her, but it was more than that. The souls with lesser awareness more times than not get pinned to where they die. I guess it's their way of trying to come to terms with their death. "How about you show me the spot where you were killed."

There was another flicker in her eyes as she again considered lying, and this time she decided to stonewall me. As straight-faced as she could manage it, she told me she couldn't remember any details of her death. The reason for her lying was obvious. Deep denial. She still wasn't ready to deal with what happened. Hell, she might never be ready for that. It would've been pointless for me to push her right then, but that was okay. I had a better way of getting the truth out of her.

"Let's walk around," I said. "Maybe something will jar your memory."

She didn't want to do that, but she had no reasonable way of arguing against it. Still, as I took hold of her arm and led her

DAVE ZELTSERMAN

through the building it was like I was dragging deadweight. When we approached the restrooms, I could feel her body stiffen. Her death didn't happen in the ladies' room, though. While she went in there reluctantly, she was still willing to go in there. When I tried dragging her into the men's room a silent scream seized her. I would've had to put her over my shoulder to get her into that room, and she would've been fighting me like a wildcat. I let her break free, and watched as she ran away in a blind panic. I caught up with her in the bar area as she stood gripping the back of a bar stool, her small, heart shaped face frozen in a pained grimace.

"Tell me what you remember," I said.

She bit her lip hard enough to draw blood and shook her head. "I don't remember much," she said in a hushed whisper. "I must've been heading to the ladies' room when he grabbed me from behind and dragged me into the men's room." Ruby closed her eyes for a solid ten count. When she talked next her voice had a dead quality to it. "I didn't see him and I had no idea who he was. Next thing I knew, he threw me to the floor. Before I could look up something hit me hard. Really hard. I must've died then, but I didn't realize it right away because I was still here, although the nightclub was empty and I wasn't in the men's room any longer. I guess I must've thought I blacked out and wandered to where I ended up inside the club before coming to. I don't know. But I didn't realize for several weeks that I was dead. It wasn't until I went outside and started seeing how different things looked that I suspected something was wrong. And then later enough weird stuff happened where I knew for certain I was dead."

She grew silent. I prompted her, asking, "Like what?"

She shrugged. "I watched a man jump off a five-story building and land face first on the concrete only a few yards from me. He was dressed in rags like he was from hundreds of years ago, and instead of the fall killing him like it should've, he just started crawling back toward the building, and I knew in my heart he was doing this so he could jump again. Later, when I walked into someone else's hell, which was a really awful place, I had a good idea where I was."

I gave her a long hard look and tried to figure out how much of what she told me was true. Probably a good part of it was, but she still could've seen who killed her. Or figured it out during her time in hell. But if she did, I wouldn't get it out of her.

"What hit you hard was a gunshot?" I asked.

"I think so. I can't say for sure. But that's the impression I have."

"Why were you killed?"

She gave me a surprised look. "If I knew that I wouldn't have hired you," she said.

"Uh uh. Most souls who hire me to find out who killed them already know the answer. They also know why. They just don't want to admit it. And I'm betting you're like those others."

"I swear, I don't know who killed me, or why."

They all swear that. It means nothing. I swallowed back a sigh and asked her why she was in hell. That question took her aback, and she flinched as if I'd slapped her.

"How am I supposed to know that?" she asked.

"We all know why we're here."

From the intense squinty look that came over Ruby's face, I could tell she was giving the question some serious thought, or at least wanted me to think she was. "It wasn't any one thing I did," she said after a while. "I wasn't really a bad person, but I guess I wasn't a good person either. If I'm being honest, I was too self-absorbed, and not as generous as I should've been. I guess you can say I just wasn't nice enough."

If she were just being honest... what a load of hogwash! You don't go to hell for being too self-absorbed or for not being nice enough. That's not the way it works. You end up here for committing sins, and serious ones. Like murder. And betrayal. And other significant transgressions. But even if she knew what the truth was, she was too deep into her denial for me to get it out of her. I accepted that and asked what she wanted to drink.

"I told you the stuff at the bar tastes awful."

"Let me give it a try."

She rolled her eyes, which made me smile. It was the first time since I'd been in her hell that she didn't remind me of a scared, trapped animal. "A cosmopolitan," she said.

"How about asking me for something I've heard of."

That coaxed a slight smile from her. "A gin and tonic," she said. "You've heard of those, right?"

"Yeah, I've heard of those."

As I walked to the bar and looked at the shelves loaded with an assortment of distilled spirits, I imagined all of them tasting like the genuine article. More than imagining it, I expected it, and I did this until it became very real to me. Likewise, I found the refrigerator where I expected it to be, and when I opened it I found several bottles of tonic water and a plate of lime wedges, just as I expected I would.

I took two tall glasses from a shelf under the bar. When I added ice from an icemaker, Ruby told me that the icemaker hadn't worked for her earlier. I shrugged, poured two ounces of gin into both glasses, filled the glasses three-quarters of the way up with tonic water, used a spoon to stir, and dropped in lime wedges. I sipped mine, liked the way it tasted, and handed Ruby hers. She gave it an apprehensive look, but tried it and gave me an astonished smile.

"This tastes like a real gin and tonic," she said. "How'd you manage that?"

"Just a knack I have," I said. "Take a seat. I've got some questions for you."

I had quite a few actually. I wore her down some and more than a few times caught her in lies, but still, I didn't get much from her that I could trust. Two hours and half a dozen gin and tonics later all I was able to squeeze out of her that felt as if it had at least a fifty-fifty chance of being true was that she grew up in the Parkchester neighborhood in the Bronx, had blue-collar parents who gave her a decent home and treated her well, at age twenty married a guy named Tyler Jane, and that her maiden name had been Harmon. While I couldn't pin her down on any specifics regarding her husband, I had the sense that he was what you'd call a knockaround guy—one of those jokers who hangs around the fringes of the mob, but would always be a nobody. Putting two and two together, as well as filling in between a hell of a lot of dots, it sounded like he did low-level shit like selling stolen sunglasses and dvd players taken from hijacked trucks. As far as her murder went, she insisted he had nothing to do with it and that it had nothing to do with him, and I couldn't shake her on that part. When I tried finding out what she did for a living, she got evasive and tried to sell me that she worked as a salesgirl at a clothing boutique, but I had the idea that what she really did was help Tyler move his stolen merchandise.

"Is Tyler dead?" I asked.

"I don't know. I don't think so."

"Okay. I need the name of a friend of yours who is dead."

"Why?"

"Because unless Tyler is dead, I'm stuck right now unless you give me someone."

She lowered her eyes from mine and bit down on her thumbnail. From the way she said the name 'Eloise Halprin' she didn't want to tell me it, but the name must've slipped out before she could stop herself. "We were friends from high school on," she said grudgingly. "Eloise died about six months before me."

"How?"

"A car accident."

"Okay. Anything else you'd like to volunteer?" I half-joked given how damn reluctant she was to tell me anything. Not that that was unusual. It's just the the way it is with every client I have. Every witness, also. My job was equal parts detective and squeezing blood from stone. When she shook her head, I pushed myself to my feet and told her we were done then.

"If you think of anything that can help me, drop by the office," I said. What I really meant was: *if you decide to stop lying your pretty little ass off to me and instead are willing to tell me what I need so I can solve your damn case, then by all means do so already.* It doesn't happen often, but every once in a while a client decides to come clean.

A dullness glazed her eyes. "I can't come to see you again," she said, a weary heaviness to her voice as if she were suddenly overcome by exhaustion. "Not with all of them out there waiting for me." She bit absently on her thumb before adding, "They weren't out there the first time I visited you, and there were less of them when I tried visiting you the second time. But even then it was difficult sneaking out of here."

The squatters. They must have her trapped all the time now. I pulled out the .40 caliber pistol that I had conjured earlier, and after showing Ruby how to chamber a round and work the safety, I handed it to her.

"You'll find a hundred fully loaded magazines in the supply closet at the end of the bar—"

"There's no supply closet there."

"Sure there is. Give it another look, and you'll find it. If you shoot a couple of the lowlifes hanging around outside the nightclub, the rest will scatter like rats. You'll be fine leaving Diablos."

She slowly, cautiously, caressed the gun. Her eyes misted up. "Thank you," she said.

"All part of the job."

She looked away from me. She tried to smile, but a slight hitch alongside her mouth ruined it. "If you want partial payment, I'll get on my knees for you now."

Ruby might've been doing better than when I first entered Diablos, but she was still mostly a wreck, and I would've deserved a far worse hell than what I had if I accepted her offer. "We'll wait until I give you what you're paying me for," I said with a wink. "And when I collect, I'll be absorbing you into my reality so that payment can be delivered over several days inside of the Plaza's best suite."

A flash of relief showed in her eyes. Whether her relief was solely over not having to provide partial payment inside of that dingy club, or the thought of eventually being absorbed into my version of Manhattan and spending time at the Plaza, I wasn't quite sure. She followed me so that she could lock the metal security door after me. As I raised the door, I could see out of the corner of my eye her grip tightening on the pistol I gave her. If any of the squatters broke in, she would've blasted them to pieces. None of them did. When I ducked under the security door, I could see that there were more squatters than before, maybe twice as many, but they hung back. I stood my ground and stared at them until Ruby pulled the metal door back down and I heard the *thunk* made by her turning the lock.

The portal to take me back to my reality was forty yards straight ahead, and I would have to make my way through a large throng of Ruby's more predatory-looking squatters to get to it. When I stepped toward them most of the throng moved back, but one of them didn't. He was a big, ugly one. A shaved skull and thick arms that would've been covered by tattoos if you could bring tattoos to hell. As he watched me an evil, malicious glint showed in his eyes. He was going to be trouble, and the thought of that made me happy. Outwardly, I expressed nothing.

He stood his ground while I approached him. With his large beefy hands hung loosely at his sides, he looked me over and smirked in a brutal sort of a way. His expression showed that he viewed me as some sort of prison bitch he was going to have his way with.

"Hey, man," he said, his accent thick, "you wanna help me out?"

I couldn't place his accent, but it sounded Eastern European, maybe one of the Slavic countries. I shook my head. "Not particularly."

That amused him. "Come on, man, why not help me get inside of Diablos?" he asked.

"I'm afraid not."

He grinned fully and showed off these overly big decaying horse teeth that were a mess. Crooked and broken and rotting, they were like fence posts that had been splintered, splattered with mud and knocked askew. His teeth were even uglier than the rest of him. Or at least the same level of ugliness.

As we stood our Mexican standoff, his grin turned into more of a smirk. "That's not being very neighborly," he said, his stare dulling as he prepared himself for violence. He moved fast then, reaching back with one of his large fists and stepping forward with the expectation of punching my lights out. I moved faster, though. Much faster. Instantly a 9mm Glock materialized in my hand and I fired three rounds into his mouth, obliterating his already ruined teeth and blasting a hole through the back of his head. He hit the pavement hard and fast. He wasn't dead, of course. As I've said before, you never fully die in hell, even after you've had your brains blown out. In his case, his eyes were still squirming around in the sockets like slow moving beetles, and they probably would continue to do so for the rest of eternity.

The other squatters had all scattered like rats at the first sound of gunfire, and Third Avenue in Ruby's version of the Bronx was now empty. All I had to do was walk ahead straight a dozen yards and I'd enter the portal to take me back to my own hell. But I didn't do that. I made a curious decision, the type of which I'd never even considered before. I decided to clean out the more predatory squatters in Ruby's hell. My thought was I'd hunt them down and put enough bullets in them so they'd never again be a threat to Ruby.

As I said, it was a curious decision. My job as a PI is to solve cases. It sure as fuck isn't to leave weapons with my clients or make their hells safer for them. At first I wasn't exactly sure why I was doing this for Ruby, but as I hunted down the most vile of her squatters I began to understand what was driving me. Empathy. As simple as that. Although I'd been trying to distract myself from it, the threat Al Zaoud represented had been weighing on me. I fully understood

DAVE ZELTSERMAN

how trapped Ruby had been feeling. Or maybe I was overanalyzing the situation. Maybe I simply wanted to make sure Ruby remained in one piece for when I collected payment from her. Because she certainly looked nice that day she came to my office.

Whatever reason drove me, I roamed Ruby's hell eliminating dozens of her vilest squatters. As it turned out, Ruby's sense of awareness was weaker than I had anticipated. Her version of South Bronx ended up being only a total of six blocks, which made it a piece of cake hunting them down. Whenever they reached the invisible boundary that would take them to either another hell or the void, they'd freeze up, somehow realizing that they were trapped. And they really were. If they moved forward even a step, they'd be forced to confront that they were only squatting in another soul's hell, which would be enough to instantly zombify them. And if they turned around they'd have to face me and my Glock with its endless magazine capacity. And so I'd either sever their spinal cords or shoot out the back of their heads. In either case it left them in no position to ever bother Ruby again.

Chapter 15

When I returned to my office I was surprised to find Olivia Danville waiting for me. This was the first time she had ever visited me in my reality.

She sat with her legs curled under her on a very comfortable-looking cream-colored silk sofa with big, plush pillows that I'd never seen in my office before. I almost didn't recognize her. Instead of her usual beach cover-up, one-piece bathing suit and sandals, she was wrapped in a full-length mink coat and wore a pair of sleek black pumps. The biggest change was how much younger she appeared. Her hair which had always been silver in her version of Maui was now a honey yellow, and she looked so much more vibrant. As I stood staring at her, her lips curved up into an amused Cheshire cat smile.

She said, "Why, Mike, I do believe my presence here has stunned you."

"Somewhat," I admitted. "You've never visited me here before. I've also never seen you as a blonde, or wearing anything other than your usual beachwear. And of course you've redecorated my office."

"You mean this sofa? Well, I didn't know how long you would be keeping me waiting, and neither did your girl up front. And I did want to be comfortable."

"I can't blame you for that. I'm just glad Vera didn't come in here. She probably would've turned into a zombie if she'd seen that sofa materialize out of thin air."

"Hmm. You haven't formed an attachment to that girl?"

I shrugged. "I'm not sleeping with her or anything. Let's say I've grown fond of her."

"That's always a mistake, Mike. Remember where you are."

"Yeah, I know." I couldn't quit staring at Olivia. I always found her attractive, but now with her wrapped up in that mink coat so that only her bare legs showed I found her so much more desirable than ever before. Christ, I was almost drooling as I kept staring at her. "That mink coat is a nice touch. I wouldn't think you'd need one in Hawaii."

She laughed at that. A nice, throaty laugh. "I thought if I was going to be visiting New York for the first time, I should be wearing something other than my bathing suit and cover-up, and so I luckily found the coat and shoes in your closet." She pulled the mink coat open so I could see that she still had on her beachwear underneath it.

I have to admit, it stung a little knowing that my awareness was so much weaker than hers that she could conjure up a sofa, coat and shoes as easily in my world as I was able to conjure up a gun and booze in Ruby's.

Olivia, her smile weakening, said, "You should know by now that we're stuck wearing the same items of clothing in hell for all eternity. Or at least while we're in our own reality. I think it has to do with the dreariness of it. The sameness."

I was well aware of that rule. I damn well should be after wearing the same cheap, old-fashioned suit since the moment I died and found myself in my version of Brooklyn. I tried, but couldn't stop myself from staring at her. "I've always found beautiful blondes wrapped in minks sexy as hell," I said.

Her eyes glistened as she smiled at me, and I couldn't help noticing the soft curvature of her throat and how nice it looked. I'd never really noticed that about her before.

"You should also know by now that hell isn't very sexy," she said.

"Sure. Whatever. But what do you say? Would you like some company on the sofa?"

"I'm flattered of course. But Mike, I value our special relationship too much to risk cheapening it like that. And besides, what would Clark think? As it was, the poor boy was nearly inconsolable when I left."

I needed a moment, but I remembered that Clark was the overly jealous squatter who had taken on the role of Olivia's gigolo when I last visited her. I felt deflated, but I understood her point. She was maybe my one friend in hell, and it wasn't worth messing that up for a quick tumble. "It's too bad you didn't bring him with you," I said.

"Mike, darling, now you're just being cruel."

I shrugged, and made my way past her to my desk. After I was seated, I asked Olivia whether I could get her something to drink. "I keep a bottle of Canadian whiskey in my desk drawer, but I'm sure you can conjure up a bottle of whatever you feel like drinking."

"Perhaps later."

"Okay. Do you mind if I have something?"

"Of course not."

I brought out the whiskey, poured myself a shot, and drank it in a single gulp. It just seemed the thing to do after spending hours gunning down squatters in Ruby's hell and then finding a stunning-looking but off-limits Olivia in my office. While the whiskey wouldn't get me drunk, I found the slow burn in my throat comforting. After pouring myself a second shot and downing it, I asked Olivia why she was there.

"We need to talk, but that can be for later." Somewhat coyly she added, "I've always been interested in seeing the Empire State Building. Would you take me there?"

"Sure." A thought stopped me. "I've had a hell of time finding any guns in my version of New York. How about helping me out and imagining a thirty-eight caliber pistol in my desk drawer along with some boxes of ammo."

"Do you need the gun right now?"

"No. It would be for later."

She smiled wanly at me as if she were realizing for the first time how far beneath her my awareness was. "It wouldn't do you any good, Mike. I would've thought you'd know that. As soon as I leave your hell, everything I create here disappears."

Shit. The gun I left Ruby wasn't going to do her a damn bit of good. And all the booze inside of Diablos that I had imagined tasting like the real stuff would already be back to tasting like horse piss. I couldn't help feeling a little queasy in my stomach, like I'd let Ruby down.

DAVE ZELTSERMAN

"Live and learn," I said. "How about I take you to see the Empire State Building?"

"That would be lovely."

I got up from behind my desk, took one of her fine, delicate hands and helped her off the sofa. As we walked out of my office, she linked arms with me, which I knew would go over wonderfully with Vera. I was right. As we walked past the reception desk, Vera lowered her magazine and I could see that she was seething with the way her face had scrunched up and her mouth had shrunk to a small, hard oval. In a way that was good. She was too mad to realize that Olivia hadn't been wearing her mink coat when she first came to the office.

"Should I know where you're going?" Vera asked stiffly.

"Vera, I'd like you to meet my sister, Olivia Danville. Olivia just flew in from London. I'm going to show her the sights. I might be back later today, I'm not sure."

Olivia held out a hand to Vera, which Vera reluctantly accepted.

"Charmed," Vera said sarcastically, not completely buying my story.

"As am I," Olivia said with a thin smile.

Later, as we used an elevator that hadn't existed before to take us down to the lobby, Olivia commented how it was a mistake to form any attachments with the souls occupying my hell. "You really shouldn't have bothered trying to placate that girl," she said.

"As I said before, I'm fond of her."

"And as I warned you before, you shouldn't let yourself be. Don't make your hell any worse for yourself by caring about any of them, especially given how tenuous their grip can be in your reality. It never takes much to send them tumbling into their own private hells."

I didn't argue any further with her. I could've brought up how she treated her boy toy, Clark, but I doubted she had any real feelings toward him. Besides, she was right. I knew she was. But it didn't matter. There was nothing I could do about how I felt about Vera. If I were to lose her, it would hurt and my hell would feel just that much lonelier.

When we stepped outside of the building, a hansom cab drawn by a chocolate-colored draft horse was waiting for us. The squatter driving the carriage was a short, round guy about fifty years old with very red eyes, patches of stringy, greasy hair covering his scalp, and a badly pockmarked face. He looked confused as he held the reins for the horse.

"I never knew horses existed in my New York," I said under my breath.

"How fortunate for us that they do," Olivia said with one of her cat-swallowing-the-canary smiles. "I always wondered what it would be like to ride in a carriage along the streets of Manhattan."

"Yeah, quite a coincidence."

I helped Olivia into the carriage, and then joined her and gave the driver directions toward the Brooklyn Bridge. I wondered how it worked with the driver. Whether Olivia, after conjuring up the hansom cab and horse, was also able to influence one of the squatters into driving it, or if the fat, little guy stumbled upon the cab and decided to take on that role in my hell. Whichever it was, once Olivia left my hell and the carriage and horse disappeared with her, it was certainly going to leave the poor sap even more confused than he currently was if it didn't turn him into a zombie.

As the cab made its way through upper Brooklyn, Olivia acted every bit the tourist as she stared at her surroundings and the Manhattan skyline as it came into view.

"Is this what New York was really like?" she asked.

"Somewhat," I said. "The buildings and streets are a close approximation, even if I have a lot of them wrong. But without the hubbub of activity I've created a mostly soulless, dead version of the city."

Shortly after that we were going over the Brooklyn Bridge. There were less zombies than usual jumping off of it. Only five of them. Olivia remarked grimly that there seemed to be a small amount of hubbub on the bridge. "They do like throwing themselves into the water, don't they?" she asked.

"Yeah, they do. They also like jumping off of buildings. We'll have to be careful when we get near the Empire State Building."

Since we didn't have to worry about traffic or one-way streets I had our roly-poly driver take us through what was pretty much a straight path from lower Manhattan to Fifth Avenue and East Thirty-third. Along the way, the driver never uttered a word, probably too baffled over how he had taken over this new role in my hell. During our ride through Manhattan we didn't see any other squatters or zombies, at least not until we arrived at the Empire State Building. We had just reached the corner of Thirty-third and Fifth Avenue

DAVE ZELTSERMAN

when a body came hurtling out of the sky and hit the sidewalk no more than fifty yards from where we were. The body made a vivid splat on impact with little left of it. As I've said before, you never die here, but when a body gets that obliterated, the soul just sinks into a lower and worse hell.

"So they jump from the top?" Olivia asked, her neck craned upward as she searched the sky for more jumpers.

"Not from the absolute top. If they did that, they'd land on lower ledges. But there are locations along the eighty-fifth floor where they can jump and make it all the way down."

Olivia gave another long look upward, her lips curling downward to show her distaste in the matter. "How do we get inside?" she asked.

I directed our driver to take us to the entrance on Fifth Avenue. We had to pass by where the last jumper landed and the bloody remains of a few others jumpers, but no one landed on us. I wondered briefly why there weren't more remains—there should've been a large pile of them—and then realized that I must've had squatters who cleaned up the area. Well, kind of a crappy job for any squatter to have taken on, but at least it made it less repugnant over there.

Once Olivia and I were inside the building's lobby, I told her that we had a long climb ahead of us since the elevators weren't working the one other time I was there. "I didn't come here that time for the view, but the portal for someone I needed to see was on the seventy-ninth floor."

"I believe we'll have better luck this time with the elevators," she said.

Of course we would. I expected as much. But I needed Olivia to make it happen. The elevator door opened right away, and once we were inside I pressed the button for the observation deck on the 86th floor. A thin smile crept onto Olivia's lips as the elevator shot up. She was enjoying the ride.

"This is the first time in ages that I have voluntarily left my hell," she confided to me. "I really should consider doing it more often." A soft sigh escaped from her, and she added, "But of course I won't. Mike, do you know what's the worst part of our existence in hell?"

I shrugged. I could've rattled off a long list of choices, but given how she had something particular in mind, it wasn't worth the effort.

"We have our dangers, of course," she said. "There's always the potential of being absorbed into a particularly malicious and violent soul's hell. But that's not the worst of it. It's the boredom and dreariness of it all. That's what ultimately robs us of everything. That's the true hell. Mike, you should consider yourself fortunate that you stumbled on your private investigation work. It gives you something to occupy yourself with."

"Yeah, I'm one lucky bastard alright. Just think without my PI business, I never would've drawn Al Zaoud to me."

"I don't believe that's true. That savage would've most likely found you regardless." Olivia shuddered and her gaze drifted from me. "Mike, I can't say this for a certainty, but I believe that Al Zaoud searches for other souls with awareness so that he can add their heads to his hideous collection."

"Why would he do that?"

"So that he can keep those souls from ever developing a stronger level of awareness than his own." A grimness had settled over Olivia's features which seemed at odds with what had been her earlier more youthful appearance. Even with her honey blond hair, at that moment she looked older than at any time previous. Ancient in a way, almost as if she could shatter into dust. "When he and his horde tumbled onto my beach, he seemed quite surprised to have found a hell that he couldn't absorb. Mike, if he didn't need to make use of your services, your head could very well be dangling from his horse's mane right now."

"Great. What you're in effect telling me is even if I solve his case, he'll still end up cutting off my head. So I'm damned if I do and damned if I don't."

"You should be looking at this more about how this has bought you time."

The elevator door opened and we walked out onto the observation deck. It wasn't as if Olivia was telling me anything I didn't already know. It was more something I just didn't want to face up to.

I wandered over to the security fence and stared out toward the East River, and it seemed as if I was looking out over the apocalyptic ruins of a dead city. And really that's all it was. Outside of a few hundred squatters and a few thousand zombies, there was no life out there in my version of New York.

Without looking at her, I felt Olivia standing to the right of me. "You came here to talk to me about Al Zaoud," I said.

"I'm afraid so," she said, her voice sounding tired. "It occurred to me that you might try to lead him into my reality thinking that you might be able to handle him there. You can't do that, Mike. At this point he might be able to absorb my reality into his. And even if he were to still tumble into my hell, it would be too dangerous to bring him there. I was lucky to survive my earlier encounter with him."

"Olivia, you don't have anything to worry about. When he enters my hell, he comes in through the south, which cuts off my path to your portal. I couldn't lead him to you even if I wanted to."

"I'm sorry, Mike. I wish I could help you with this problem. I really do."

She reached out and laid her hand on top of mine. It felt as smooth and cold as a piece of glass. We stood quietly like that for several minutes until the peace was broken by a zombie jumping out of a window one floor below us. I tried to ignore it and not watch the body fall.

"Have you had enough of my New York yet?" I asked.

"Yes, I believe I have."

The hansom cab was waiting where we left it. No jumpers had fallen on it, and it looked fairly clean without any blood splashes. Other than the directions I needed to give the driver, we rode in silence. I was mostly lost in my own thoughts, as I'm sure Olivia was as well. What I kept going back and forth over was how I was going to deal with Al Zaoud, because I knew my time was running out. And what I kept coming back to as much as I hated the idea of it was that I was going to have to see the White Devil.

Chapter 16

Nicolaus Bratianu. The White Devil of Wallachia. An apt name if there ever was one.

While his fellow countryman, Vlad the Impaler, got all the press in the history books—no doubt because of Bram Stoker's novel—you'd have to give the edge for pure cruelty to Bratianu. Roasting children alive and force feeding their corpses to their mothers. Check. Burning down villages. Check. Wholesale slaughters. Check. Impaling tens of thousands of enemy soldiers on the battlefields. Check. But where Bratianu won out was the unbridled fervor and inventiveness he demonstrated in torturing his prisoners. Bratianu looked at it as if he was doing God's work, that it was his duty to squeeze every drop of pain that he could out of those poor unfortunates. And now that he was dead and in hell, he was continuing to do what he considered God's work.

Whenever you have a religious zealot as mad and powerful and ruthless as Bratianu, the smart thing to do is keep a safe distance from him even if he owes you, and Bratianu owed me for a job that had so far gone unpaid. It seemed like centuries ago since he demanded from me that I discover the person who murdered him by poisoning his wine. Even though all of the suspects turned out to be in hell, which allowed me access to them, and further, none of them had any awareness, it still wasn't an easy case by any means. When I visited them in their private hells there was no threat I could make that scared them as much as incurring Bratianu's wrath. It was only through pure dumb luck on my part that I was able to trick Bratianu's eldest daughter, Alina, into admitting that she had used crushed berries from the nightshade plant to murder her father.

All of this is to help explain that I didn't come to my decision lightly to visit the White Devil. Not by any means. More than most I know what you buy when you make a deal with the devil, but I didn't see how I had much choice on the matter.

Nicolaus Bratianu's hell could've been taken from one of those Hammer *Frankenstein* movies from the sixties. Permanently dusk. Large full moon showing on the horizon. Wolves baying. A foreboding stone castle on a hilltop surrounded by dark woods.

The portal left me at the edge of the woods about a mile's walk to the castle's front gate. One of the wolves howling sounded so close that it set my skin crawling. A normal wolf would be bad enough, but I'd have to imagine that any of them in Bratianu's hell would be some sort of demon beast, like the horses in Al Zaoud's reality, and the thought of spending eternity being ripped apart by a pack of them didn't appeal to me. I moved as fast as the worn out soles of my shoes allowed me to along the rocky terrain.

I'd made it a half mile to the castle when a troop of soldiers surprised me. Even with their gray, dreary uniforms, I should've seen them given that they were carrying torches, but they seemed to come out of thin air. I didn't realize they were there until a tip of a lance pushed into my chest almost knocking me over.

"Who are you and why are you sneaking here?" the soldier with the lance yelled at me. "Speak or I will run you through!"

Of course he wasn't speaking in English. It was instead some sort of ancient version of Romanian or whatever language was used in fifteenth century Wallachia. But as what happens in hell, I understood him the same as if he'd been speaking English with a stilted accent. He was certainly an excitable one. His eyes were liquid and wild, his ragged face tense, and a tremor showed in his hands as he gripped his lance. I glanced quickly at the other soldiers with him, and they looked just as excitable. I could understand it. When you had a boss like Bratianu you were going to be constantly on edge.

"Hey friend, put the lance down and relax," I said speaking in the same language the soldier had used. "I'm here to see the Prince. We're friends."

He didn't quite believe me, but there was enough doubt to keep him from running me through. "You had better not be lying to me," he said. "God pity you if you are."

I had to give this squatter credit. He played the role of one of Bratianu's soldiers admirably. Any of my squatters in that same role would've been laughable. I had a theory why that was. The souls that drift about are attracted to hells that they can relate to, and when they find one that's roughly the same time period as their life and in an area of the world they're familiar with, they're able to become squatters. The zombies are the ones that stumble into hells that are too foreign to them. At least that was my theory, although I've never really cared enough to try to prove it.

The squatter pulled his lance back, and the soldiers quickly buffeted me as we made our way toward the castle. I was glad I came across them. While I hadn't seen any wolves, I had the sense that several of them were tracking me at the very end. The soldiers with their torches and lances would keep the wolves at bay.

I was surprised the White Devil wasn't in his dungeon. I would've thought he'd be there every possible second, but instead we found him in the great hall. You could've fit St. Patrick's cathedral inside that hall. The walls were decorated with what must've been forty-foot paintings of the Wallachian kings and princes that preceded Bratianu, and at the very end of the hall Bratianu sat gloomily on his throne, a goblet that I presumed was filled with wine by his hand. As Bratianu sat staring at me he reminded me of a hawk perched on a stone ledge. Not because of his nose, which while large and fleshy wasn't really hawk-shaped, but more because of his piercing black eyes, his sunken cheeks, his long black hair that was as fine as silk, and his equally long black mustache and beard. It was more than just that, though. He had this raptor-like quality about him that was creepy as hell.

Two of the soldiers brought me to Bratianu while the others hung back. Those two were shaking noticeably, and it only got worse the closer we got to the White Devil. I couldn't blame them. One misstep or wrong word and their roles within Bratianu's reality would

DAVE ZELTSERMAN

be changing dramatically. As we got within fifteen feet of Bratianu a glint of recognition showed in his coal-black eyes.

"The great inspector," he noted, a twitch of a smile showing.

"Good evening, Prince Nicolaus," I said, bowing my head deferentially. "I trust that you remember the debt that you owe me."

He lifted a hand to his chin area and began stroking his long, black beard, his eyes turning blacker by the second as he studied me. "I have thought of that from time to time," he said. "The decision I've made is that there could be no greater repayment than for me to help you atone for your sins." He looked away from me and commanded his two soldiers to take me to the dungeon.

An icy panic seized me. As much as I didn't want to admit it to myself, I knew this risk existed. Fuck. Spending an eternity being tortured by the White Devil was possibly a worse fate than having my head lopped off and added to Al Zaoud's collection.

I tried to break free of the two soldiers gripping my arms, but they held on for dear life as their own fear gave them greater strength. If I broke free, they'd also be spending eternity paying for the transgression.

"That wasn't the repayment I had in mind!" I yelled out to Bratianu.

"No doubt," he said, frowning as he stared at his goblet.

One of the soldiers had me in a bear hug while the other was trying to grab my legs. I kept fighting them, but it was pointless. As they were dragging me away, I yelled, "What I wanted for payment was for you to spend eternity cleansing the soul of the greatest heathen in hell!"

That perked Bratianu's interest. He signaled for his soldiers to let go of me. I collapsed onto the stone floor, my chest heaving wildly. My exertion from struggling with them had left me badly out of breath. When I could I pushed myself back to my feet and desperately tried to suck oxygen into my lungs.

"Tell me about this heathen," he commanded.

I shook my head on reflex. Maybe that gesture meant the same in fifteenth century Wallachia as it did in my world, maybe it was meaningless to Bratianu. I had no idea since he reflected nothing in his expression. Between gasps I first insisted that he not repay me through forced atonement, but rather with what I asked of him. He made a face as if he had just bitten into a bad piece of fruit, but agreed. "Fine. I will repay you under your terms, even if it means leaving you unpurified in the eyes of God."

He barked out orders to two of his servants who had been standing in the wings, and both of them hurried off. One of them returned carrying a great red velvet chair that looked like it could topple him over at any moment, the other rushed over with a goblet of what passed for fifteenth century wine that had been poured straight from a barrel. After I was seated in the chair and handed the wine, I told Bratianu all about Al Zaoud.

"Once I have that unbeliever in my dungeon, you will consider my debt to you paid in full?" Bratianu asked.

I nodded.

"And how should I cleanse his soul? Should I break him on the wheel? Or house him within the iron maiden? Or should he be introduced to the Judas Cradle?"

I said, "Whatever you wish."

DAVE ZELTSERMAN

Chapter 17

After surviving my trip to Nicolaus Bratianu's hell I headed straight to the Gotham Lounge. If it was possible to get drunk in hell, I would've stayed holed up in that dive for at least a week, but since it wasn't I had to settle for Jim pouring me bourbons over the next three hours. It was all really pointless, but I guess I did it out of habit.

Eventually my nerves calmed down and I found myself buzzing with a hyped up sense of elation. Why wouldn't I? Having my Al Zaoud problem solved was an enormous weight off my shoulders. I hadn't realized how much it had been dragging me down until then. I also knew I didn't have to worry about the White Devil taking his time to deal with Al Zaoud. When I left Bratianu's hell, he was palpably itching to get his hands on the worst heathen in hell. I had no doubt that Al Zaoud was now his top priority and that he would be quickly taking care of that crazy barbaric sonofabitch.

After I left the Gotham Lounge I headed back to my office and with only a little effort was able to coax Vera to put down her romance magazine and flirt with me. Early on she was as stiff as a month-old corpse and gave me a bit of the stink eye, but by the time we were done I had her blushing a nice pink. Any jealousy she had been feeling toward Olivia was forgotten.

For the first time in a long time I found myself eager to get to work, and as I headed down to the building's basement I whistled a happy tune, or at least as happy as any tune can be in hell.

There weren't any Tyler Janes in hell, which was odd. Usually there'd be dozens of entries for any given name. The last time I checked there were a hundred and thirty-seven Mike Stones here, and I'm sure a few more must've been added since. So either Ruby Jane's husband was still alive, which was what she had thought, or he had died and gone to the other place, which seemed unlikely given what Ruby had told me about him. As far as her friend Eloise Halprin went there was only a single entry, but I knew as soon as I saw it that it was the soul I was looking for.

The address for Halprin's portal was in Brooklyn Heights and only a few blocks from my office, and as I made my way there I couldn't help thinking that the address seemed awfully familiar. When I got within a block of it, I started to get a sick feeling in my stomach. I tried to hold out hope that it wasn't going to turn out the way I suspected it would. That the address would be for a neighboring building. But of course it wasn't. I ended up back in front of the Gotham Lounge. The address I had for Halprin's portal was the same that was stenciled onto the glass entrance door.

I had never before needed to track someone down who turned out to be a squatter in my own hell, but Eloise Halprin had to be Candy, the young hooker who hung out all the time in the bar. The usual crowd at the Gotham Lounge included other women squatters who had slipped into the roles of degenerate alkies, but they were all too old to have been Ruby's high school friend. So it had to be Candy, and if I were to cross through the portal and slip into Eloise Halprin's reality I'd be dragging her out of my hell and into her own. And I knew her private hell had to be a lot worse, even if she would otherwise be spending eternity turning tricks in a squalid little bar like the Gotham Lounge.

I sat down on the stoop of the building adjoining the bar so I could think it out. While I had no problem sending predatory souls into worse hells, that wasn't the way it would be with Candy. There was nothing predatory about her. She was more someone you wanted to protect. A sad girl with godawful sad eyes and an even sadder smile. But I never asked her to squat in my hell and I had a job to do. If I didn't question her I'd be pretty much stuck on Ruby Jane's case, at least until her husband died, and I didn't want to keep her waiting, especially knowing how slowly time dragged in her reality. Besides, nobody ever said hell was fair.

I made my decision and headed toward the Gotham Lounge. As I crossed over the entranceway threshold, I concentrated on slipping into Eloise Halprin's world, and in the blink of an eye I was stepping into a foul-smelling dungeon cell with Eloise Halprin tumbling out of thin air alongside me. The girl who I used to know as Candy cried out as she fell onto the rough stone floor and tore up her knees.

She was in too much pain and too confused to notice me right away, and I stood quietly next to her and watched as she sobbed. When she finally realized I was there, she jumped a little in her skin as if I had yelled *boo* in her ear, and began crawling away in a mad panic. She stopped once she recognized me. Her mouth became a wide gaping hole as she stared at me and tried to make sense of what had happened.

"You're that private investigator who comes into the bar sometimes," she stammered out in a dumbfounded sort of way.

"That's right."

She blinked several times and rubbed a hand under her nose. She was still struggling to keep from crying any further from her pain and shock. "People there say you're a good guy," she said with a tragically hopeful smile.

"Yeah, okay. Do you remember yet who you are?"

She remembered then. I could see it in her eyes that she remembered she was really Eloise Halprin. And then fear froze her face as she noticed the bullwhip that I had conjured up and was holding in my right hand.

"The whip's not for you," I said. "It's to keep them away from us."

At first she didn't understand who I was talking about. Then she noticed the demons lurking in the shadows. They were a nasty looking bunch. There were at least a dozen of them scattered about the edges of the cell, and when the light from one of the torches hit them you could see that they were blood red in color, stood six feet tall, and had arched backs that gave them a particularly feral quality. It was their large razor sharp fangs and claws that made me think of them as hairless werewolves. Eloise Halprin should've noticed them earlier since from the start they were making these angry snarling noises as they tried to decide how much they needed to fear me, because they badly wanted to get to the girl. As fierce looking as they were, they were pretty much gutless. With their numbers, they should've tried charging me. It wouldn't have done them any good, but they couldn't have known that.

Eloise mouthed "Oh fuck" as she caught a glimpse of one of them who had moved briefly out of the darkness. Any questions she might've had about how she went from the Gotham Lounge to materializing inside of this dungeon cell were forgotten.

"I'll keep them away from you as long as you tell me what I want to know," I said.

One of those butt ugly demons had worked up enough courage to try sneaking up behind me. I would've known he was doing this even if the girl hadn't screamed, and in a flash I was cracking the bullwhip against the demon's face knocking out one of his eyes. The creature let out a blood curdling howl as he slunk back into the shadows, his claws brought up to cover his now empty eye socket. If any of the other demons were trying to build up their courage to attack me, the quickness and deadliness I displayed with the bullwhip brought that to an end.

"If you lie to me once I will leave you to them," I said. "Do you understand me?"

She nodded.

"Tell me your name."

"Eloise Halprin," she said in a near breathless voice, her head jerking wildly as she desperately tried to keep track of where the demons were.

"Forget about them for now," I said. "Just look at me."

It was hard for her to ignore the demons, but she forced herself to meet my stare. Her face was as white as any I'd ever seen. It was completely, utterly bloodless. She was beyond terrified. I'd seen plenty of fear before when I visited souls in their private hells, but nothing like this. It made sense. These other souls had been suffering in their hells long enough to accept what was happening to them. In Halprin's case, this was all very new to her, and it was probably just beginning to dawn on her what was in store.

I asked her when she first met Ruby Harmon. If the two of them had met when Ruby was in high school as Ruby had told me, then

DAVE ZELTSERMAN

Ruby's name would've been Harmon then, but from the confused way Eloise Halprin stared back at me, the name seemed to mean little to her. "I don't know who you're talking about," she said.

Her confusion could've been an act, or it could've been genuine. I wasn't sure which. "I warned you what would happen if you lied even once."

"I'm not lying! I swear it! I knew someone named Ruby, but her name was Ruby Jane. We were in foster care together. I was thirteen, Ruby was a couple of years older. That's the only Ruby I've ever known!"

"Where was this foster home?"

"In the Bronx."

"What neighborhood? Parkchester?"

She shook her head. The demons growling in the shadows got to her, and she jerked her head nervously in their direction before staring wild-eyed back at me. "The home we were placed in was in Port Morris," she said.

Christ. That was an even worse neighborhood than Mott Haven. An idea came to me about why Ruby told me her maiden name was Harmon. "What were the foster parents' names? Harmon?"

"No. McClechan."

The look that came over her face when she spat out that name told me everything I needed to know about how they were treated in that house, but I asked Eloise Halpin anyway. "It was rough there?"

She bit her lip and nodded.

"Did McClechan abuse Ruby?"

"The old man? No, he was a useless drunk. It was his wife who hurt us." She relaxed enough to show that she had forgotten about the demons lurking around. "Sometimes she'd sell us out to these disgusting old men in the neighborhood," she said.

While she might've forgotten about the demons, they hadn't forgotten about us. Two of them on my right started edging closer to me as if they were going to attack. It was a ploy. They were trying to lure me after them so others could grab Halprin. I could've cracked the whip in both of their faces before they'd even realize what was happening, but instead I chose to ignore them.

"Did you stay in touch with Ruby after the two of you left the foster home?"

"We'd see each other now and then," she said. A shadow fell over her eyes. "We weren't exactly close, but after what we went through at that house we had a bond."

"Was Ruby ever married?"

"Not that I know of."

"Did she know someone named Tyler?"

She shook her head. "Ruby never mentioned anyone named Tyler to me."

"How about a boyfriend?"

"Yeah, back in foster care she was seeing a boy named Dickie Racsine." Her lips curled into a sneer when she said Racsine's name. "She was still seeing him later when I knew her."

"What was wrong with him?"

The shadow covering her eyes darkened. Her mouth closed shut as if she weren't going to tell me anything, but one of the demons at that moment let out an unholy growl which spooked her pretty good, and she quickly answered me after that. "He wasn't good for Ruby. He used her to do some rotten things. Like robbing people."

"Any specifics?"

"Ruby never told me exactly what he had her do, but I was able to figure out enough that it wasn't good."

She was telling the truth about all of it. It was Ruby who had lied to me. There were no loving, supportive blue-collar parents, no family home in Parkchester, but instead a foster home filled with abuse and misery. There was no husband, only a slime-ball boyfriend named Dickie Rascine. I wondered briefly where the name Tyler came from, but only briefly. It was just one of Ruby's lies to keep me from finding out about Rascine.

I kept at it with Eloise Halprin but couldn't get much more out of her. It wasn't because she was intentionally lying or holding back. The hope that I would save her from the demons had her cooperating. But it was just that she couldn't tell me much more. She didn't know whether Ruby had a job, or where she lived, or who she hung out with other than Rascine, or really much of anything else about Ruby's later life. She'd occasionally see Ruby at clubs in Mott Haven, and sometimes in Port Morris, and they'd talk a little, and that was about it. The only other possibly useful information I got out of her were the McClechans full names, although I didn't know what good it would do me seeing them other than making their private hells worse than they already were. I found myself dreading have to tell her we were done because she was expecting me to rescue her, and there was nothing I could do to help her. Once an unaware soul settles into their private hell they're stuck there until they sink into an even worse private hell.

"I'm sorry," I said. "I truly am."

Like an absolute coward, I turned quickly from her and hurried towards the portal that would take me back to my reality. An excited cackling noise erupted from the demons as they realized Eloise Halprin was now theirs. The split second before I entered the portal I heard Eloise's tortured screams, and then it was all gone as I stepped into the Gotham Lounge as if I had just walked through the door. I sat at the bar, and when Jim came over to pour me a shot, I told him instead to leave me the bottle. One look in my eye and he didn't bother arguing with me.

As I'd mentioned before time is relative in hell. What can be only seconds in the real world may end up seeming like decades to any of us in our realities. Similarly, hours in Eloise Halprin's private hell could only be seconds in my own, and from the look on the face of one of the degenerate alkies who stumbled out of the men's room, I was pretty sure that must've been the relationship between Eloise's hell and mine. Eloise, as Candy, must've been in the act of servicing this guy when she was dragged out of my version of New York and into her private hell. Having her disappear on him wasn't enough to turn him into a zombie, but from the way his gumby face had contorted it must've still been a shock.

Over the next hour I emptied the bottle shot by shot, and genuinely felt rotten about what I did to that girl. The fact is Olivia was right when she scolded me about forming any sort of emotional attachment with any of my squatters, and the reason is we're like water here—as much as we might fight against it, we're always seeking the worst and lowest hells we can sink down to. Every squatter, whether its Vera, that poor putz, Edwin, who had acted as my cabbie, or Olivia's jealous lover, Clark, eventually they all either get dragged into their own private hells or become zombies. It's inevitable. And I suspect after that happens they'll eventually end up in an even worse hell.

It's not that much better for those of us with awareness. Eternity is a long time. Even after what might seem like centuries of existence, we will still be left with an eternity for things to be made worse for us. This is the real reason Olivia spends every day lying on a lounge chair at that Hawaiian beach nearly crippled with paralysis. She knows that eventually a worse soul than even Al Zaoud will absorb her into his or her hell and transform her existence into a hellish nightmare. The same is true with Al Zaoud, and that's why he was so desperate for me to find him a way out of hell, and in his case his worst fears were about to come true, if they hadn't already. Even the White Devil was vulnerable. Somewhere in hell there had to be even more powerful and more ruthless souls than his own, and eventually he'll suffer the same fate that's waiting for all the rest of us.

I know sooner or later the same will happen to me. I've bought myself some time with my PI work, but that won't last forever. Eventually some malevolent soul who will make the White Devil and Al Zaoud look like pussycats will absorb me into his world and then I'll be truly damned. As hard as I try not to think about it, I know it's only a matter of time. The true hell of this place is understanding just how long eternity really is.

After working my way through the bottle of bourbon, I decided to quit beating myself up over Eloise Halprin. This shit was going to happen whether I intentionally caused it or not, and there just aren't enough tears to shed for every soul here in hell that I end up fucking up.

When I got up to leave, Jim suggested halfheartedly as he always does that I settle up, and I told him to put it on my tab. I didn't get an argument from him.

Chapter 18

Unfortunately Iris McClechan wasn't dead yet, but her husband John was, and he had settled into a private hell that consisted of a boiling lava pool. In all my journeys in hell, I hadn't yet seen anything quite like I did with McClechan as he lay in the middle of this pool screaming in anguish, his flesh bubbling off him while new flesh simultaneously regenerated. There was nothing I could do to get information out of him. Even though he was staring straight at me I doubt he knew I was there, or could hear what I was saying. It was too bad. I was hoping he could give me names of other friends Ruby might've had since Dickie Rascine wasn't dead yet.

Even though I couldn't find Dickie Rascine in the directories, I found pages of other Rascines, and my palms itched when I went through them and saw an entry for a Brad Rascine. It made me think that Eloise might've had the name wrong—that Rascine might've used the name *Dickie* as a nickname, but that his real name had been Brad. The problem was I didn't get that strong gut feeling I always got when I knew I had the soul I was looking for, but still, I couldn't just ignore the way my palms itched. The address for this Rascine's portal was all the way out in Brookhaven on Long Island, which was a haul and a half, but I decided I needed to check it out.

Rascine's portal turned out to be the ladies' room at a gas station. I found this out by trial and error. When I tried slipping into Rascine's hell by walking through the gas station's front office doorway nothing happened. I have to admit that confused me at first, but then I was struck with inspiration and tried first the men's and then ladies' room before I found myself stepping into a backroom of some dive bar where a thin, ratty-looking man shot pool by himself. He was about thirty-five, had a sallow complexion and dark, furtive eyes, and looked like the type of guy who should've always had a cigarette dangling from his lips. Of course he had to have awareness for him to be existing in this kind of hell, but from the surge of strength that I felt I knew his awareness was far weaker than my own, although not nearly as weak as Ruby Jane's.

He must've noticed me materializing out of thin air, but he acted as if he hadn't. After he sank the shot that he had been lining up, he moved nonchalantly around the table to size up his next shot.

I stood and watched him, and after he rattled the ball in and out of the pocket, I asked, "Rascine?"

Without bothering to raise an eyebrow, he muttered, "What of it?"

I didn't like the guy. And it wasn't just because he might've been the same Rascine who went by the name *Dickie* and helped screw up Ruby's life. I just didn't like the way he looked, and I didn't like his attitude, and I considered conjuring up a gun so I could shoot the sonofabitch in the knee. That would sure as fuck get his attention. But I didn't want to act rashly, and instead tried to calm myself down. I was still doing this when Rascine's world disappeared. In the blink of an eye we were no longer in the backroom of some dive bar, but were standing on a dusty narrow brick street in a foreign land with bombed out buildings all around us. Rascine stared at all this dumbly as if he had no idea what was happening, or why a dozen or so of his squatters lay catatonic on the street while others were embedded in the buildings that had sprung up around them. All at once he turned on me, enraged, his eyeballs nearly popping out of their sockets.

"What did you do?" he demanded in this crazy excited way, spit flying from his mouth.

"Shut up," I ordered. I thought I had heard car engines off in the distance, and I was right. Whoever was in those vehicles were coming our way and they were coming fast.

Rascine grabbed me by the shoulders and tried to shake me as he again demanded to know what I did to him. Unbelievable. The guy was not only too dense to realize that another soul had absorbed his hell, but that the two of us had been speaking in German since that happened. If I didn't dislike him as much as I did I might've handled things differently, but what I did was punch him as hard as I could in the stomach. The blow dropped him to his knees and left him clutching where I'd hit him.

"I didn't do a damn thing to you," I said in a low, hushed voice, and again speaking in fluent German. I had never studied the language, but I guess I recognized it from all the Word War II movies I had seen as a kid. "Look, I don't have time to educate you. You hear those trucks coming? We have to get off the street."

I grabbed him by the collar of his wife beater and half-dragged him through the opening that had been blown out of a storefront wall of what I was guessing had once been a bakery. While a good part of the building lay in ruins, enough of it stood where we'd be able to hide ourselves. Besides, it wasn't as if we had any other choices. If we made a run for it, we'd be caught. Once I got Rascine inside the building I shoved him behind a pile of rubble and told him to stay put. He didn't fight me on it. I think it was beginning to dawn on him that his reality had been absorbed into someone else's hell, and whosoever it was, it wasn't going to be pleasant.

I positioned myself behind the crumbling remains of the front wall so I could hide myself and also look out onto the street. When Rascine's world first disappeared and I saw the bombed out buildings and the strange, foreign lettering on the storefront windows that hadn't been destroyed, I thought we might've been in a version of war-torn Bosnia, but once I heard the two of us speaking German I had a better idea of what kind of hell we were sucked into.

I didn't have many options here. The portal back to my reality vanished with Rascine's world. Somewhere inside of this new hell, there'd be another portal to take me back but I had no idea where it was. If I could make it past the boundaries of this hell, I'd stumble into a new one, but it most likely wouldn't be my own, and if I tried doing it now I'd be hunted down in the street before I made it very far. My best bet was to hide out with Rascine and hope that whoever this invading soul was he would leave at some point and that Rascine's world would then pop back into existence. I swore to myself over this mess that I had fallen into. Nothing like this had ever happened before, and I had no idea what the rules were. I felt lost, and the thought occurred to me that I might never make it back to my own hell. And to make matters worse, whatever soul's hell we were now stuck in, his awareness was at least equal to my own because I had no power here. Ever since Rascine's world vanished, I had tried imagining a pistol tucked away in my waistband without one materializing.

A shot rang out. I was expecting it so I was braced for it, but from the way Rascine's head jerked up and the startled, panicked look that froze his face, the guy probably would've croaked from a heart attack if it was possible in hell. Over the next several minutes there were four more shots, and Rascine reacted to each like he'd been kicked in the groin.

"What's happening out there?" he asked in a desperate, pleading sort of way.

I could've told him the obvious. That whoever it was that invaded his hell was putting bullets into the heads of all of his squatters as they lay catatonic in the road. Instead I gave him a smartass answer that someone was firing a gun. In a way I was relieved to hear those shots. It meant that it was going to take at least a few minutes for this murderous bastard to make his way to us. It wouldn't give me enough time to make a run for it, but at least it would give me time to question Rascine.

"In case you haven't figured it out yet," I said, "we've been sucked into a Nazi's hell, and he's coming for you. If he gets you, maybe he drags you back to a concentration camp and spends the rest of eternity torturing you, or maybe he just puts a few bullets in your head. Whichever it is, you're not going to like it much—"

"Why is he coming after me?"

"You realize you're in hell, right?"

He tried to give me a tough guy look, but he was too scared to manage it. "I know where I am," he forced out.

"Then you know there are a lot of truly evil souls here. They enjoyed their time killing and torturing when they were alive, and now that they're dead they invade other souls' realities so they can keep on doing it. And that's what this Nazi bastard is doing now

DAVE ZELTSERMAN

with you. But here's the deal. You answer questions for me right now without giving me any lip and I'll help you survive this. First question, are you the same *Dickie* Rascine who knew Ruby Jane?"

He was scared half out of his mind, but he still couldn't help himself from sneering at me. "Sorry, pal," he said. "You've got the wrong Rascine. And my name's not Dickie. It's Brad, you dumbass."

"What did I tell you about giving me lip?" Two more shots rang out, and these wiped the sneer off Rascine's lips. "If you're not the Rascine I'm looking for, you at least know the guy. One more smartass comment from you, and you're on your own."

"Alright, relax, already," he said in this rapid-fire way. "Yeah, I know Dickie. He's my brother. And yeah, he got involved with that crazy bitch when she was in that foster home on East 137th, if you can call a cruddy three bedroom apartment a foster home."

More gunshots sounded. These were louder, and so were the engine noises. The Nazi was probably only a couple of blocks away. As I stared at Rascine a coolness filled my head. "Why was Ruby a crazy bitch?" I asked softly.

"Why? Because she was." A sourness twisted Rascine's lips the same as if he had sucked on a lemon. "I'm not saying Dickie was any sort of saint. He might've had a wild streak to him, but it was her fault he ended up sentenced to eight years at Dannemora."

Dannemora was a maximum security in upstate New York. It was damn cold up there in the winter, and was about as harsh as New York had for prisons. You had to be a pretty bad dude to get sent there. "How'd he end up there? And why was it Ruby's fault?" I asked.

"The two of them were running a game where that cunt Ruby would lure a hapless sap into a motel room, and after the two of them got naked and started screwing, Dickie would break into the room acting like he was the jealous husband, beat the crap out of the sap, and rob him. Dickie told me the reason he'd work over the sap as much as he did was that Ruby got off on it. One of the saps got worked over a little too much and ended up in intensive care, and that got the cops looking into it." He wiped a hand across his mouth, his black eyes shining with meanness. "I can't prove it," he continued, his breath heavy with anger, "but I'd still bet my left nut that Ruby sold Dickie out to the police to keep herself out of prison.

EVERYBODY LIES IN HELL

I can just imagine her crying to the detectives how Dickie abused her and forced her to screw those men so Dickie could rob them. What a bunch of bullshit. Running that game was all her idea to begin with. But yeah, I can just about see those crocodile tears of hers when she sold them that crap—"

He stopped in midsentence because I signaled for him to shut his mouth. An old-style touring sedan and a transport truck rumbled into view and stopped about a hundred feet from the shop where we were hiding. I couldn't help groaning as I watched all the squatters dressed as German soldiers file out of the transport truck, each with rifles slung over their shoulders. There were six of them. A dread filled me when they brought three Rottweilers out of the truck. These weren't normal Rottweilers but some sort of demon dog. Their eyes were burning red, their bodies larger and more muscular than any Rottweiler I'd ever seen, and their heads grotesquely misshapen. Without those dogs we might've had a chance, but those dogs were going to find us.

I took stock of what was around me, and there wasn't much other than some loose bricks that I could try using, although I didn't think those would help much against one of those demon dogs. I was guessing their skulls were thicker and harder than the brick. What could help was that there was another room in the back of the shop, and if this was a bakery like I thought, maybe I'd find knives there, or something else I could use as a weapon. Something that would give me a better chance than a damn brick.

I stopped my inventory as three men got out of the touring sedan. It was obvious which one of the three owned this hell, and not just because of the dull slack-jawed look of the other two dressed as soldiers. But with the third one there was no question about it. When I was alive I was never any sort of war buff or had any great interest in World War Two, but I'd seen enough Nazis in hell to recognize that he was an officer with the SS. Shiny black boots that went up to his knees, black uniform, red armband with the swastika. A shiver ran down my spine and continued all the way to my toes when he turned his pale blue eyes in my direction. It seemed as if he was looking straight at me, but he couldn't have seen me. Still, though, I sucked in my breath and kept it held until he turned away so he could walk to one of the catatonic squatters lying nearby. As he did this he took out his sidearm.

DAVE ZELTSERMAN

This gave me the opportunity I needed, and I started crawling with my belly flat on the floor toward the backroom. Rascine gave me an alarmed look as if he thought I was abandoning him. I signaled with my hand for him to stay put. By the time I reached the door a shot rang out, but this was the Nazi officer delivering a *coup de grace* to one of the squatters. There were enough other squatters lying in the street to keep him busy for a few minutes.

While still flat on the floor, I reached up and tried the door. It was unlocked. At least I caught one break to make up for all the godawful luck I'd had since entering Rascine's reality. There was a chance one of the squatters acting as a Nazi soldier would see me opening the door, but I didn't think it likely. Their attention would be drawn to the Nazi officer as he exterminated more of the catatonic squatters. I doubted any of them would be watching the buildings now for movement. That would be for later.

Oh hell, it wasn't as if I had any choice in the matter. I gritted my teeth and opened the door enough so I could squeeze my way through, then pushed it closed behind me making damn sure I didn't make a sound, at least nothing I could hear over the pounding of my heart. I caught another break that part of the roof overhead was gone since there were no windows in the room and I was sure the electricity was dead. At least I'd be able to see what I was doing instead of having to fumble around in the dark.

I was right. This place had been a bakery. Buried under debris were ruined ovens and iceboxes, and lining the back wall were rows of drawers and cabinets. I went quickly through the drawers pulling out anything I could use. Rolling pins, a cast-iron frying pan, and plenty of knives. I was feeling the weight in my hand of a particularly deadly-looking butcher's knife when a ruckus broke out in the front of the store. Shit. The Nazis must've finished up dealing with Rascine's squatters and started searching the buildings with this being the first. Or maybe those damn demon Rottweilers led them here. That was probably what happened because I could hear the dogs snarling ferociously as if they were trying to tear apart a side of beef. Over those sounds I heard Rascine selling me out, screaming that I was hiding in the backroom.

I shoved several of the knives into my jacket pockets, moved over to the side of the door, and after first dropping a meat cleaver by my feet I brought up a frying pan with both hands so I could swing it with as much power as I could generate. The door opened and one of the soldiers peered into the room with a pistol held at his side. I swung the frying pan like a baseball bat and a solid *clanging* noise rang out as I hit him smack in the face. He dropped to the floor hard, and I dove after him for two reasons: first, to avoid the bullets being fired at me by one of the soldiers (before diving to the floor, I noticed that the soldier shooting at me stood by the damaged front wall alongside another soldier, this one holding back two of the demon dogs), and second, so I could grab the pistol the soldier dropped when I bashed his face in.

I was busy searching for where the pistol had fallen, but knew the dogs had been released from the hellish noises they made as they charged after me. I had the meat cleaver in one hand and was reaching for the pistol with the other when I caught out of the corner of my eye one of the Rottweilers leaping at me, its fangs dripping yellowish strings of drool. I swung the meat cleaver with everything I had and buried it in the dog's muzzle. The beast let out what only could be described as an unearthly scream and somersaulted over me as I fell to the side. I tried to scramble back to my feet when something heavy bowled into me knocking me back to the floor. And then it was as if a bear trap had clamped onto my left arm. The second demon Rottweiler.

I thought this was it for me. That with the way this beast was shaking and pulling on my arm that it going to rip my arm off from its socket, and that I would be existing for eternity as a bloody stump torn to pieces by this demon. I still had the knives that I collected, but with the way this demon Rottweiler was pulling on me I couldn't get any leverage. I was able to cut it, but not enough to do any real damage.

As I looked into those burning red demon eyes, I started to laugh. I couldn't help it. Even with how badly my arm hurt I couldn't stop from laughing. Because he wasn't trying to tear me apart. The damn dog was only trying to drag me through the door and back to where the soldiers were waiting with Rascine. And so I laughed in a hysterical sort of way, and I let the beast drag me through the door. Hell, I helped him by moving with him as much as I could. And when I passed the pistol that had been dropped, I picked it up, fired two rounds at the soldiers waiting for me, and leapt forward

DAVE ZELTSERMAN

and shoved the gun muzzle into the Rottweiler's ear. For the split second before I pulled the trigger the skin surrounding the demon dog's eyes folded into a look of confusion as if he had no idea what I was planning. Then when the explosion happened and the bullet entered his brain, the dog went limp and he collapsed onto the floor dragging me down with him. The demon dog wasn't dead—nothing ever completely dies here, not even these unholy beasts, but the bullet to the brain loosened his grip on my arm enough so I could pry myself free.

After firing those two shots at the soldiers all my attention had been focused on the demon Rottweiler, and I looked up expecting to find myself in a gunfight, but instead I saw only one of the soldiers, and he was sitting on the floor blinking stupidly at me with a big bloody hole in the middle of his chest. Rascine and the other soldier were gone.

I stumbled to my feet and had to clench my teeth over the pain that jolted me from my torn and broken arm. I moved in a slow jog to where the soldier sat on the floor and looked out of the opening in the wall. Rascine's hands were tied behind his back and a soldier was taking him to the touring sedan where the SS officer waited. Four of the Nazi soldiers were milling about by the transport truck with the remaining Rottweiler held by a leash. The Rottweiler must've sniffed me out because he started snarling like a demon possessed and alerted the soldiers about my presence. If all four of them went after me in a coordinated sort of way, I would've been caught by them, but these weren't trained soldiers. They were simply souls attracted by the Nazi officer's evil, and had taken on their role. And so when one of them panicked on seeing me and pulled the pin from a hand grenade, I fired a shot at him that missed wildly but it was enough to make him drop his grenade. Again, these weren't trained soldiers. If they were they would've dove away from the live grenade instead of bending over and searching for it. The explosion that followed ripped one of them in half and separated the others from limbs as they were tossed in the air like rag dolls. The demon Rottweiler, however, survived the blast and came running at me, but as I stood my ground and aimed my pistol at it, the beast did a quick U-turn, grabbed one of the soldier's severed legs in its jaw, and ran off.

A bullet chipped the wall only a few inches from my face, and that caught my attention. It was the Nazi officer. I saw him with his arm outstretched aiming his pistol at me so he could get off another shot. I ducked back behind the wall and grabbed the rifle from the wounded soldier. When I peeked back out from behind the crumbling wall, Rascine was being loaded into the back of the sedan. By the time I stumbled through the opening in the wall, the car was driving away. I aimed the rifle at one of the rear tires and missed badly. My next shot hit the gas tank. If a professional soldier was behind the wheel instead of some joker playing one, he would've ignored the shot and kept driving. Instead he panicked and turned the wheel sharply and ended up driving into a building. The front of the car crumpled on impact and smoke poured from the engine. They weren't going anywhere.

My left arm hurt too much to move quickly so I took my time walking toward the car, the rifle raised so I could get off a quick shot if needed. The driver side door flung open and a soldier tumbled out of the car and onto the sidewalk, and I nearly cut him in half with the rifle shot when he got to his feet. I dropped the rifle and took out the pistol from where I had stashed it in my waistband. From where I was I could see the last remaining squatter playing soldier slumped face forward. The crash must've knocked him unconscious. I kept limping my way toward the car until I was outside the passenger window. The Nazi officer looked dazed. He must've bumped his head against the dashboard. I waited until he turned to face me before I fired the last three bullets in the clip at him. Right before the first bullet entered his forehead I could see terror register in his pale eyes.

I tossed the empty pistol, then opened the passenger door and pulled him onto the ground, which wasn't easy given how messed up my arm was. With his brains mostly blown out the back of his skull there was no chance he was going to be able to use his pistol on me, but I took it from him anyway, checked how many rounds were left in the magazine, and shoved it in my jacket pocket after dumping out several knives that I was still carrying around. I knelt down beside the Nazi officer and gave him a quick search, and pocketed a gold lighter. I then pulled one of his knee high leather boots off of him.

I went back to the car. Rascine looked groggy, but awake. He must've also bumped his head in the crash. I pulled him out of the car and brought him to a spot a few feet from where the SS officer lay. His eyes were unfocused as he looked at me, but he whispered thanks. I brought the Nazi's boot back with me and put it under the hole in the gas tank that was leaking out brown diesel fuel. Once I had enough of it collected, I brought it back to the SS officer and poured it over his face. His eyes were rolling around in the sockets, but otherwise he was incapable of movement.

"What are you doing?"

That was Rascine. He was grimacing as if he had a killer headache but his eyes were more focused than before.

"The only way to get back to your world is to obliterate this Nazi bastard."

"You shot him three times in the face. That didn't kill him?"

"You can't kill anyone here. But if I set him on fire and burn away enough of him, I'll knock him into another level of hell. And that level won't be much fun for him."

I used the Nazi's lighter to set him on fire. As he burned, Rascine asked whether his world would come back once the Nazi burnt up enough.

"Yeah."

"Man, that's pretty cool." Another grimace creased his face. "How about helping me out and untying my hands? That goddamn dog, or whatever the creature was, went to town on my arm."

I just stared at him for a long moment before telling him the obvious, which was given how gingerly I was holding my left arm and how torn up it was, I'd have little chance of untying the rope, or even cutting him free with any of the knives I had taken from the bakery. "Once this Nazi burns up and his world disappears, so will the rope they used. Just be patient and your hands will be free in a couple of minutes."

"Alright, sure," he said.

As we waited Rascine must've started to feel more like his old self given the meanness that glinted in his eyes and the way his lips twisted into a nasty smile.

"Ruby's dead, huh?" he said. "I had no idea. She sent you to see me?"

"Not exactly. I'm looking into something for her."

"How does that work? You're some sort of private eye in hell?"

"Something like that. After Dickie went away, do you know who Ruby hooked up with?"

"Sorry, I couldn't tell you. I did my best to forget about that cunt after that. But I'll tell you, even though she was a cunt and a half she was a nice piece of ass. Maybe I'll look her up sometime." He winked at me and something truly nasty shone in his eyes. "Ruby and me weren't strangers biblically speaking. Sometimes when she would pass out Dickie would call me over so I could have fun with her. Even though she'd be dead to the world, she could still grind those hips—"

I pulled the Nazi's pistol from my waistband and unloaded what was almost a full clip into Rascine's belly. By the time the gun clicked empty I had blasted a hole through him bigger than my fist. Even though I didn't realize it until then, I must've been planning to do that to him. There was no other reason for me to have grabbed that Nazi's gun since I was going to lose it once his world disappeared.

I left Rascine to pour more diesel fuel on the Nazi and keep the fire burning hot. Only minutes later Rascine's world popped back into existence, and I found myself standing out on the sidewalk in front of the bar that I'd been in when I first entered his world. Rascine was lying a few yards from me in a puddle of his guts and blood as he'd be doing for the rest of eternity.

I left Rascine so I could walk into the bar and find the portal that would take me back to my world.

DAVE ZELTSERMAN

Chapter 19

Yeah, I know, I've got to learn to control my temper better. It was just plain stupid shooting Rascine like I did, or at least shooting him when I did. I should've questioned him more before I emptied a clip into his gut because there was a lot more I could've gotten out of him. Like names of Dickie's associates. Or pushed him into telling me about other people who knew Ruby. But I let him piss me off, and I acted rashly, and it made no sense for me to do that. So what if he turned out be a reprehensible piece of human sludge who bragged about routinely taking advantage of Ruby all those times when she was passed out? You're not going to find any boy scouts here, and if you dig deep enough with many of the denizens in hell, you're going to find souls every bit as ugly as Rascine's. So why'd I take what he said so personally? Damned if I knew. All I could figure was I must've been cranky from how much my arm was hurting, which was a hell of a lot. When that damn Rottweiler grabbed my arm in its mouth, it must've clamped down hard enough to do some serious damage. At the very least, my arm was broken.

The first thing I did when I got back to my version of Brooklyn was fashion a sling for my arm. It didn't help much. I needed a powerful opiate to take the edge off the pain. Morphine, heroin, Oxycontin—it didn't matter which. I thought about heading down to Red Hook and seeing what I could pick up there, but with my arm useless I couldn't afford to tangle with any of the lowlifes who made my version of Red Hook their home. So instead I headed back to my office, all the while berating myself for how I handled Rascine. On the way, I stopped at a liquor store and loaded up with Canadian whiskey. The booze wasn't going to help with the pain, but at least I was hoping for some sort of psychological crutch.

When I returned to *Stone Investigations* Vera was at first too engrossed in her romance magazine to pay me any attention, but as I was opening the door to my private office she must've caught a glimpse of my sling and my torn up suit jacket because she lowered her magazine and commented in a deadpanned voice, "You fall into an alligator pit, or something?"

"A crocodile pit," I mumbled as I closed the door shut behind me.

I felt bone tired as I got seated behind my desk. If sleep was possible in hell, I would've put my feet up and taken a nap. But sleep was never possible here, so instead I stored away all but one of the whiskey bottles I'd picked up in my bottom desk drawer. The next thing I did was break the seal on the bottle I'd kept out and started emptying the bottle shot by shot. It didn't help at all. Not even the muscle memory of it. My skin still felt every bit as damp and feverish as before, and a dull ache continued to radiate from my injured arm. Of course I knew this was only illusionary, but I couldn't do anything about it. No matter how many times I repeated to myself that I didn't have any bones, broken or otherwise, I couldn't fix myself. I just didn't have the level of awareness to do it.

I had just about decided to visit Olivia and see if I could convince her to once again heal me up when the temperature in my office dropped twenty degrees. It was so sudden that it dumbfounded me, and I thought it was because I was going into shock even though my injuries were only imaginary, and it pissed me off thinking that my awareness was so pathetically low that something like that could happen. But then I heard the door to my outer office open. Even before I heard him telling Vera that he should skin her alive for her insolence, I knew what had happened. The White Devil had visited my hell.

I stumbled out of my chair in a mad rush to get to the reception area before Bratianu carried through with his threat. It was disorienting hearing his ancient voice speaking English instead of whatever long ago forgotten version of Romanian that I've heard

DAVE ZELTSERMAN

from him previously. All the other times Bratianu had absorbed me into his world so Vera and the rest of my squatters all ended up comatose and incapable of offending him. But now that wasn't the case. Just the way she was dressed would leave him seething. There was some more back and forth between them and I cringed when I heard her giving him lip, and then even more when she yelled out to me, "Mike, some freakazoid is out here all hot and bothered because I wouldn't kiss his feet!"

I flung my office door open to see Bratianu glaring at Vera in a murderous rage while she defiantly stared back at him, her eyes narrowed to slits and her mouth moving slowly as she chewed her gum. She had no idea that Bratianu with his level of awareness was like a god in my reality. An angry, vengeful god.

"Prince," I said, bowing my head reverentially, "I am of course honored by your visit."

"The great inspector," Bratianu said, his voice dripping with ice and death. At no point did he turn to look at me as his stare remained focused on Vera. He was dressed in the same getup that I've always seen him in: a red satin hat emblazoned in the front by jewels and a silver cross, a decorative red satin coat with black silk sleeves, silk black pants and brown leather boots. I could tell he was trying to decide between skinning or gutting Vera, and given the curved dagger that he wore at his side, he could've done either without needing to conjure up anything. I don't know what Vera could've possibly been thinking, but she continued her staring contest, all the while slowly chewing her gum with the same deliberateness of a cow chewing its cud.

"Prince, please, join me in my office."

At first he seemed incapable of movement as he stared with bitter contemptuousness at Vera, but miraculously he turned from her without harming her and walked stiffly into my office as I held the door for him. He continued on to one of the windows, and he stood for a minute brooding in front of it, reminding me of a peregrine falcon searching for something to kill. When he turned around again a great wooden throne materialized along with a golden chalice lying on the armrest. A barrel of wine lay on the floor next to it. He walked to his throne, sat on it, and continued his brooding. Of course he was expecting me to fill his chalice with wine.

"Instead of wine would you like to try a drink from my time called whiskey? I think you'll find it enjoyable."

He grunted out something that I took as a yes. He was still brooding too heavily to otherwise acknowledge me. I filled his chalice with a pint of whiskey and handed it to him. He sniffed the whiskey, sipped it, and then drank down half of it. The drink seemed to mollify him somewhat, although his piercing black eyes were still enflamed.

"Prince, I was surprised to see you," I said. "If I knew you were visiting I would've prepared for it."

"How? By hiding that wretched whore from my sight?"

"For starters."

That didn't even crack a smile from him. Instead he turned to look at me, and I could see the disdain in his expression as he noticed my injured arm and realized that I lacked the ability to heal myself. He turned away from me and continued staring at nothing in particular.

"I needed to send you a message," he said, "and I couldn't very well send a servant to deliver it as he would have become addled-brained the moment he set foot in this godforsaken land. So I decided to deliver the message personally." A harsh smile wrinkled his face. "I was curious how the great inspector lived."

I caught a glint in his dark eyes that scared the shit out of me, or would've if my body was still capable of producing shit. I knew I had to distract him from whatever thought had entered his mind, and I asked him if I could pour him more whiskey. He made a face as he looked into his mostly empty chalice and handed it to me. I poured him another pint, and after I handed the chalice back to him he drank down a good amount of the whiskey.

"This drink is good," he said. He turned his head again to stare at me, his eyes glinting maliciously. "Your world is an abomination."

I held my breath waiting for what he would say next. I didn't dare look away from him, and my heart became an icy sludge.

His eyes wavered and he let out a sigh. "But this drink does please me. And I gave you my word. While I would like to crush this blasphemous abomination of yours, I will not do so. Instead I will simply relay my message. That heathen has been secured in my dungeon."

"Prince, thank you. That is a great relief."

"You will follow me back to my castle so that I may show him to you."

This wasn't said as a question or request, but as a demand, so I told Bratianu that I would of course do so. He grunted at that, finished off his whiskey, and appeared as if he were about to raise himself from his throne. I spoke quickly, apologizing for Vera's behavior.

"She had no idea what she was doing earlier," I said. "She doesn't have the capability of understanding. Let me go out there and send her away so that you don't have to lay eyes on her again."

He waved away that idea. "Do not bother," he said. "Leave her where she is. I will be bringing her back with me."

"Prince, please don't do that."

"Why not? I should instead let that godless harlot go unpunished?"

"I beg of you."

He made a face as if he had something extremely unpleasant to spit out. "You could not possibly have feelings for that wretch?"

"She amuses me," I said.

I left it at that. The White Devil's eyes dulled as he decided to think the worst of me, which nine hundred and ninety-nine times out of a thousand is going to be the right way to go here in hell. That I wanted her only as a sex toy.

"Very well," he said, "you may keep her in this vile world of yours. That will be punishment enough for the wretch. But you will be in my debt."

I would've been in his debt regardless since I would never be in a position to turn down an assignment from him, but I played my part and fell to my knees and bowed my head. "Of course," I said.

He made a grunting noise and left his throne so he could stand once again by one of the windows. That was a signal for me to send Vera away, because if he saw her again he was going to take her regardless of what he might've promised. I got to my feet and rushed out to the reception area. Vera had put down the romance magazine she'd been looking at earlier and was filing her nails while trying to appear unconcerned, but I could see the anxiety eating at her. She might have been an unaware squatter playing the role of a PI's sassy receptionist but she must've sensed Bratianu's power and the danger he represented to her. As I'd said several times before, all squatters tend to show a keen sense of self-preservation.

"He's really royalty?" she asked in a hushed tone.

"Yeah, he's an important man. Look, Darling, I need you to go to Brentwood's on Clark and Willow and order us some lunch. Sirloin steaks. Mine well-done, the Prince's rare. Have them put it on my tab. Okay?"

She gave me a squinty look. "You're just trying to get rid of me because he doesn't want to see me again," she said, her voice tight with emotion.

"That's about right, Darling."

"It wasn't my fault, Mike. The first thing he did when he came in here was call me a slut and tell me I should be whipped. Actually it was much worse than that. I'm cleaning up what he really said." She made a face. "But really, me? With how conservatively I dress? He's going to call me that? It wasn't my fault what I said back to him."

"He's from a different place and sees things differently. But you really should go now."

She blew up her cheeks like a chipmunk to show how much she didn't like what I was saying, but she grudgingly nodded. All at once she looked very vulnerable, and she asked, "I'm not fired, am I? Because if I got you in trouble and you need me to apologize to him, I'll swallow my pride and do so."

"Darling, everything's fine. Just come back with the steaks, and don't worry about a thing."

"Okay."

She looked uncertain as she got to her feet and headed for the exit. It was possible that since she took up the role as my receptionist that she hadn't left the office a single time. Before she walked out she gave me a desperate, pleading look, but I ignored it and waved so long to her. Once she was gone, I went back for the White Devil.

Chapter 20

Bratianu arranged for a troop of a dozen soldiers to meet me at a location a few hundred yards from where my portal left me, and I was glad to see them. Within minutes of entering Bratianu's hell I began hearing wolves skulking nearby, and if I didn't have Bratianu's squatter soldiers escorting me those wolves would've gotten me and used me as a chew toy.

The mile walk to Bratianu's castle was done in a tense quiet with the only sounds coming from our labored breathing and the scurrying about of unseen creatures. Maybe these were wolves also, but I had the sense that they were something more vile. Whatever they were, the soldiers' torches kept them at bay as they stayed hidden in the dark, although I'd catch occasional glimpses of their flaming red eyes.

When we reached the castle, two of the soldiers stayed with me and brought me down the dank and shadowy stone steps that led to the dungeon far below the castle. Both of these soldiers shook noticeably as they flanked me, their complexions having dropped to a sickly milk white. When Bratianu absorbed me for the first time into his hell he gave me a tour of his dungeon to let me know where I'd be residing for the rest of eternity if I failed him on his assignment. These two soldiers had to know that for any arbitrary reason the White Devil might decide to change their roles in his world and keep them forever inside that dungeon as prisoners or torturers, and either one would be pure hell.

The dungeon really was a place of nightmares. An enormous honeycomb-like space carved out of rock that held a malignant chill in the air and made you feel as if you'd walked into a freezer stacked with rotting corpses. Of course that wasn't too far off, except instead of rotting corpses the dungeon was overflowing with rotting souls. Each turn in the maze would send you past a cell holding a soul being tortured. Maybe it was a prisoner chained to the rack while his torturer slowly turned the wheel to extract the most possible pain. Or the prisoner was bound to a wagon wheel while his torturer broke his bones over and over again with a cudgel. Or chained to the wall with spikes having been pounded into his eyes, knees and shoulders. Or sealed up within an iron maiden. Or flogged while hung by his toes. Or in some cases Bratianu took advantage of the rules of hell where people never fully die and he'd leave prisoners hung by their necks to forever suffocate, or crushed under hundreds of pounds of rock. In all of the above I used the pronoun *he* in a gender neutral way as almost as many women were being tortured as men.

Torches hung along the walls provided just enough light to show the horror taking place inside of each cell. As I passed by them I could tell whether the souls being tortured were originally squatters that Bratianu chose for his dungeon or unfortunates that Bratianu dragged to this hell. The squatters would scream in anguish, the others had long since turned into zombies and took their torment silently showing nothing on their faces. Even the torturers at times reflected the horror they faced with some of them openly weeping while they performed their duties. Any squatter drawn to Bratianu's hell had to be exceptionally evil, but spending centuries involved in this horror proved too even much for them.

As devious and horrific as these tortures were, I'd seen worse just about every time I visited an unaware in their private hells, but the sheer volume of it wore me down as we made our way deep into the dungeon's labyrinth. It got to where I didn't think I could take much more of it, and I had to give Bratianu credit for his inventiveness. He came up with levels of sadism that I wouldn't think possible for the human mind to devise, and every time I'd think he couldn't be topped for pure sick twistedness, I'd soon be proven wrong. I tried not to look into the cells as we passed by, but hearing their screams without knowing what was causing them soon became unbearable.

DAVE ZELTSERMAN

And so I looked.

We must've walked several miles through that dungeon before we found Al Zaoud and the White Devil in one of the cells. I noticed Bratianu first. If the sea of torment that he created within this massive dungeon of horrors bothered him, he didn't show it by his manner or expression. If anything he looked serene as he stood in front of the opening of the cell, as if all this agony he was responsible for soothed him. I looked past him and spotted Al Zaoud. The barbarian was manacled to a stone wall and had a leather gag silencing him, but otherwise appeared unhurt. He was no longer a giant. He was still a large man, but more how Olivia had described him. His expression turned livid as he caught sight of me, and this alerted Bratianu of my presence. A glimmer of satisfaction showed in his eyes as he turned to greet me.

"The great inspector," he said. "As you can see, the heathen has been captured. Now that you have arrived I will start him on his path to God."

From the moment Al Zaoud saw me he began straining against his manacles in a frenzied attempt to break free. Even though I knew there wasn't any chance of that happening, the sight of him caused the hairs on the back of my neck to rise. Fuck, I was glad to see that maniac in shackles. Even though I knew logically Bratianu would get him, it was a huge relief to see that it happened.

Bratianu moved into the shadows of the cell and picked up a contraption that I hadn't noticed earlier. The White Devil appeared especially proud of this device as he held it up for my inspection. It appeared to be an iron box the size of a small toaster oven with thick leather straps attached to it on both sides. The bottom of the box had a round hole carved out of it about the size of my fist, and the top of the box had a metal grate that could slide open or be locked closed. Bratianu asked me if I knew what the device was for. I had a good idea but I played dumb and shook my head.

"For such a great inspector you seem to lack imagination," Bratianu said with a thin smile. He barked out a command to the two soldiers who had brought me to him to bring back spikes and hammers. They rushed off, and during the two minutes while we waited for them to return, the White Devil paced impatiently. The spikes these soldiers brought back were one-foot long and had been sharpened to where they could be driven through rock, and the hammers were more like mallets. Bratianu was not happy with how long it took them, but the sight of Al Zaoud desperately straining to break free seemed to mollify him.

"Hold this flush against his stomach," Bratianu ordered me. "And you will soon learn this device's secret."

I did as Bratianu demanded, using my good arm to push the bottom of the box with the fist-sized hole against Al Zaoud. Of course this enraged the barbarian, and he strained his neck toward me as if he were struggling to bite me; probably in his rage forgetting that he had been gagged. While I kept the box pushed hard against Al Zaoud's stomach, the two soldiers stretched out the leather straps against the wall and drove spikes through them. When we were done, the box had been secured tightly against Al Zaoud. Bratianu spent several minutes examining our work and seemed satisfied with it. He barked another order to the soldiers, which I didn't quite get. One of the soldiers hurried away, and when he returned he was carrying a cage holding two rats.

As you have probably guessed, these weren't normal rats, but some sort of demon rats with blood-red eyes, grossly misshapen skulls, large and deadly looking claws, and piranha-like fangs. Bratianu slipped on a leather glove, and then had one of the soldiers open the grate on the metal box. With the grate open, Bratianu reached into the cage, pulled each of the rats out, and placed them in the iron box attached to Al Zaoud. Once this was done the grate was locked closed. Instantly I heard the rats scratching furiously against the metal.

Bratianu stroked his black beard while observing this, then in an almost giddy tone, said, "They need some encouragement."

He took one of the torches from the wall and held it close to the iron box. Soon the scratching against metal stopped with the sound replaced by a more frantic scratching against hardened flesh, and soon mixed into this were grunts of pain from Al Zaoud.

"Within hours they will have dug their way into his stomach cavity where they will nest," the White Devil explained. "The agony that this heathen will suffer will be excruciating, and it will only become more unbearable over the next several years as they hollow him out completely from the inside. This agony will be his salvation.

DAVE ZELTSERMAN

His pathway to atonement. As these creatures consume him, so will they also consume all of his godlessness."

I didn't know whether Bratianu believed the nonsense he was spouting, but I didn't care. Nor did it bother me that I brought Al Zaoud to this horrific fate. Hell, if I could've thrown another demon rat or two into that box, I would've done so gladly.

From the way Bratianu was looking at me, it was clear he was expecting some sort of response. While staring into Al Zaoud's rage-filled eyes, I mustered up all the false sincerity I was capable of and told the White Devil that all of us were grateful to him for his devotion. "You're doing God's work here," I said with a straight face.

Chapter 21

The White Devil's portal was located at a mausoleum in Cypress Hills. When I stepped out of Bratianu's hell and into my own, I was glad to see that my squirrely new cabbie, Paulie, had waited for me. If he hadn't it would've been a long seven mile walk back to my office. When I got in the back of the cab, Paulie while in the midst of a nervous spasm blinked out a Morse code message. "These places give me the willies," he mumbled under his breath.

"You don't know the half of it."

He squinted in a confused way as if what I said didn't make any sense to him, but he didn't bother asking what I meant by my crack. I had to control myself from reaching out and mussing up his hair. That's how fucking fantastic I was feeling. *On top of the world*, as Jimmy Cagney from *White Heat* might've said. If I was in a Disney cartoon I would've broken out whistling a happy tune. Who could blame me? Al Zaoud and his threat to do horrible things to me had been weighing on me ever since that first time he invaded my reality. I knew eventually a soul as dangerous or more so than Al Zaoud would put me under a similar threat—and who knows, maybe that soul would turn out to be the White Devil. But I didn't care. With that psychotic barbarian out of commission, at least for now, I was safe.

Thoughts buzzed through my mind like an angry nest of hornets as I sat in the cab and watched my version of Brooklyn pass by me. With a start I realized my arm no longer hurt. I didn't have a sling for it anymore—I'd lost that when I entered Bratianu's reality. That's the way things work here; when you move between different hells the only thing you keep are the clothes on your back. I flexed my arm several times. The sleeve on my suit was still torn to ribbons, but my arm was fine. Maybe that was a parting gift from Bratianu. Or maybe finally having the weight of Al Zaoud's threat off my back allowed me to progress to where I was able to heal myself, even if I didn't realize I was doing it. Whichever it was, I couldn't keep from grinning.

I was far too hyped up to go back to the office, and I was feeling too good to want to sit among the usual group of degenerate alkies at the Gotham Lounge, so instead I had the cabbie let me off in front of the Busted Grill Diner. Like all the other times I'd been there, I was the only customer. After I sat at the counter I nodded to Doris. She was in the same generic waitress uniform that she always wore, her bluish-gray hair molded into its usual beehive. She moved quickly over to me so she could mop up the counter. As she did this she gave me a wink, and asked, "What will it be, Hon?"

"Coffee, black, and a grilled ham and cheese."

Doris twisted her neck back toward the grill area and yelled, "You got that, you deaf old fool?"

The grotesquely-scarred scarecrow, Max, who had taken over for Charlie, looked out from the grill area, a hurt expression showing on his nightmare face. A few seconds later I heard the sizzling of ham slices on the grill, and as I smelled the meat cooking I found myself salivating. You never really get hungry in hell, or thirsty for that matter. It's more that you trick yourself into thinking you are, and at that moment I was doing a good job with both. Doris brought over a mug of coffee, and I took a long sip, savoring it.

"Whatever happened with that murder case?" Doris asked. She tried to act as if she were just making casual conversation, but the way her tongue darted out and wetted her lips betrayed her interest in this. "You nail that mob enforcer for it?"

I stared at her blankly, at first confused, and then I remembered that weeks ago I had told her about Vogel's case and how I suspected Borelli of killing him. It surprised me at first that she remembered it as well as she did, but I guess she wasn't going to be chewing the fat with too many other customers, nor did Max look like the talkative type. My conversations with her were probably the only ones she ever has.

"It turns out the mob guy didn't do it," I said.

"Huh? How's that possible? Didn't that sleazebag lawyer send him up the river so he could keep banging the guy's wife?"

"Yeah, well, I was able to confirm he didn't know about the affair. Also the lawyer worked his ass off to keep the sentence as short as it was. At least the mob guy believes that's what happened. He's not the killer. But I've got another lead."

"Yeah, Mike, really? So who's the new suspect?"

Doris had rested her thick forearms on the counter. She leaned closer to me, her expression tense as she eagerly waited for any tidbit I could give. As I looked at her I started seeing her as she really was. I no longer saw a friendly, gossiping, grandmotherly-type who waited on me at the diner, but a severely twisted soul who when she was alive made her living by exploiting young girls and robbing them of any future. And now she was little more than a parasite feeding off my reality.

My good mood quickly soured and I ended up losing my appetite even before I saw how Max had burnt the grilled sandwich to charcoal. Just as earlier I had tricked myself into feeling hungry, for years now I'd been tricking myself into believing that I had some sort of bond with squatters like Doris. But now that I no longer had to worry about Al Zaoud, I could see things clearly. None of it was real before. It was all only an illusion, something I had tricked myself into believing. The truth was I had no connection with them, no camaraderie, nothing, and I was as isolated from them as they were from me. But unlike them I had an escape from this god-awful eternity. My cases. Those were my salvation.

Doris placed the blackened sandwich in front of me. "I hope you don't mind but it looks like Max might've burnt this a little. It ain't so bad, though. If you use your knife you can scrape off the burnt parts. Now what were you telling me about your new murder suspect?"

I stumbled off the counter stool desperate to get out of there and away from her. A hysteria edged into Doris's voice as she yelled out, "Hon, wait! I'll get him to grill you up another, and this time it won't be burnt! I promise!"

I mumbled something about needing to meet with a client, and continued toward the door. As I was leaving the diner Doris screamed at Max, "Goddamn you! Can't you grill anything without burning it! Your lousy cooking chased him out of here! I'm going to take that cleaver and chop you into fish bait!"

I quickened my pace to get the hell away from there.

I guess it's possible to have breakdowns in hell because I must've been having a mini one, but I don't see how anyone could blame me. When I was sitting there with Doris less than two feet away from me and edging closer, it was like I could see all of the evil rotting away inside of her. It was almost like I could taste her evil in the back of my throat.

As you can probably guess, I wasn't in the best state of mind as I walked the three blocks back to my office. And things didn't improve any when I was half a block away and looked behind me to see a demon Rottweiler racing after me. I don't know what caused me to look back, but all I could do was stare dumbly at that beast for a good three seconds before it clicked in my mind what I was seeing. Once I realized it was the surviving Rottweiler from the Nazi Colonel's hell, I started running as if my life depended on it. Of course, that beast wouldn't have been able to kill me, but it wouldn't have been much fun spending the rest of eternity after being torn apart by him.

I couldn't even begin to guess how that demon Rottweiler survived the obliteration of that Nazi's world, but somehow he did and he had tracked me down to my own reality. Goddamn it, it was always something in hell. If it wasn't a psychotic ancient barbarian threatening me it was two hundred pounds of snarling demonic fury chasing after me. Needless to say seeing that dog scared the bejesus out of me. I doubted whether I could've run any faster right then even if Satan himself was chasing after me with a pitchfork.

If I'd had more than half a block to go, that demon dog would've gotten me. I had no doubt about that. But somehow I made it inside my building a couple of seconds before that Rottweiler could reach me, and watched as the dog bumped his head against the glass door. The beast let out an angry yelp and backed up a few feet, his head cocked to one side as he stared at me, his eyes blood red. Damn, he was an ugly creature. Bigger and more muscular than a normal Rottweiler, his head grossly misshapen, a yellowish-greenish foam dripping from his muzzle. For the next minute we both stood on our respective sides of the glass door staring at each other. Me, so I could catch my breath and wait for my heart to slow down, that beast, God knows why. Once I felt steadier I headed for the staircase.

I wasn't about to stay locked up in the building forever because of a vengeful demon dog. I was going to have to find something in the building that I could use to kill him, and then hunt him down. Those were the thoughts running through my mind as I climbed the stairs, and I'd made it up two flights when I heard the crash from below. At first I wasn't sure I really heard what I thought I did, and wondered whether I'd only imagined it. After all I was kind of jumpy right then, and could've blown out of proportion any creaking or other noise that building might've belched out. But when I heard the Rottweiler scampering up the stairs after me, I started running.

I had two flights of stairs ahead of me before I'd reach my office. The demon dog was able to run faster than me, but he wasn't doing so well keeping his footing on the wooden stairs, and I could hear him sliding into the wall every time he tried rounding a corner. I was going to make it, but then what? If the dog could crash through the building's front door, he should be able to do the same with the frosted glass door of my office. But maybe not. With the other door he was able to get a running start, and he wouldn't have that chance with my office. Yeah, he could build up some speed running down the hallway, but then he'd have to take a sharp ninety degree turn to hit the door.

I got an idea then of what I could use to kill the damn thing.

The Rottweiler was still a full flight of stairs behind me by the time I reached the floor my office was on. I knew it was only a trick of the mind, but it felt as if a burst of adrenaline was pounding through me pushing me harder. I just hoped I had time to do what I needed to do. When I flung open my office door and Vera looked up at me startled, I realized the revelation I'd had with Doris didn't fit with her. Vera was more of a broken soul than evil, and I found that I still cared about her. I certainly didn't want to see her torn to pieces by that demon animal.

"Get into my private office now," I told her as I gasped for breath.

"Mike, what's the gag?"

She didn't move. Instead she stayed seated behind the reception desk and stared at me wide-eyed. I had upended the coatrack, and I stomped on it breaking it in half. The coatrack was made of oak, and the splintered end of the piece I held might've been sharp enough

DAVE ZELTSERMAN

to ram through that dog's hide. At least I hoped it was. I growled at Vera to get a move on. "I mean it. Go in there now and barricade the door. It's not safe here."

"This isn't funny, Mike. You're scaring me."

While still holding onto my makeshift spear, I moved toward her with the intention of dragging her out of her chair and throwing her into my office if I had to, but I was interrupted by the Rottweiler crashing through the outer door. Shards of glass exploded into the room as the beast landed on all fours. I lifted my makeshift spear, preparing myself to drive it into the beast when he jumped at me. The demon dog, though, let out a couple of snorts, took a few steps toward me, and then lay down on the floor and stretched his legs.

"Ah, he's a cutie," Vera cooed. She finally got out of her chair, but this was so she could kneel next to the dog and scratch him behind his ear. While she did this the beast let out another snort. She looked up at me and asked what the dog's name was.

While the dog lay on the floor he kept one eye glued on me. The damn thing hadn't been chasing after me for revenge. Instead it was simply because he needed a new home and decided to adopt me as his new owner. It looked like I now had myself a demon dog. I dropped my makeshift spear and let out my breath. The last few moment I'd forgotten that I'd been holding it.

Vera had lifted the demon Rottweiler's head off the floor so she could wrap her arms around his neck and give him a hug. The beast consented to let her do this and only let out an embarrassed grunt in response. After a minute of this, Vera scrunched her face, annoyed at me. "Come on, Mike," she said. "What's this handsome lug's name?"

I continued to stare at the damn beast while he stared back at me. "Bob," I said.

Chapter 22

Bob was a dumb name for a dog, even if it was for a demon beast. I knew that as soon as I told it to Vera. But I never had a pet before—not when I was alive and certainly not since I'd been dead. I didn't want to come up with a cutesy name tied to hell, like Cerberus, and names like Spot or Rover didn't fit. I guess I could've given the beast a German name like Hans or Siegfried, but I decided to name him after Bob Mantero, a PI from the same firm where I worked when I was alive. Mantero was a big, ugly sonofabitch, and neither of us ever fully trusted the other. From the wary looks the demon dog and I were giving each other, the same was still true.

Before this I had always wondered whether the demon animals I encountered in other hells were simply imagined for their hells in the same way that my New York landscape was imagined for mine. Now I had my answer. Bob had to be real, otherwise he would've faded from existence with the rest of that Nazi's hell when it was destroyed, and he damn well wouldn't have been able to jump from one hell into another. He wasn't a dog, but instead something spawned here in hell. And now he appeared to be mine. Or Vera's. If she wanted to spend the rest of eternity hugging that beast, that was okay with me.

I started toward my private office, and the moment my hand touched the doorknob I heard a grunting noise and then what must've been Bob pushing himself to his feet. So he was going to follow me wherever I went. Fine.

I left the door open. There was no reason to have him smashing his way through that door also.

Of course, the throne, chalice and barrel of wine that Bratianu had conjured up earlier in my office were all gone as those objects would've disappeared the moment Bratianu stepped out of my hell. I was surprised, though, to find two steak dinners sitting on my desk. Vera knew I was just getting rid of her when I sent her out for them, and I didn't think she'd bother with them. I tossed one of the steaks to Bob and started on the other myself. The steak was cold, but it didn't matter. I was eating just to give myself something to do while I thought about my two open investigations.

Vogel's case had pretty much hit a dead end once again, at least until Thomas Hilliard becomes worm food. That would happen eventually, and when it did I had little doubt that he'd end up here in hell, but until then I was stuck. If I could get the name of the girl killed in the jewelry store robbery maybe that might lead somewhere, but I wasn't going to get it from Vogel. I could see when I visited him that I had no chance of prying that out of him. It didn't matter. For now I was more interested in working Ruby Jane's case, and with the information I had gotten from Eloise Halprin and that dirtbag Rascine, hers was wide open. It was time for Ruby and me to have another chat.

I tossed Bob the rest of my steak which he swallowed whole without chewing. After knocking back two thick fingers of whiskey, I headed out to the reception area with Bob tagging close behind. I winced when I saw the busted up coatrack and all the broken glass scattered along the floor, and even more seeing the office door. A piece of jagged broken glass remained attached to the top of the door frame, and my name was cut down the middle leaving the outline of a lightning bolt. It was a mess. Vera didn't seem to mind. She sat at her reception desk absorbed in one of her romance magazines as if nothing had happened earlier. If she was at all interested in her new best pal, Bob, she didn't show it by bothering to look up once from her magazine. Then again, Bob didn't pay her the time of day as we made our way through the reception area and out of the office.

If there was any sort of symmetry in hell, the portal to Ruby's reality would've been located in the same Bronx neighborhood that made up her world, but instead it was at a Laundromat in Queens. Fortunately Paulie had his cab waiting at the usual spot as otherwise it would've been a long walk to Ruby's portal. Bob barreled into the cab taking up a good part of the back seat, and I squeezed in next to him. It was obvious from the way Paulie was squirming around in the driver's seat and sneaking peeks at Bob in the rearview mirror that he didn't like having a dog in the cab, but he waited until we had gotten out of Brooklyn before complaining about it, saying how the dog was slobbering all over the seat and making a mess back there. "That dog smells bad also," Paulie added in an excitable voice. "I don't want him in my cab."

Paulie was right, of course. Along with the same yellowish-greenish foam dripping from Bob's muzzle, thick strands of drool also oozed out of the side of his mouth, and all of it smelled like a bad mix of ammonia and pungent body odor. What happened next surprised me. Before Paulie had said that, the Rottweiler had been lying on the seat curled up, but all at once he reared up snarling, his fangs bared. It was almost as if he understood what Paulie had said. And maybe he did. After all, he was something demonic that only resembled a dog.

Paulie was squirming and blinking so hard I thought he was going to crash the cab. He was too scared to spit out any words, but he let out a high-pitched scream. This was a guy who normally sounded like a bullfrog on downers and now he was screaming like a teenage girl. He had every right to be scared out of his mind. He must've thought the demon dog was about to rip his head off, and I thought so too, and there was nothing I could've done to stop him. Bob was two hundred pounds of muscle spawned in hell, and if I tried grabbing him he would've dragged me along. But I had an idea of something to try.

"Relax," I said. "The dog's just smiling. Nothing more. Because he knows I don't want him to hurt you."

Bob grudgingly lay back down after that. He continued to show his fangs, but his snarling subsided to more of an ill-tempered growling. There was no question anymore about it. Bob understood what was being said. And it appeared he was on the touchy side. I told him to stop his growling. He didn't look too happy with the request but he did as I asked.

DAVE ZELTSERMAN

Once the demon Rottweiler settled back down, Paulie stopped his screeching. He continued to blink like crazy, but we made it in one piece to the address in Queens where Ruby Jane's portal was located. By the time we left the cab, it was pretty rancid in the backseat from all of Bob's foam and drool and other odors he had released. I told Paulie to find a cleaning supply store so he could deal with the mess, and to wait for me back at the Laundromat. His small dark face showed a dozen different nervous twitches as he reluctantly nodded.

This time when I crossed Ruby's portal instead of slipping into her world I absorbed her hell into mine, and as soon as I did I saw one of her squatters lying catatonic in the middle of the Laundromat. I was sure if I looked out in the street I'd see others, but I didn't bother. I yelled out for Ruby without getting any response. She wasn't in the main area of the Laundromat, but she had to be someplace nearby. Bob cocked his head to one side as if he were listening for something, and then he raced toward the back of the building. A few seconds later I heard him barking, if you could call the hellish, guttural noises he made barking. I followed after him.

His barking led me down a staircase and to the basement where I found him making his god-awful caterwauling. I opened the door for the room he seemed so keen on and muscled my way past him. Ruby was standing in the middle of a utility room looking scared out of her mind. Her face was as pale as the moon and her mouth was frozen into something resembling a knife gash, and while she still had on the same black dress I'd first seen her in, it was torn from her collarbone area to halfway down her waist and was barely hanging onto her body. As she stared at me, her knees began knocking so badly that I was sure she was going to collapse, but then she recognized me and seemed to steady herself.

"Mike, is that you?" she asked, her voice so feeble that it got to me.

"Yeah, it's me. There's nothing to worry about. I absorbed you into my world so we could talk, that's all."

She bit her lip and nodded, but I wasn't a hundred percent convinced that she understood me. She had regressed so much since the last time I saw her, and all of her cockiness from our first meeting was gone. Something had happened to her.

Bob bulled his way into the room, and when Ruby saw him she stepped back and almost toppled over in her stiletto heels.

"He won't hurt you," I said, more for Bob's benefit than Ruby's. She didn't seem so sure of that, but when the Rottweiler plodded over to her she stood her ground and gave him a halfhearted pat on top of his grossly misshapen skull.

"You have a dog here?" Ruby asked.

"Yeah, I guess I do."

"I don't remember seeing him before. You didn't have him earlier, did you?"

"Nope. He adopted me only recently."

Ruby gave Bob another unenthusiastic pat. "How come you brought me here this time?" she asked.

I smiled as pleasantly as I could manage, which is no easy task in hell. Wicked, nasty, and vicious smiles were no problem, but a pleasant smile is an entirely different matter.

"I thought it would be nicer this way so I can take you to a diner and get you some decent food while we talk."

She accepted that, or at least seemed to. That wasn't my real reason. I had a better chance of shaking the truth out of her if I got her off her home turf. Ruby didn't look too sure on her feet so I offered her my arm and she accepted it. I thought about asking her what had happened, but decided to wait. As we made our way out of the room Ruby asked me if she was going to get sick again like the first two times she entered my reality.

"This is your third time in my world, so probably not. If you are going to get sick it will take longer to happen this time. And if you start feeling that oncoming vertigo let me know and I'll get you back to your world."

"I don't want to go back." She said this in such a meek little girl's voice that it made wonder again what the hell had happened to her. Her grip on my arm tightened. "What would happen if I stayed here in your version of New York?"

"It wouldn't work. After a few days you'd lose yourself and become a zombie, which would be a far worse fate than whatever right now is going on in your world."

Ruby's face darkened as if a storm were brewing, and while she still tightly clutched my arm she didn't say another word as we made our way up the stairs. There wasn't much room on those steps, and her slender body had to press firmly against mine for the two of us to make it up the stairs together, but she wasn't about to let go of me.

It was when we walked into the main part of the Laundromat that I felt her body stiffen. I gave her a quick look. The muscles along her jaw and mouth were rigid and her eyes had narrowed to harsh slits. I realized she was staring at the comatose squatter lying in the middle of the room. The squatter was in his thirties, and wore a sleeveless muscle shirt, jeans, and black biker boots. He was on the short side, but thick in the body, and as we continued toward him I got a better look at his abnormally large shaved head and thick, dark rat's nest of a beard.

"Do you know him?" I asked.

We were about five feet away from him when Ruby came to a stop. She let go of my arm and stood with her hands clenched into small fists at her side. For a good ten count she seemed incapable of talking, then she told me how she had left Diablos with the gun I had given her.

"This was a couple of hours after you left me," she said in a robotic-like voice, almost as if she were in a trance. "I had been trapped in that nightclub for so long that I felt like I had to get out of there, even if it was only for a few minutes. I thought I would be safe with the gun you gave me. But I was outside for only a few minutes when he came at me."

Her mouth clamped shut, and for several long seconds her mouth moved as if she were chewing gum. I had a sick feeling in my gut what she was going to tell me, and when she could talk again she told me how she was holding the gun out in front of her with both hands, and that the guy just kept running toward her.

"I didn't want to miss him, so I waited for him to get only a few feet from me before I pulled the trigger. But just as I was feeling the trigger pull back the gun disappeared. No bullet was fired. Without a gun to protect myself he easily overpowered me and dragged me back inside of Diablos. Since then he's been doing things to me. At least until a few minutes ago."

"I'm so sorry, Ruby."

She turned to me, her eyes brimming with pain. "Why did that gun disappear like it did?" she asked.

"It was my fault. I didn't realize at the time that the things I created inside of your world would disappear the moment I left it, and I guess I must've crossed back into my world just as you were firing the gun. I'm sorry that happened. I wish it hadn't."

I felt sick to my stomach over what I had inadvertently done to her. It wasn't just because of bad timing that things worked out the way it did with the gun and that lowlife scum. In hell, the only luck you ever had was the worst possible kind. Once I had conjured up that gun for Ruby, I had set all of that in motion without realizing it. Fuck.

"I don't want him coming back to my New York," Ruby said.

"He won't. At least there won't be enough left of him to ever hurt you again. He's going to remain comatose like that until after you return back to your world. If it will help you to see what's done to him I can take care of him now, or I can wait until later. Your choice."

Ruby squeezed her eyes shut causing thin lines to crease her brow. The memory of what she had suffered through seemed to weigh down her features as she shook her head. "I don't want to see it," she said. "I want him hurt badly, and I want him to never be able to hurt me again, but I don't want to see it. At least not now."

"Okay, later."

We sidestepped past the thug scumbag and walked out of the Laundromat. Paulie had parked his cab across the street. As we walked toward it, I was explaining to Ruby how we were in Queens when I caught a shadow of something large flying at me out of the corner of my eye. I reacted by turning away from it and shielding Ruby. Bob, though, reacted differently. He sprang into the air and grabbed the thing. It turned out to be a winged creature, except much bigger than I first thought. It must've had a good six-foot wingspan, and its hairless body was the size of a large alley cat, its face somewhere between a rat's and a baboon's. It was a demon of some sort, and it tried to fight back as Bob went at it, but it had no chance even with its razor-like talons. Within seconds Bob had ripped off one of its wings, and then seconds later bit the demon in half. After that he tore apart the other wing and gobbled up what was left of the demon.

Whatever that thing was, it wasn't from my world. I must've absorbed it from Ruby's. I searched the sky to see if there were any others flying around, but there didn't appear to be. When I looked over at Ruby there was an expression of horror on her face, but also recognition. She knew what that thing was.

"What was it?"

DAVE ZELTSERMAN

She shook her head, her lips pressing into two bloodless lines.

"Uh uh," I said. "That demon came from your hell, and I know you recognized it. So you're not going to get away with stonewalling me this time."

Ruby's mouth weakened as she stared numbly at Bob crunching on the demon's talons. They were the only parts still remaining from the demon other than some fragments from its wings, and Bob chomped on those talons as if they were chicken bones. Ruby told me that she used to have nightmares about that demon. "This was when I was maybe eight or nine," she said. "I hadn't thought about those nightmares in years, and I never saw that thing in my New York."

The demon attack left her shakier than before. I had to help her to the cab, and after I got her in the backseat, I brought Bob back to the Laundromat. There was no time like the present to take care of the squatter who had tormented Ruby and was singlehandedly responsible for her regressing as much as she had. I had previously only seen unawares manifest nightmarish demons for their hells, and for Ruby to have done so must've meant she was on the verge of slipping into unawareness. That was how dire her situation had become.

I had Bob rip the head off of the squatter, but I decided that wouldn't be enough. When her hell reconstituted itself, the odds were good that that squatter's remains would end up inside of Diablos, and I didn't want Ruby having to keep stumbling across it. Bob was more than up to the task, so I had him devour the head. Normally something like that would've been gruesome to watch, but in this case I didn't mind one bit, and at some point while Bob was crunching the skull into bone meal he succeeded in obliterating the squatter enough to where the remains faded from sight. That meant the squatter had sunk into a private hell. I took a small bit of satisfaction in knowing that whatever that hell ended up being, he was going to suffer far worse than what he'd put Ruby through.

Chapter 23

Years ago I had stumbled across a diner in the Astoria section of Queens, and like the Busted Grill Diner it had a squatter acting as a waitress and another as the short order cook. I had Paulie take us there. The place cooked up roughly the same fare that the Busted Grill did, but the cook didn't have a nightmare face and he didn't burn everything.

The same two squatters were still on the job, and Ruby and I took a booth while Bob lay down next to it. The diner had another customer; a short, heavyset guy who sat at the counter and dug away at an apple pie topped off with what must've been a gallon of vanilla ice cream. He was sweating as he ate, and didn't look particularly happy, but he kept shoveling the food in. Every minute or so he'd twist his thick neck around to give Bob an annoyed look, but whatever he wanted to say he held it in.

The squatter acting as the waitress was a bone thin, skittish woman of about fifty with bulging eyes that looked like they could pop out of the sockets. She was nervous when she took our order, and even more so when she brought the food. Maybe it was because she felt as if she was auditioning for our business, or maybe it was the way Bob licked his chops when he looked at her.

Ruby had ordered a hot turkey sandwich and a chocolate milkshake while I stuck with black coffee. Her eyes opened with amazement when she bit into the sandwich.

"This tastes like real turkey," she said, as if awestruck.

I waited until she ate more of her food before telling her that she had to quit lying to me.

She reacted to that almost as if I'd slapped her. Half under her breath she muttered that she hadn't been lying to me.

I leaned back and sipped my coffee while she fidgeted uncomfortably. She knew I was looking at her, and she tried to meet my gaze, but couldn't do it.

I let a deep sigh rumble out of my chest. "Ruby, all my clients lie to me, and I really don't care. It's certainly not something I take personally. The thing is they're so filled with self-denial that they can't help themselves. And it doesn't much matter to me. I know when they're lying, and I'm going to end up at the truth no matter what they tell me."

She was trying hard to look at me, but she still couldn't force herself to do it. Watching her made me think of a magnet being repelled. "Everything I've told you has been the truth," she said in a dead-like voice.

"Come on, Ruby, I'm not an idiot. You wouldn't have hired me if I was an idiot. I've talked with Eloise Halprin and Dickie Rascine's charming brother, Brad. I know you didn't have the family life you told me you did. I know you grew up in foster care, and I know what those sick fucks the McClechans did to you. I know you were never married to anyone named Tyler Jane. And I know what you and Dickie Rascine did to make money."

She was shaking her head, her stare frozen onto her clasped hands. She looked utterly lost, but still she persisted in telling me that I was wrong.

"Look, Ruby, normally I wouldn't care about this," I said. "I would just wait for Dickie Rascine to die and end up in hell, because I'm pretty sure I'll be able to get out of him what I need to solve your murder. But the problem is by the time that happens I won't be able to collect payment from you."

"Why's that?"

"Because you're heading in the wrong direction, and if things keep going the way they are you're going to lose all awareness and end up as a zombie, or worse, sinking into a private hell that will be infinitely more horrific than anything you could imagine."

What I said stunned her enough to look at me. Her voice trembled as she asked, "How can you say that?"

I could've explained to her how all the brashness and confidence that she exhibited the first time she came to my office was gone and had been replaced by confusion and fear, but instead I kept it simple and more direct.

"Unaware souls manifest demons to torment them. The fact that you had brought that winged demon into your hell shows that you're on the brink of slipping into unawareness, and if that happens I won't be able to collect payment from you when I solve your case. Well, technically I'd still be able to collect, but it would be about as much fun as sleeping with a corpse, which is something I'm just not into."

That got her angry. That was obvious from the heat flaring up in her eyes. Good. I needed her angry. The angrier the better.

"So that's all you care about. Fucking me."

"You got it, baby doll. I told you when you hired me that I'm no white knight. When I take a case I expect to be paid."

She was simmering in her anger now. I had a chance of turning her around. "You're such an asshole," she said.

"I'm an asshole who collects what's owed me."

"If you're so fucking brilliant, then what do I do to change things?"

I had to fight to keep from smiling. She was pissed enough now to show flashes of her earlier self. As nonchalantly as I could manage, I told her how denial was a killer here in hell. "Look, it sucks here," I said. "I mean, it's hell, so it's going to suck no matter what. But the more aware you are, the better chance you have of it sucking just a little bit less. And the path to greater awareness is to cut through your denial. If you can tell me one true thing that can help me in solving your case, it would go a long way in helping with your awareness."

She dropped her knife and fork. Her mouth was pinched with anger and her eyes were little more than chunks of dark emerald ice as she stared at me with this white hot intensity as if she were trying to burn a hole through me. Again, all this was good. I felt better about her chances now.

"I had a fiancée," she said in a voice that was meant to cut to the bone. "Bruce Dudley."

"Yeah? Tell me about Dudley."

An exhaustion seemed to wash over her features, and whatever

DAVE ZELTSERMAN

heat had been burning inside her died out then. "He was a good man," she said. "An honest man. Nothing at all like Dickie. He was going to take care of me. But he died."

"How'd he die?"

"He got sick. Okay?"

Ruby pushed her plate away. "I'd like to get the hell out of your hell," she said, her eyes glazing and growing distant. "The doorway back to mine is in Brooklyn. How about being a sport and giving me a lift in that taxi? You can add it to your bill."

"Sure. But why don't you eat the rest of your food? It could be a while before you get a chance to eat again."

A spark of anger again flashed in her eyes as she glared at me. "Why would that matter to you?" she demanded.

I shrugged. "No real reason. But I like the girls I bang to have a little meat on their bones."

She whispered *asshole* loud enough for me to hear her, but she also picked up her fork and knife and somewhat reluctantly continued eating her food. She wasn't about to give me the satisfaction of further acknowledging my presence other than by what she had whispered, but that was fine.

Of course what I told her was utter nonsense. Eating and drinking are only illusions in hell, and it's certainly not something you're going to gain any weight from. But nothing cuts through denial like anger. If I pissed her off enough to tell me something with a kernel of truth in it, then it was all worth it. I was sure that what she told me about Dudley wasn't entirely true, but there was something to it. Maybe it would help me in solving her murder, maybe not, but I had the sense that she was no longer on the verge of slipping into unawareness, so it was all good. The illusion of eating was also good for her. The deep-seated memories that it triggers can provide additional comfort, which Ruby needed right then.

As Ruby was finishing up her sandwich and milkshake, she looked like she had a question for me, but didn't want to give me the satisfaction of asking me anything. I couldn't help smiling, and I asked her if she wanted anything else to eat.

She shook her head.

"What's troubling you?"

That actually got a small smile out of her. "Other than having to spend eternity in hell?" she asked.

"Yeah, other than that?"

"These souls who take up residence in our hells, like that fat slob over there stuffing his face with pie and ice cream—"

"Hey, for Chrissakes, I'm sitting right here! You think I'm deaf and can't hear what you're saying about me?"

That came from the fat pie-eating slob sitting at the counter. At first he just stared incensed at Ruby. But then as his round face started turning a bright beet red he slid off his counter stool, and with his pudgy hands folded into fists came charging our table like a mad bull. At that moment he must've been blind to everything in the diner except Ruby. "Goddamned little cunt!" he swore, pie crumbs tumbling from his ice cream smudged pie hole. "You're going to call me a fat slob?"

Up until then Bob had been resting quietly with his eyes closed. I guess it must've been tiring for him locating me and traversing hells. But the fat slob's yelling had him rearing up and showing his fangs. A snarl that sounded as if it had been unleashed from the bowels of hell roared out of him. The fat slob stopped dead in his tracks, his eyes opening wide as he remembered about the demon Rottweiler. He turned and ran for the door. He almost made it but Bob caught up to him at the last second and sank his fangs into his right thigh, and then dragged him screaming out of the diner. The screams continued for another thirty seconds and then stopped abruptly. The bone-thin waitress wandered over to where the pie-eater had been sitting and cleaned up the counter area. She acted as if nothing had happened. I did the same. Ruby's expression had turned ashen.

"Aren't you going to do anything?" she asked.

"Nope, no reason to. This is hell, right? The guy is only getting what he deserves."

"Because he yelled at me?"

"If it was up to him he would've done a lot more than just yell at you. But no, it's because of a life of evil acts. His soul was rotten to the core. Forget about him. Let me guess, though, what you were going to ask me before he interrupted you, and that's how come unawares like him get to spend his eternity eating pie and ice cream while your hell is no picnic. Is that what you were going to ask?"

She blinked at me several times still shaken up by what she saw.

DAVE ZELTSERMAN

She said, "Something like that."

I leaned over the table toward Ruby and kept my voice low as I explained the truth about squatters to her. I saw no reason to let the squatters acting as waitress and cook overhear me and possibly freak out and turn into zombies.

"It pretty much sucks being a squatter. They have no identity to lean on, and until things turn south for them, their existence is soul deadening monotony. And as you just witnessed, things can turn south for them in a heartbeat. How about we get out of here?"

I noticed Ruby had started to look a little green around the gills. It had to be the vertigo illness. Usually you didn't get it your third time visiting the same hell, but her awareness was so damn weak. She looked unsteady as she got to her feet, but she wouldn't take my arm for support. She wasn't about to forgive me. As long as it kept her from sliding into unawareness, I was fine with that.

When we stepped out of the diner, Bob and the pie-eater were nowhere in sight. Bob must've dragged the guy someplace private where he could eat in peace. It was going to be a heavy meal, and maybe the demon dog needed to take a nap afterward. I had no doubt that he'd be finding me later.

I got Ruby into the passenger seat of the cab. After I had her give me the address where her portal was located, I directed Paulie back to Brooklyn. Along the way I asked Ruby where her portal would leave her.

"What do you mean?"

"Whether it leaves you inside Diablos or outside of it."

"Why would that matter?"

"I'm assuming Diablos is locked up. If your portal leaves you outside of it, then I'll need to go to your reality so I can help you find a way into the nightclub."

"Why would you bother doing that?"

"I've got to protect my investment."

There was a good minute of stony silence from her, then, "You really are rotten through and through."

"I never said I wasn't."

Chapter 24

Ruby now despised me, but that was okay as long as I kept her from slipping into unawareness, and I was pretty sure I did. When I left her at her portal she was closer to being the same tough, brash version of herself that I had first met. And it would be better for her to simmer in anger toward me than to spend her time dwelling on what that lowlife scum did to her after dragging her back into that nightclub.

When I returned to my office building, I went straight to the basement and the Hell directories. There was almost a full directory of Dudleys, and ninety-three of them were named Bruce, but none of them was the guy I was looking for. Assuming Ruby had leveled with me, that meant the Bruce Dudley she was engaged to really was a decent guy and ended up in the other place. Which meant I'd hit another dead-end.

I went over those ninety-three Bruce Dudleys a dozen times hoping I'd missed something, but I didn't feel anything with them. If I tried visiting them I'd only be wasting my time. While I sat in that musty basement room wondering what I could do next to solve Ruby's case, I started thinking about the other guy she claimed was her husband, Tyler Jane, and wondered where that name came from. Then I started thinking of what she told me her maiden name had been, and that's when inspiration hit. I put back the directory listings for Dudleys, and found the book that would list all the Harmons in hell, and sure enough, there he was. Tyler Harmon. A hard grin twisted my lips as I stared at his listing. Whatever it is that lets me know when I've found the soul I'm looking for was now going off like a fire alarm. I touched Harmon's name in the directory and had to pull my finger back to keep it from burning. As it was I singed the skin. Yeah, he was the one I wanted. This damn case wasn't cold yet.

Tyler Harmon's portal was located in a crumbling, fire-damaged tenement building in the Port Morris section of the Bronx. All in all it was a pretty crummy neighborhood teeming with squatters acting as drug dealers and thugs and I wouldn't have minded having Bob keeping me company, but he hadn't come back by the time I left. It turned out not to matter. While the squatters gave me their thousand yard stares, they kept their distance.

The interior of the building smelled heavily of smoke and the walls were charred black, but at least I didn't have to deal with any squatters as I made my way up three flight of stairs. It was almost a relief when I got to escape the heavy stench of smoke and slip into Harmon's private hell. The portal left me standing hidden in the shadows where I could observe what appeared to be a game of darts between two ape-like demons with Tyler Harmon acting as the dartboard. They weren't actually throwing darts, but daggers, and at first I wasn't exactly sure what I was watching.

Harmon stood naked against a wall, his wrists and ankles in manacles. His body was covered with knife wounds and scars, and bits and pieces of him were missing, the most prominent being his penis and testicles. Even with the damage that had been done to him, it was easy to see that he would've been a good-looking guy in his early thirties when he died.

The two demons were standing near the wall opposite Harmon, about thirty feet away from him. Earlier I called them ape-like, but as I watched them arguing, I decided they were more like orcs from the Ralph Bakshi *Lord of the Rings* cartoon I saw in the seventies. They were each about five feet tall, muscular, squat, hairless, and with rough gray skin that made me think of an elephant hide. Their faces, squarish and flat, were disproportionately large compared to their bodies, and long needle-shaped fangs protruded from thick frog-like lips.

When I first entered Harmon's hell, one of the demons was screeching at the other, all the while excitedly pointing at the demon's feet. It wasn't until the other demon let out an angry burst of his own garbled noises and took a step back that the first demon stopped his screeching. All appeared calm, and then this second demon lifted a dagger, aimed and threw it at Harmon hitting him flush in the cheek. The first demon let out a whoop and pumped his fist in what looked like a celebratory gesture while the knife-throwing demon barked out angrily. They then traded places, and when the other demon threw his knife and hit Harmon square in the nose, he started jumping up and down whooping and hollering while the first knife-thrower angrily cursed himself, or at least that was my take on what he was doing. That was when I figured out they were playing a form of darts with Harmon as their dartboard.

There were several more minutes of gloating from the winner and angry, bitter screeching from the loser, and then the two demons headed toward Harmon to retrieve their knives so they could play their next round. This game must've been going on for years, and Harmon should've been little more than hamburger meat by now, but those demons had to be healing Harmon's wounds quickly so they could keep the game going for the rest of eternity.

The demons didn't make it to Harmon. I had conjured up a net trap large enough to capture a Bengal tiger, and when one of the demons stepped on the trigger, it snared both of them.

The trap must've surprised the hell out of them. For a good thirty seconds they remained mute and motionless as they hung four feet in the air trapped in the netting, then they started struggling furiously and making a hellacious racket for all the good it was going to do them.

I stepped out of the shadows then. When the demons saw me they went ballistic, and their screeching rose to a migraine-inducing level. I needed to shut them up or I probably would've started bleeding from my ears and eyes, so I conjured up a baseball bat and took a dozen or so healthy swings at them, and by the end they stopped their screeching. I always find it satisfying to smack demons around, and this time proved more entertaining than usual. Nostalgic too. For the briefest of moments it fooled me into feeling like I was a kid again at my tenth birthday trying to break apart the piñata except this time I didn't have to wear a blindfold. I decided I would have to use this net trap trick on demons more often.

Once the demons grew mostly silent other than some occasional moaning and groaning, I heard Harmon's voice drifting in from behind me, asking if I could do him a favor and pull the knives out of his face. He talked in a painfully slow cadence and his voice had a weakness to it that made me think of a balloon losing air. Of course, the two knives stuck in his face probably had a lot to do with how he sounded.

Up close I could see that his eyes were a mass of scars and it was doubtful he could see me, at least more than as a shadow. The knife buried in the middle of his nose came out easily, the one in his cheek was stuck in bone and took some muscle to yank it out. There was less blood than I expected, and the wounds seemed to start healing the moment the knives came out.

"Thanks, buddy," Harmon said in his soft, wheezing, whispering-like voice. "Mucho appreciation. I can't see much anymore, just shapes really. Are those two bastard demons hanging upside down in a net like I think they are?"

"Yeah."

"You do that?"

"Yeah, I did."

"I owe you, buddy." He gave me a weak smile that made me think of a clown's smile given how his mouth seemed quite a bit larger than it really was thanks to all the knife wounds and scars at the edge of his lips. "I try not to give them any added satisfaction by showing them how much those knives hurt, but they hurt like a mother, although the anticipation of when the next one is coming is the worst." His voice slowed down to a softer hiss and he had to breathe in more air before he'd be able to leak out any more words. His chest was a relief map of wounds, and one or more of the knives thrown into him must've punctured a lung. Once he finished sucking in more air he told me how he knew those demons made him heal faster than normal, but he also knew that pieces of him had been lost over the years. "I know parts of my fingers are gone and both earlobes and other little bits here and there. Can I ask another favor? Do I still have my dick and balls, or are they gone like I've been imagining?"

"I'm sorry, they're gone."

"Ah shit, I thought I felt a little lighter down there." There was more breathing in and filling up so he'd be able to spill out more words. When he was able to he said, "I guess there's no use crying over spilt milk. How about another favor, and you free me?"

"I'm sorry, I can't do that."

He gave me another grotesque clown smile. "Is it that you don't want to or you're unable to?" he asked.

"Unable," I lied, because it would've been a piece of cake to free him, but if I did he'd keep asking for more and more, and I'd never get anything out of him. "Those manacles are solid iron, I don't see any key, and I have nothing to break them open with. You realize you're in hell, right?"

"I know where I am." All of Harmon's easy chumminess from before was gone, his face becoming as cold and harsh as a block of ice. "Those bastard demons have been using me for target practice for centuries, so yeah, I know where I am alright." More sucking in air. "I'd have to think if you're able to trap those bastards in a net, you'd be able to break me free, but whatever. What do you want?"

"Tell me about Ruby Jane."

That brought a crooked little smile to his lips. "Sweet Ruby," he said. He sucked in air to refill the tank. "That was so long ago. She must've been damned to hell ages ago also, huh?"

I ignored his question and asked, "Who killed her?"

"Ah, I'm sorry, buddy, I can't help you there seeing that as far as I know Ruby was alive and well at the time of my own death."

"How did you die?"

Another of his clown smiles, but there was more of a nastiness to this one. "In a very unpleasant way, but unrelated to Ruby."

He was holding back on me, and I considered pushing him for more details regarding his death, but decided to keep my questions focused on Ruby for the time being. After all, it wasn't as if he was going anywhere.

"Did you know Ruby before or after Dickie Rascine?"

"Ah Dickie, what a charmer he was. I knew Ruby while she was with that Neanderthal, and later after he got shipped off to Dannemora. I'm sure Dickie must be rotting in hell also."

"Tell me about Bruce Dudley."

It always happens with the unawares. At some point while I'm interrogating them in their private hells, they start thinking they can bargain with me. At that moment I could just about see the wheels spinning behind Harmon's badly scarred eyes, and I knew he was about to reach that same poorly conceived conclusion.

He smiled apologetically and said, "I don't want you to think I'm ungrateful for what you've done for me." There was more air sucking, then, "I mean, that was a neat trick capturing those two bastards. But it doesn't seem fair that I tell you everything you want to know when you won't get me out of these chains." He took another break to breathe, then, "Until you free me, I'm not telling you anything else."

He braced himself expecting me to try torturing the information out of him. When I conjured up a samurai sword sharp enough to cut brick, Harmon either saw enough of a shadowy outline to figure out what I was holding, or he was able to guess it from the way the demons broke out jabbering excitedly. In either case he braced himself even more.

"The sword's not for you," I said. "If you're not willing to help me out, I'm going to cut down your demon friends and leave you to them. From what I can tell, they're pretty damn pissed right now. I know it's not fair, but I'm guessing they're going to blame you for what happened, and when they restart their game it's going to be done with quite a bit more vigor and enthusiasm than before, if that's even possible."

"You won't do that. If you do you won't get what you want."

This was said with a false bravado. I walked over to where the demons were so I could cut down the rope and free them. Their jabbering became more excited and I had to shake a finger at them to quiet them down.

"Tyler, where you're screwing up in your thinking is not recognizing that I've got all the time in the world," I said. "Whether I get the information from you now or a few hundred years from now, it doesn't matter to me. I could end up getting it elsewhere so I never have to come back here. So maybe I'll see you in a few hundred years and we try this again, or maybe not."

He was defeated. That was evident from the way his face fell slack and how his body slumped in his chains. Still, he waited until the last second before pleading with me to wait.

"If I tell you what you want, you won't cut them down?" he asked

"You've got my word. As long as you don't play any games with me and answer me honestly, they'll still be trapped in those nets when I leave here. But if you lie to me once or act cute in any way, I'm cutting them down without giving you a second chance. And Tyler, I'll know if you're lying to me. Tell me about Bruce Dudley."

Harmon showed a faint smile. Or maybe it was a grimace. It was hard to tell with how distorted his lips looked. "He was our meal ticket. Ruby and I were going to get rich off Dudley." A soft sigh eased out of him. "It almost worked out."

"What was the plan?"

"For Ruby and me to score half a million dollars, and for the two of us to live happily ever after. Or at least as happily as two people like us could live."

"You didn't answer my question."

He offered me another faint smile. Or grimace. I still wasn't sure which it was. "I'm trying," he said. "But it's complicated. Or maybe not so much. You see, Bruce Dudley was a sad, lonely putz. And an exceptionally ugly one, too. Big and lumpy and with a face only a blind woman without hands could love. But he had money. Or at least his family did." His voice had died down to a thin wheeze, and he had to stop to refill his lungs, then, "The plan was for Ruby to use her feminine wiles to lure Dudley behind an abandoned warehouse in Queens where I'd be able to grab him—"

"Wait a minute. Slow down." I had to get my mind wrapped around what Harmon was telling me, because it wasn't what I was expecting. I was convinced their plan was going to be for Ruby to marry and divorce Dudley, and to do so without a prenup, or worst case, a prenup that would pay out half a million. I thought the kicker was going to be that Dudley got sick and died before they could get married. Their kidnapping scheme caught me off guard. "Did Ruby know that you were planning to kidnap Dudley?"

"Of course she did. It was her idea. Setting marks up to be robbed in hotel rooms, like she did with Dickie, was nickel and dime stuff. She was sick of it. She wanted a big score. And so did I." There was more sucking in air before he could tell me how they spent months looking for the right target. He offered me another of those smiles or grimaces before saying, "And then we found Bruce Dudley."

"How did he die?"

DAVE ZELTSERMAN

"Ruby slit his throat with a box cutter."

This just kept getting worse and worse. I was hoping at least that Dudley's death had been accidental; that maybe things went badly when they tried abducting him. My voice sounded detached and hollow to me as I asked him if Ruby knew from the start that Dudley was going to be killed.

"Well, yes, that was the plan. Dudley might not have known Ruby's real name, but he could still describe her to the police, so Ruby, bless her heart, insisted from the beginning that we kill him once we no longer needed him." There was another long pause while he refilled his lungs, and I was shocked to realize that outside of his breathing how quiet it had gotten in his hell. Even the two demons had stopped their moaning and other gibberish sounds as if they were listening intently also.

Once Harmon was able to continue, he said in his soft, slow, air-leaking-out-of-a-balloon voice, "I was the one who was supposed to kill him, but I didn't want to do it. Dudley was such a sad case and it seemed so unnecessary. We had him tied up inside that same abandoned warehouse, and nobody was going to find him until we wanted them to. Our plan was to flee to Sao Paulo, and any description Dudley ended up giving the police wouldn't have helped them in tracking Ruby to Brazil. But after we got the money and I refused to do the honors, Ruby grabbed the box cutter and did it herself before I could stop her."

I had to back him up, because something he said didn't make sense. "You told me that it almost worked out. Now you're saying you did get your half million dollars?"

Harmon's mouth twitched as he gave me a bleak nod. "We collected the ransom and everything would've worked out as planned, except Ruby tried ripping me off. If she hadn't, we would've gotten to Brazil and everything would've been hunky dory, except for Dudley who'd still be in that warehouse with a slit throat. But those four days we lost while Ruby and I were playing hide and seek ruined everything."

His voice broke down again into another slow wheezing hiss, and while I waited for him to breathe in more air it took every bit of self-control I had to keep from fleeing from Harmon's private hell. I didn't want to hear any more. I don't know why I hadn't realized that

Ruby's soul was so utterly broken, or why it mattered so much to me, but it did. And it sickened me to hear how she was the driving force in Bruce Dudley's kidnapping and brutal murder.

"I did catch up to her," Harmon continued when he was able to. "Ruby, double bless her black larcenous heart, had tried setting me up to be killed the same night we collected the money. But it didn't work out the way she thought it would, and so she had to go into hiding instead of flying off to Brazil, or wherever else she was planning to go. The funny thing was I couldn't work up any real outrage toward her. I wanted to because I was royally pissed at her, but I just couldn't." He stopped again, but this time it was for reflection instead of needing to fill up his lungs. "How much do you know about what Ruby went through as a kid?" he asked somewhat wistfully.

"I know she was put into an abusive foster care situation."

"To put it mildly. The McClechans did a real number on Ruby, but she didn't get dumped into foster care until she was twelve, and what was done to her before that was far worse." There was more sucking in air, then, "Ruby never had a chance from the beginning. There was never any dad in the picture to protect her, and her mom was this high-strung, neurotic piece of work who blamed Ruby for everything that had gone wrong in her life, and made her young life a living hell." He smiled then, and added, "And I know what I speak of. But then when Ruby was eight her nutbag mom married Lewis Jane, and that was when the real fun began."

The demons started their wild screeching and jabbering again. It was as if they could understand what Harmon was saying and Ruby's tales of woe excited them. I told Harmon I'd be right back, and I used the baseball bat on the demons with every ounce of strength I had until they stopped their racket. I was glad for the break, and smacking the hell out of those demons proved to be a good release. Hearing about the misery Ruby Jane suffered as a young child had gotten to me, and I needed some time away from it. For a while there it was like I was dipped naked in ice water the way I started shivering like a dope fiend needing a fix. But spending ten minutes or so swinging for the fences on those demons helped.

By the time I returned back to Harmon my shivering had stopped. I still felt an uneasiness worming its way deep into my gut, but at least that intense coldness was gone. In his soft, air-hissing voice, Harmon told me the little he was able to get out of Ruby about what Lewis Jane did to her. According to Harmon whenever he'd try getting her to talk about her stepdad, Ruby's face would usually darken and tighten up like a clenched fist, and then it would be like trying to pry open a clam with his fingers. But every once in a while she'd let slip about what happened, and it was the horrifically awful stuff you'd expect, with the worst being that for almost her entire time with Lewis Jane she was terrified that he was going to kill her and her mom. But while she'd let those things slip out she always refused to tell him how she ended up in foster care.

"Ruby never had a chance," Tyler said after another long pause so he could breathe in more air to fill up his leaking lungs. "But even knowing all that there were times I'd look at her and I'd see her smiling in this carefree way, and I'd imagine how different things might've been for her. And sometimes I'd think the same about myself." His voice once again died down to a soft hiss, and after filling up his lungs he continued, saying, "And then I would talk myself into thinking that it wasn't too late for Ruby and me. That we could actually be happy and sort of normal if we had enough money to start fresh someplace far away from the Bronx. I guess that was pretty delusional of me, huh?"

"How about slowing down for a minute. You told me you got the half million back from Ruby, but you also told me that things ended up not working out. Why was that? Were you arrested?"

He gave me a blank stare with his badly scarred eyes and in a slow, methodical movement shook his head. "I honestly can't remember," he said. "Do me a favor and don't go cutting down those demons because you think I'm stonewalling you, because I'm not. It's funny, I can remember so much about my life but when it comes to what happened after I got the money back from Ruby, it's all one big haze. All I know is things didn't work out. I don't know how I know that, but I do. I'm sorry, buddy, that's all I can remember."

That's the thing with these unawares. It's usually awfully damn convenient for them what they can't remember. "You killed Ruby didn't you?" I said. "You caught up with her inside of Diablos, took the money from her, dragged her into the men's room and shot her in the chest."

He laughed weakly at that. "Oh man, you are so wrong. That part of it I remember. I don't know where you came up with this Diablos shit, but I caught up with Ruby at a fleabag motel off US 1 in Jersey City, and I wasn't kidding when I told you I felt sorry for her." More sucking in air, then, "Even though she betrayed me and tried to have me killed, and even though she ripped me off, I still felt sorry for her."

"Yeah? I guess you're the forgiving type. All you did was take the money from her and leave her in one piece, huh?"

"Mostly. I had to do something to Ruby after what she did, so I gave her a beating, but nothing too severe. I mean nothing that she couldn't walk away from. I didn't break any bones or knock out any teeth. But considering what she did she got off easy."

I found myself despising Harmon right then with a white hot intensity, especially given how cavalierly he justified what he did to Ruby. If he could've seen more than shadows, he would've seen my contempt for him burning in my eyes. I was able to keep my voice flat and unemotional, though, when I told him to tell me how he died. I was guessing he was going to try telling me it happened during a shootout with the police.

He gave me more of his blank stare. "I don't know," he said. "Seriously, I don't."

"You told me before you died in an unpleasant way."

"I was lying," he admitted somewhat sheepishly. "You hadn't threatened to cut those bastard demons loose yet, so I was lying. But since then I've been telling you the truth and I don't remember anything about my death."

Of course, I knew he was lying earlier. Unawares never remember anything about their deaths. I asked him that to see if he had any obvious *tells* when he lied, and I asked him it a second time to see if he was still lying to me. I'd had enough of him and his private hell, but I had one last question, and I asked him the name of Ruby Jane's mom. He shook his head and told me he didn't know it.

"You knew the name of Ruby's stepdad but not her mom?"

"Ruby never told me it. She always referred to her only as her *bitch mother*. Never anything else."

I didn't bother saying anything else to him, but turned and headed to the portal that would take me back to my hell. I heard some panic in his hissing voice as he asked me if I'd keep my promise about not cutting down the demons caught in the net.

Without looking back at him, I said, "I gave you my word, didn't I?"

I didn't bother mentioning to him that as soon as I left his private hell, everything I had conjured up inside of it, including the net, would disappear. It wasn't worth the breath for me to tell him that since he'd be discovering it for himself soon enough.

Chapter 25

Paulie's cab wasn't waiting outside the tenement building in Port Morris where I expected it to be. Bob, though, had somehow tracked me down and was standing guard by the front door, and given how much larger and surlier the crowd of squatters had gotten, I was glad to see that slobbering demon Rottweiler. Without Bob I might've had trouble making it out of the area, but as it was, the squatters wisely kept their distance.

I had a long walk back to Brooklyn Heights, at least thirteen miles. But as Bob and I made our way toward my version of the Robert F. Kennedy Bridge, it felt good being in the open air after Harmon's more claustrophobic private hell, even though it was all illusionary, and the walking helped clear my head and settle down my thinking. As I thought about what Harmon told me, I couldn't believe I'd bought the swill he was selling me as completely as I did. For whatever reason my brain must've just turned off while I was with him. More than almost anyone, I know how souls here in hell can't help themselves from lying, especially the unawares, and I had no idea why I'd been so eager to buy Harmon's story. For the life of me, I couldn't figure it out.

Harmon might've been scared out of his mind that I'd cut down those demons if I caught him lying, but that still wouldn't keep him from sneaking in whatever lies he thought he could get away with. And even when he sincerely believed he was telling me the truth, I couldn't be able to trust what he was saying, at least not completely. He needed to reimagine himself as someone very different than who he was, so he built himself up in his mind as a decent guy who went along with the kidnapping only so he could rescue Ruby from a miserable existence. But his playing the martyr was complete bullshit. The odds were that he used Ruby the same as all the other lowlife scumbags before him. The kidnapping was most likely his idea. And he probably flipped around the rest of the kidnapping story. The more I thought about it, the more I liked him as the one who did the throat slitting and Ruby as the one who tried to talk him out of it.

Bob and I had hiked about two miles, and we were on the Robert F. Kennedy Bridge when I saw a yellow cab idling a half a mile down Route 278. As I got closer to it I could see the driver's window had been smashed and that there was no one in the cab. Then I saw Paulie's legs sticking out of the water, at least I assumed from how short and slight the body was that it was Paulie. As I stared at his legs I realized they were twitching slightly, as they would be for the rest of eternity. One or more of the squatters back in Port Morris must've broken the driver's side window and pulled Paulie out of the cab and beat him to death, at least as much as you could beat anyone to death here. For a reason I couldn't figure out, these squatters decided to drive out here to dump Paulie's body and abandon the cab. When we got within twenty yards of the cab and Bob started snarling in his demonic Rottweiler way, I understood what was going on.

I quieted Bob down. We approached the cab quietly after that, and sure enough two thuggish squatters were hiding in back waiting to ambush me. I opened the back door, and the shock on both their faces when they found themselves staring directly at Bob with his demon fangs bared and yellowish-greenish foam dripping from his muzzle was like something out of a Bugs Bunny cartoon. They had no chance. Bob sprang into action, dragging one of them out of the car and ripping him open from throat to sternum. While he was doing this the thug's partner had crawled out of the other door and was trying to get away, but he had nowhere to run other than back toward the Bronx. He didn't get very far before Bob chased him down and crushed his head into a bloody pulp.

I waited until Bob returned and settled onto the backseat before I got behind the wheel. It looked as if I was out of squatters to chauffeur me around and that I was going to have to drive myself. Given what had happened to the last two squatters serving as cabdrivers for me, it was appearing to be too high risk an occupation, and it was probably going to be a while before another squatter would willingly take on that role.

When I returned back to the office, it was still the same mess as before with shards of glass and the broken coatrack littering the linoleum tiled floor. Vera seemed oblivious to it as she sat in her usual spot behind the reception desk with her nose buried in one of her romance magazines, and once again she ignored Bob while he ignored her. I didn't get that given how nuts they were about each other that one time earlier, but there were certain things about squatters that I still hadn't figured out. She did, though, consent to lower her magazine before I reached my private office so that she could tell me I had that horrible freakazoid waiting for me.

This stunned me the same as if I'd been smacked in the face with a sledgehammer. There was only one reason Nicolaus Bratianu would've returned. He was reneging on our deal, and he was going to be taking Vera back with him. The fact that he was waiting for me meant he was trying to decide whether he was also going to be purifying my soul in his chamber of horrors, regardless of our agreement. It was pointless trying to run. Anytime he wanted he could suck me into his hell and have me. The only chance I had was to talk him out of whatever plans he had in mind, and I felt numb as I continued on to my office with Bob following at my heels.

I had to blink several times when I saw who was waiting for me, because it wasn't the White Devil, but the mortuary man. As I stood gawking at him, his very red lips tried to twitch themselves into a smile, but his nose wrinkled in disgust as smelled Bob. Then he caught sight of the demon Rottweiler rushing in behind me and his attempted smile dropped completely, an anxiousness pinching his face.

"Ah, Mr. Stone," he said, his voice squeakier than I remembered, "I see you have a new companion. Quite an impressive dog. Yes sir. I hope he's friendly?"

Bob continued on until his head was pushing into the mortuary man's lap. With little effort he'd be able to eviscerate this man. I

DAVE ZELTSERMAN

thought about ordering Bob to do just that. My gut was telling me I'd be better off with the mortuary man ripped to pieces. But I didn't do it. Instead I made my way to my chair and signaled for Bob to join me. He did so reluctantly, and continued to give the mortuary man the evil eye.

I said, "Are you here to waste my time again, or do you have a job for me?"

The mortuary man's lips grew twitchy again. I wasn't sure if he was trying to smile or if Bob was making him nervous. "I came here to sell you information."

"Yeah? And what would that be?"

This time his lip twitching succeeded in forming a short-lived smile. Given how unnaturally red his lips were, it looked like two quivering, blood-saturated leeches curling up over his mouth.

"The name of the hit man who killed Sam Vogel."

There wasn't much in hell that surprised me anymore, but I have to admit that did the trick. When he was alone in my office the other time, he must've gone through files. That had to be how he knew I was looking for Vogel's killer. But still, I'd been struggling with this case for what seemed like centuries. How the fuck did he figure it out this fast?

"Why should I believe you know who the guy is?" I asked, a slight stammer in my voice.

He giggled then and steepled his fingers together, holding the tip of them under his chin. It had been a long time since I'd heard anyone giggle. It wasn't something souls in hell usually did, even when it was as insipid as his.

"Because Mr. Stone, gathering valuable information is what I do," he said, sounding overly pleased with himself. "I listen for whispers and rumors, and collect what I hear. And then I find buyers for it."

"What do you want for this?"

More lip twitching. "Nothing too outrageous. Only that you owe me, and if ever need you to investigate something for me or one of my clients, that you handle it for me. Not only that, but that you make it your top priority."

"Only one investigation?"

"Just the one."

"Do you have one in mind?"

"No." He winked at me, and did so without the skin surrounding his eye ripping. "I trade in futures, Mr. Stone. Collecting and trading in obligations."

He could've been lying. He could've already been planning to sink me into some swamp of a case, but if that was his game, I couldn't tell.

"Here's the thing," I said. "If I accept your deal I'd be at best breaking even. While I'd be able to collect payment from Vogel, I'd have to work my ass on your case without any compensation. Actually, I'd be worse off since I'd have to take your case no matter how much of a dog it was."

His lips twitched downward into a slight frown. "That's one way of looking at it," he said. He pursed his overly red lips, then added, "Another is you'd be collecting payment from Sam Vogel that you might not be collecting otherwise. So I would say you'd be winning here. You'd also be clearing from your desk a case that has proven extremely difficult for you. I would have to think that would be a second win."

As much as I wanted to close the Vogel investigation, I didn't like the idea of making any deal with this man. I also made the educated guess that my awareness was stronger than his, otherwise he would've conjured up a weapon when Bob threatened him. And if he could've, he certainly would've sucked me into his world so he'd have the upper hand negotiating with me on his own turf.

"I could just force the information out of you," I said.

Bob rose to his feet when I said that and showed the mortuary man his fangs while a demonic growl rumbled out of him. The man unsteepled his hands and gripped both armrests of the chair, his eyes ping-ponging between me and Bob.

"You wouldn't do that for three reasons," he said, his voice more nervous and twitchier than before. "Number one, you have to know that I couldn't give it to you no matter how much you threatened me. If I did, my business would be finished. Number two, you should expect that I took the precaution of arranging for one of my clients to pay you back in kind if you were to do anything to me. And number three, the intel that I gathered about you shows that you are at worst only borderline evil and it would be outside of your character to try something like that."

"Only borderline evil, huh? I guess I should take that as a compliment." I pushed down on Bob's neck to send him back to the floor, and he grudgingly complied, his growling dying down to more of a disappointed grumble. "How about you? Are you only borderline evil?"

More of his lip twitching, and this time it formed an opened-mouthed smile that revealed piss-colored and badly cracked teeth. "Mr. Stone, I assure you I'm far further down the evil curve than that, although I haven't reached the same level as your friend, Nicolaus Bratianu."

This guy turned out to be full of surprises. "You have dealings with the Prince?" I asked.

"Certainly not. I only know of him by reputation and rumors. It would take a very reckless man to make any sort of deal with the White Devil. And I am certainly not reckless." His eyes seemed to glaze over as he looked at me, and then there was another lip tremor that caused a slight smile to form. "Mr. Stone, will we be doing business today?"

Against my better judgment, I found myself nodding.

"Very good," he said. I'd only seen rattlesnakes in the movies and on TV, but at that moment that's what he made me think of, or more specifically, a rattlesnake on the verge of striking. "In that case, can you swear to me that in exchange for what I'm about to tell you that you will owe me an investigation, and you will carry it out to the best of your abilities?"

"Is that really necessary?"

"I'm afraid so."

"Do I need to make it a blood oath?"

He giggled at that. "No, your word will be enough."

I didn't know what he could possibly get by having me swear an oath, so I did, although I added in that he was entitled to his investigation only if the information he provided me proved correct, and that I couldn't guarantee results. When I was done, his lips spasmed into a smile that caused an icy shiver to run up my spine.

"Ernest Bush," he said. "That's the name of the hit man you're looking for. Although he goes by the name of Ernie. And to confirm our deal, you now owe me one investigation."

"Yeah, okay, assuming that this Ernie Bush checks out."

"Fair enough." He unfolded his nearly seven-foot frame from the chair and wandered over to the farthest window from where Bob was lying. He appeared unnaturally stiff as he stood looking out the window.

"If you don't mind I think I'll enjoy this New York city view for a few minutes," he said. A giggle escaped from him, and he added, "Even if it is only Brooklyn."

I didn't like the idea of leaving him alone in my office, but I didn't see what additional harm he could do given that he'd already had plenty of opportunity to search through my case files.

"Knock yourself out," I said.

DAVE ZELTSERMAN

Chapter 26

I heard the rattling noise behind me, and when I turned I saw a rattlesnake coiled up in the dirt. Or really, a demonic rattlesnake given its blood red eyes and what looked like a malformed head and larger and deadlier fangs than I'd expect to see on a normal rattlesnake. If I'd had time to think about it, I would've found it an interesting coincidence that I was seeing my first rattlesnake, even if it was a demonic one, after only a half hour earlier thinking how when the mortuary man was smiling with his mouth open he resembled that same type of snake.

Anyway, I had no time to think since it scared the hypothetical crap out of me seeing that snake shaking its rattler only five feet from me. I had no idea how fast the damn thing could move or whether I'd have any chance of outrunning it, but at least I had enough presence of mind to try conjuring up an Uzi submachine gun with a full clip, and when it appeared in my hands I had the answer to the question regarding whether I had greater awareness than Ernie Bush.

Before the snake could strike, I sprayed it with bullets blowing it into pieces, and then I shielded my eyes from the far too bright sun burning overhead and searched the dusty plains I was standing in for more rattlesnakes. I saw more of them and blew them into pieces also. Then I stood and listened to the stillness around me. If there were other demonic rattlesnakes nearby they weren't rattling.

If I had to guess Ernie Bush's hell was a facsimile of some remote part of West Texas. The sun overhead was far too bright and big and hot, and it baked the dying grass the same dull brown as the dirt. Up ahead about a hundred yards was a small cabin, and outside of that in all directions were miles of plains.

It was like an oven in Bush's hell, I took off my suit jacket and loosened my tie. I'd only been in his hell for several minutes, and I was already drenched in sweat. As I squinted and looked over the plains I could see bodies lying on the ground. Most likely these were zombies who had made their way into Bush's hell so they could be baked to death for the rest of eternity.

Bob had been right next to me when I slipped through the portal to Bush's hell, but the demon Rottweiler must've needed a different portal and he didn't end up coming over with me. That was okay. I didn't need him now that I had the Uzi. As I headed off toward the cabin I searched the ground for more snakes. I was glad I chose to slip into Bush's hell instead of absorbing him into mine, otherwise I would've also sucked those damn snakes into my New York.

When I reached the cabin's front door, I knocked and called out Bush's name. "I'm just here to talk, nothing else," I yelled out.

I got no response. I tried the door and found it locked. It didn't look very sturdy, and a kick with my heel broke the door open. The cabin was made up of a single room with an interior no more than three hundred square feet. Bush sat on a rickety wooden chair leaned up against the back wall wearing only a sleeveless undershirt and a pair of boxers. There was no kitchen or food in sight, but it smelled like cooked pig fat in there.

Even with the slack jawed, dull eyed way he looked at me, I could tell there was a toughness and hardness to him. Still, with the way he sat there without blinking his eyes or uttering a sound, I wondered whether I was wrong about who he was, and that maybe he was only a zombie who had stumbled into the cabin.

"Ernie Bush?" I asked.

Still no response.

I took several steps into the cabin. I said, "I'm just here to ask you a few questions and then I'll leave you alone."

"Go to hell," he said in a slow drawl, and then he started making wheezing cackling noises as if he were laughing at something other than the lamest joke there was.

DAVE ZELTSERMAN

I lifted the Uzi so it was pointed at him. "Kind of a stupid way to treat someone who's aiming a submachine gun at you."

That a drew a smile out of him. "Pal, you want to shoot me, go right ahead," he said. "If you haven't noticed, I'm already roasting for eternity in this godforsaken hell. So go ahead and do your worst."

"You don't think you'd be worse off having your knees shot up?"

He hawked up something from his throat and spat it onto the floor. Or at least I thought he did. I wasn't sure whether coughing up phlegm was possible here in hell. Since I didn't see what he spat out, he could've only been going through the motions. Some sort of muscle memory thing.

"It don't matter to me," Bush said. "Have yourself a blast and shoot me wherever you want for all I care."

He was serious. I wasn't going to get anywhere shooting him. I'd only make him more obstinate.

"I'll see you again real soon," I told him, and I left his cabin.

Chapter 27

I wasn't kidding Bush when I told him I'd be seeing him again real soon. When I left his cabin I made my way back to my portal while keeping a watchful eye out for more rattlesnakes. Stepping through the portal left me back in the hallway of the eighth floor apartment where Bush's portal was located. Bob was lying on the floor moping, and he let out an unhappy grunt on seeing me. I found the keys for the cab where I had hidden them—I didn't want to bring them with me when I slipped into Bush's world since they would've disappeared the moment I stepped onto those sunbaked plains and been lost forever. After I had the keys back in my pocket, I again stepped through Bush's portal, this time absorbing his world into mine.

Yeah, I was going to be sucking into my New York any of those demonic rattlesnakes still slithering around Bush's reality, but I figured Bob could go on a hunting spree and take care of most of them, and the ones that survived would probably either end up in the sewers or find their way into other hells better suited for them.

I still had to find Ernie Bush in my hell, but given where the portal was in relation to his cabin, I had a good idea where to look. The problem was it was going to take me a few minutes to make my way down eight flights of stairs, and it was doubtful Bush would sit still and wait for me, but I didn't think he'd get too far. And besides, I had Bob to track him down if needed.

It turned out Bush was leaving the store across the street at the same time I was walking out of the apartment building. Our eyes met and I could see an angry glint in his. He took several steps toward me with his fists clenched, but then he spotted Bob and he stopped in his tracks, and his hands relaxed to his sides.

He looked around quickly to get his bearings before facing me again. "If you were going to try beating me into talking, you should've just done it back at the cabin instead of dragging me to this Jew city," he said in his West Texas drawl, his eyes small slivers of flint. "'Cause nothin' you do is going to get a word out of me."

A hit man and an anti-Semite. Great. The pricks I had to deal with here in hell. If I didn't care about what he had to tell me I would've had Bob rip him a new one. But I did care, so I gave him an easy smile and told him that I decided to use the carrot instead of the stick on him. "I'm going to see if I can win you over with kindness. It's probably been ages since you ate anything. How's a burger sound? And maybe afterwards a dozen or so boilermakers?"

He gave me a dubious look. "I can hold my alcohol better than any New Yorker," he said, overemphasizing it as *Noo Yorka*. "If you think you're going to get me drunk and talking, you're making a mistake there, pal."

"That's not what I'm thinking, Ernie. Only that you'll show some appreciation by answering a few questions."

"You want to make a fool bet like that, that's your problem."

I had left the cab in front of the apartment building, and Bush got into the vehicle without an argument. Before Bob joined him, the dog's head shot up and he turned to stare down the street. He probably spotted a demonic rattler brought back from Bush's hell, but he didn't give chase. Instead he let out an angry sigh and jumped onto the backseat, and for the entire ride the two gave each other wary looks.

Bush's portal was located in the Jackson Heights neighborhood of Queens, and for the next several blocks I came across a dozen or so bodies lying in the street that had to have been zombies that came from Bush's version of West Texas given how blistered and red their skin had gotten. I tried the best I could to avoid them but it wasn't always possible.

I had a twenty minute drive back to Brooklyn Heights, and besides me asking Bush whether he'd like to skip the food and go straight to the bar, and him saying how if I wanted to twist his arm first with some food that was entirely up to me, neither of us talked. Given that, I drove to the Busted Grill Diner and parked in front.

Bush and I took a booth with Bob curling up on the floor next to it. As I expected Doris was still working the counter and booths, but I was surprised to see Max and his nightmare face handling grill duties. If I'd had to place a bet on it, I would've put money on Doris having already followed through with her threat of cutting Max into fish bait. Given her swollen lip and the purplish-red bruise under her eye, maybe she tried but Max proved to be tougher than he appeared.

Doris first looked at me with surprise, but as it dawned on her that I was really there, she shuffled over to our booth as fast as her swollen, arthritic ankles could take her.

"Mike, I wasn't expecting to see you today," she said breathlessly. She eyed Bush in an anxious, eager sort of way, her tongue wetting her lips. If it bothered her at all that Bush was only wearing a badly stained undershirt and a pair of boxers, she didn't show it. "Who's your friend, a client?"

"Hardly. His name's Ernie Bush. He's a hit man I suspect of killing that lawyer I told you about. I'm trying to get him to answer a few questions, but he's not being very cooperative so I thought I'd try plying him with food and booze. I'll have a coffee, and get Ernie whatever he wants."

Bush looked royally pissed, and it took him a moment to cool down enough to ask for a burger cooked rare and a plate of onion rings. I had to bite my tongue to keep from laughing seeing the murder raging in his eyes and the frozen smile on Doris as she tried to decide whether I was playing a gag on her or telling her the truth. From the queer look stuck on her face she was still trying to figure it out by the time she shuffled back to give Max our order. I spoke up then, asking her to remind Max to make sure the burger was cooked rare.

"You hear that, you damned fool!" Doris screamed at Max with a hysterical edge in her voice, most likely thinking this was her last chance to keep me coming back to the diner. "If that burger ain't rare, I swear I'm going to cut your arm off with that cleaver, and you ain't going to stop me this time!"

"Charming place, isn't it, Ernie," I said.

He leaned closer to me, and he kept his voice a soft growl as he said, "If you didn't have your guard dog protecting you, I'd stab you in the eye with my knife before you ever knew what happened."

I broke out laughing. I couldn't help it. "Ernie, for a hit man, you're awfully damn sensitive. You need to lighten up."

He sat back in the booth with his arms crossed over his chest and his glare amping up from a hundred to three hundred watts. "You're a funny guy," he forced out through clenched teeth.

We waited in silence for my coffee and his food with me smiling amiably, and Bush stewing in violence. When his burger was brought over, it wasn't anywhere near rare, but amazingly it hadn't been burnt to charcoal and was something edible. I didn't bother drinking my coffee, but instead watched Bush as he slowly chewed away at his food while he stared back at me with dead eyes.

"Ready for some drinking?" I asked when he was done. He smirked at that and said, "Whatever you say, boss."

We left the diner, and Bush's rage over me telling Doris about him was mostly gone. He now acted amused over the fact that I was treating him to food and booze when as far as he was concerned I was going to get nothing back in return. I drove to the Gotham Lounge and we sat at a table in the back, and I had Jim start bringing us boilermakers, the kind where the whiskey is poured into the beer instead of being served in a separate shot glass. We were on our seventh round when Bush squeezed his eyes tight and grasped his forehead.

"You doped up my drinks," he grunted out, accusing me, his breathing labored. When we walked into the bar, I noticed he was listing a bit, which was a telltale sign of the sickness. He must not have noticed it then, but he certainly was at that moment.

"Nothing's been slipped into your drinks," I said. "You haven't been around much in hell, have you? What you're suffering is an illness every soul suffers when they get sucked into another hell. And it's going to get far worse. It will soon make your life sweltering daily in a hundred and twenty degree heat in that cabin seem like paradise. There's only one way to stop this illness, and that's to get you back to your own hell. Which I'll help you do if you answer my questions."

"You sonofabitch," he spat out, his eyes woozy as he tried looking at me.

"And that surprises you?" I said, arching an eyebrow. "I'm in hell, aren't I? So what do you say, Ernie, are you willing to cooperate or do you want to keep sitting there until it's too late for you?"

Bush tried standing up but collapsed back onto his chair. Given that the symptoms first showed up an hour ago, he had to be suffering far worse than simply his head swimming with vertigo. By now it must've felt like every nerve in his body was on fire.

"You'll make this stop if I tell you what you want to know?" he said, his drawl completely gone, and his voice groggy and weak.

"Yeah, I'll take you back to the portal in Queens and go through it with you. You're not going to be able to stop it otherwise, and it's going to get far worse than it is right now. You did the hit on Sam Vogel?"

He nodded.

"Explain to me how it went down."

The only thing keeping Bush from collapsing face forward was that he had his elbows planted on the table and was holding his head in both hands. "I flew out to Los Angeles," he murmured, his words blurring together. "Once I got there I waited until I got word that the target was on his way to an East Hollywood address to meet up with his girlfriend. Then it was easy. After he parked, I walked up behind him, tapped him on the shoulder, and shot a hole through his heart when he turned around to see who I was."

"Who put the hit on him?"

"A nobody named Ben Tulley."

"For what reason?"

Bush let out a soft murmur of pain. "Jesus, this hurts like hell," he groaned out in that blurry voice. "Can't you get me back to my cabin, and I'll tell you what you want then?"

"Uh uh. We tried that already. You need to talk first, then I'll take you back. Why'd Tulley want Sam Vogel dead?"

"The man was grieving. He blamed that Jew lawyer for his boy's death and he wanted him iced."

That didn't make sense, at least not with what I knew. A girl died in the jewelry store robbery, not a boy.

"Because he got Tommy Hilliard off?"

"Yeah."

"Vogel proved in court that Hilliard was innocent of that jewelry store robbery, so why'd Tulley blame him?"

"That's bullshit. Hilliard was guilty as sin. That shyster knew it and threw money around to buy off witnesses and buy a not guilty verdict. If he hadn't done that, Hilliard would've been in prison and wouldn't have killed Tulley's son while driving drunk." Even with as much pain as the hit man was in, he forced a hard bare-fanged smile. "I never cared why a hit was being ordered. Why would I? But Tulley did his homework, and he had enough evidence where he could've sent that shyster away for obstructing justice if he wanted. But I'm glad instead he paid me to put a bullet in that Jew lawyer's chest. You got what you wanted. Are you going to help me already?"

So that was it. Tommy Hilliard was at the heart of it like I'd thought, but a different grieving parent had ordered the hit. I didn't need to find Ben Tulley to verify what Bush told me. I knew it was the truth. No matter how much he might've wanted to lie to me, he wasn't capable of it with the level of pain he was in. As it was, I could see him struggling to hold it together. If he wasn't such a tough bastard he would've been screaming his head off right then.

I told Bush to have himself a nice rest of eternity. When I got up from the table and started walking away, he lifted up his head and actually looked surprised that I was abandoning him and not living up to my end of the deal.

"You sonofabitch," he forced out, his voice slurring as badly as if he'd just chugged a quart of whiskey—at least if he'd still been alive. "You lied to me?"

"That's what we do here in hell, you dumbass. We lie."

Bob joined my side. Bush tried to get up, but he instead collapsed onto the floor as if his feet were dead. He flopped around for half a minute before becoming still. The only thing that was keeping him from screaming now was that he didn't have the strength. I waved Jim over and pointed out the hit man.

"This is a nice place," I told Jim. "You shouldn't have customers falling drunk on the floor like this. Especially jokers like this one only wearing his underwear."

Jim nodded to me grimly. He didn't bother mentioning that only minutes before I was sitting with this same severely underdressed drunk.

"Why don't you grab his wrists, I'll grab his ankles, and we'll take him out the back door and let him sleep it off in the alley."

Ernie Bush was mostly dead weight as we carried him out of the bar and into the alley. We found an inconspicuous spot behind the dumpster and we left him there.

Chapter 28

The mortuary man was still in my office. He had moved from the window back to the chair he'd been sitting in earlier. His far too red lips twitched when he saw me, but didn't quite make it into a smile or anything else concrete.

"I thought you would've left by now," I said.

"Oh, I did," he said. "But as you can see I needed to return—"

Bob, who had followed me into the office, began snarling, his fangs glistening in the dull light of the room. The mortuary man's eyes opened wide as he focused on the Rottweiler, and whatever twitching his lips did was now out of fear. His voice rose an octave as he said, "I assume you'll control your dog?"

"Yeah, don't worry about it."

From the way the fur rose on the back of Bob's neck, I could tell he wanted to tear the mortuary man apart, but he behaved himself and followed me to my chair. The mortuary man relaxed seeing that.

"I trust you were able to confirm the information I gave you?" he asked.

I nodded.

That caused enough lip twitching to form what I assumed was a smirk. "Ernest Bush is such an obstinate, and might I add, unpleasant soul. I'm curious how you were able to coerce him to talk."

"A trade secret," I said. "What do you want?"

He giggled at that, but it was a nervous giggle given the way Bob's hackles were raised. "This is purely coincidental," he said.

"But shortly after I returned back to my hell I was met with a client needing an investigation."

Yeah, right. I didn't buy his earlier talk about trading in future favors. He already had this in the works when he made his deal with me. "What do you want?" I said.

"It's not what I want. It's what my client wants. He is looking for a soul who appears to be missing, and has presumably been absorbed into another soul's hell. What he wants from you is to find this missing soul."

"Give me a name."

The mortuary man's lips started spasming so much right then they made me think of two bloody worms fighting. When they calmed down a bit he said, "Al Zaoud."

All I could do at first was stare at him. It was no accident about him earlier mentioning Nicolaus Bratianu to me. This had been a setup from the beginning. What I wanted to do was punch him enough times in the mouth so I could pound out all that blood stuck in those lips, and then I wanted to keep punching him until I turned his face to pulp. I didn't do that, though. Instead, I stayed seated where I was, and with my voice sounding distant and detached as if someone outside of me was speaking, I told him how Al Zaoud was a guest in Bratianu's dungeon.

He opened his eyes in a mock look of surprise, but not wide enough to tear the surrounding skin. "I find it remarkable that you already know this," he said, giggling. "You certainly got the better of me on this deal, but a deal's a deal, and our business appears to be concluded."

He got out of his chair, and as he walked woodenly toward the door on his long, stilt-like legs, Bob rose to his feet snarling ferociously, foam dripping from his muzzle. I was once again seized with the impulse to sic him after the mortuary man and have him tear this ghoulish stick-like man to pieces, but instead I held Bob back and otherwise didn't move.

I know it shouldn't have bothered me. The mortuary man suspected where Al Zaoud was before he contacted me, and all I did was confirm his suspicions. So what. It wasn't going to change anything. Still, it put me in a rotten enough mood that when I went to see Vogel I absorbed him into my hell instead of slipping into his.

As soon as I did this Sam Vogel and two women in their twenties tumbled to the floor, all three of them naked. Their clothes also fluttered to the floor.

The two women went comatose, Vogel was startled and agitated by the reality shift. He kept yelling out "What the hell!" as he disentangled himself from the blonde he was on top of, and once he was free of her, he jerked his head around to try and orientate himself. He caught sight of Bob before he saw me and grasped his chest, and for a second it looked like he was going to pitch forward. I spoke up then telling him to calm down. He turned quickly to me and relief flashed on his face as he realized whose hell he was in.

"Jesus, Stone, you could've given me a little warning before dragging me here. You interrupted me in the middle of the act!"

"Yeah, what were the odds of that happening? Nine out of ten? Put your clothes on. I've got your case figured out, but I'll wait until you're decent before giving you the lowdown."

Again, this was only because of my rotten mood, otherwise I would've just told him what he wanted to know instead of making him fumble around for his clothes. His face became rigid with anticipation and he got so anxious he didn't seem capable of buttoning his shirt. He accidentally pulled a button off, and he stared at it as if he were going to cry.

"Stone, please, just tell me already," he begged.

He wasn't looking at me, but still, I nodded. This was my oldest open case, and I took some satisfaction in finally having solved it even if I needed the mortuary man to point me to the hit man.

I said, "Ben Tulley hired a hit man to kill you."

He gave me a look as if he had no idea who Tulley was, but a flicker of recognition showed in his eyes. Still he persisted in his ignorance act, saying, "I don't know what you're talking about. I never heard of him before."

"His son was killed by your client, Tommy Hilliard, in a drunk driving accident. Tulley blamed you for his son's death because of the way you subverted justice to get Hilliard exonerated from that jewelry store heist and felony murder charge."

"That's ridiculous! I did no such thing. Tommy had nothing to do with that jewelry store, and it's not fair to blame me for that boy's death!"

Vogel was making a lot of noise, but he wasn't being very convincing. In fact, he looked sick to his stomach. The truth can do that to you sometimes.

"Why don't you sit down," I said.

He moved over to a chair, walking the same as if he'd been heading to the gallows. Since I told him Tulley's name he hadn't looked at me once. I waited until he lowered himself to the chair before telling him that Tulley knew about him buying Hilliard's acquittal for the jewelry store robbery. I had a good idea what the answer was going to be, but I asked him anyway why he did it. "Everything before this pointed to you being an honest lawyer, so what did Hilliard offer that was so important to you?"

The logjam of self-denial that had built up inside of him broke free then. "Three million dollars," he said in a tired, defeated voice. He looked at me for the first time since I gave him his murderer's name and offered me a queasy smile. "Half of his take from the jewelry store heist."

I was expecting that, just as I was expecting his answer to my next question, which was why he was willing to sell himself out for Hilliard's money. He shrugged and stared morosely at his clasped hands.

"I told you before that I loved Nina," he said. "What we had wasn't something cheap and tawdry, but the real thing, and I wasn't going to give her up. Even though Vincent was in prison, sooner or later he was going to find out about us, and when he did we were dead. I needed the money so we could disappear."

His mouth clamped shut. I thought he was done, but after a few seconds his lips began pushing in and out, and he started up again, saying, "Part of the deal I made with Hilliard was for him to quit the heist game so no one else would get hurt. Since he was going to walk away with three million I thought he'd live up to that part of it. But only five days after his acquittal he got drunk celebrating and killed that boy. I still hadn't gotten my three million yet, and he wasn't going to pay me until I got him out from under this new vehicular homicide charge. So I was stuck. I couldn't run off with Nina like we had planned. And now here I am."

This time he was done. His face had become as drawn and lifeless as a corpse's, his eyes rimmed red as he stared vacantly at his hands as if they could provide him an answer for why things worked out the way they did. All of his denial had finally been stripped away and he was forced to come to terms that no mistake was made. That he was where he was supposed to be.

"I'll visit you sometime soon for payment," I said.

He nodded bleakly but couldn't look at me.

A young actress who committed suicide at the age of twenty-five had taken up residence as a squatter in his hell. I was only thirteen when she killed herself, but before then I watched her religiously on TV, and continued to watch her in reruns after her death, and for most of my teenage years I had a major league crush on her. As payment Vogel was going to set me up to spend some quality time naked with her. Yeah, I know, it's not what you'd call very honorable on my part, even for hell, but as I keep telling people, I'm no saint here.

I was going to just leave Vogel where he was, but in his state of mind he was never going to make it back to his hell, and that would've meant I'd never get paid. As much as I didn't want to spend another second with him at that moment, or see his Los Angeles version of hell, I left the apartment, and then walked through the portal again, this time slipping into Vogel's hell so I could bring him and those two naked women back to his office.

DAVE ZELTSERMAN

Chapter 29

Ever since I met with Tyler Harmon I had a good idea how things were going to turn out with Ruby, and it took me several days before I could get myself to look through the Hell directory book that listed all the Dudleys. When I came across the listing for Jonah Dudley I knew I had the soul I needed to see. The address for his portal was located in the Brooklyn neighborhood of Fort Greene, which wasn't too far from me, and I decided to walk it.

Bob tagged along next to me, although at times he'd run off, but several minutes later would come trotting back, usually chewing on something. I didn't care enough to find out what it was he was eating. It seemed like a good example of ignorance being blissed.

It wasn't too hard to figure out why I'd put off searching through the Hell listings for Dudley, and why I was feeling so much dread now. I had been hoping for a less ugly reason for Ruby's death than what it was going to turn out to be. But she was hiring me for the truth, and sugarcoating it wasn't going to help. Denial was a disease here that would only lead to you sinking into an even worst hell than the one you were currently in. The best I could do for Ruby was to get her to accept what really happened. That was the only path possible to greater awareness, and that was the only hope any of us in hell had.

When I reached the portal for Jonah Dudley's reality, I stood outside of it for a good ten minutes before I was able to build up enough resolve to step through it and slip inside of Dudley's hell.

The portal left me standing in the middle of a lawn of weeds outside of a small mansion. The mansion looked like one that would've been built in the early nineteen hundreds, and like the lawn and the rest of the grounds, was in disrepair. Not only was the sky a dreary gray, but everything in Dudley's hell seemed muted in color, and the gloom that hung in the air was thick enough that you could almost taste it. Like the last time I had stepped through a portal with Bob, he didn't come with me, and I was there by myself. I looked around and didn't spot any squatters or zombies.

The front door was unlocked, not that it mattered. I imagined a forty caliber pistol, and felt the heft of it in my jacket pocket. Since I had greater awareness than Jonah Dudley, if the door had been locked all I would've needed to do was imagine finding the key in my pants pocket.

I entered the mansion without knocking or ringing the bell. The dark wood paneling and the mostly barren rooms made the gloom even more pervasive inside. As I made my way through the first floor, the pit in my stomach seemed to grow heavier and more uncomfortable.

I found Jonah Dudley sitting in what must've been a private library, except there were no books on the shelves. He was a big, hulking man in his sixties, his hair white and messy and probably several months past where he normally would've got it cut, or given the money he must've had when he was alive, styled.

He looked up at me with haunting eyes and told me he'd offer me a seat, but it appeared as if he was already sitting on the only chair in the house. "At least it was the only one the last time I looked," he said in a voice every bit as hollow as his eyes. He attempted a bleak smile and added, "But it's been a while since I've last checked."

"That's okay. Was Bruce Dudley your son?"

His eyes welled up with tears. "Yes."

"Would you mind if I asked you some questions about him?"

He tried another bleak smile, and this one stuck a little better than his earlier attempt. "If you came here years ago asking me that I would've told you to go to hell, but that was then. Go ahead and ask me what you want."

Not that it mattered, but I was curious how long he felt as if he'd been in hell, and I asked him that.

DAVE ZELTSERMAN

"I've lost track of how many centuries I've been here." Another bleak smile as he added, "You're the only soul I've seen since I died." He tragically waved a hand around the room. "I used to love my books and used to think an eternity without them would be pure hell, and as it turned out I was right."

As I noted earlier, time had no real meaning in hell, and each soul was going to feel the passage of time differently. I was guessing Dudley died sometime after Ruby, and couldn't have been in hell for more than a few years at most, but it already felt like centuries to him. Even though I was fairly certain about the role he played in Ruby's death, I felt sorry for him.

"Did you smoke cigars when you were alive?" I asked.

He raised an eyebrow at that, surprised by my question. I was surprised by it also. "Why yes, I did," he said. "I would look forward to spending an hour each evening inside this very library with a good book, a good cigar, and a glass of cognac."

The only cigars I ever smoked when I was alive were cheap ones, and I never so much as had a sniff of cognac. I asked him to give me the brands of both which were his favorites and to describe them, and after he did, I imagined as best I could two of those cigars sitting on one of the empty shelves, as well as a bottle of cognac, two glasses and a lighter. Sure enough when I looked all of it was there. He seemed surprised when he saw it also, but he didn't ask me how that happened.

I handed him a cigar and the lighter, and poured out glasses of cognac. After we were both puffing on our cigars and sipping the cognac, I asked if they tasted like the real thing.

"They're close," he said. "Thank you."

I realized then the real reason I conjured up the cigars and cognac. It was yet another attempt to delay the inevitable. I couldn't put it off any longer, and I asked Dudley how he discovered Tyler Harmon was behind his son's kidnapping and murder. Because I knew that had to be the reason Harmon died within days of the ransom being paid.

A pained looked squeezed Dudley's large face and he put down the cigar. "The police found Bruce less than twenty-four hours after I paid the ransom. Before they cut his throat, they beat him so badly that they cracked the eye socket for his right eye, fractured his cheek bone, broke his jaw, and knocked out six teeth. Bruce was a good boy. Awkward, but good and kind, and if he'd had a chance to grow more into a man he would've outgrown his awkwardness. I couldn't let what they did to Bruce stand. I had connections with certain people in New Jersey, and I hired them to find out who did this and to make them pay."

Jonah Dudley was overcome with a surge of emotion. I waited until he battled it back before asking how his contacts in Jersey found out Harmon was involved.

"They knew about some thieves looking to fence a million dollars' worth of stolen diamonds, and it turned out they were approached after Bruce was kidnapped about working out a deal for half a million dollars. I guess the kidnappers thought it would be easier to smuggle diamonds out of the country than half a million in cash. The diamond thieves didn't have names, but the Jersey people let them know what would happen if they didn't call when the kidnappers made contact again, and that was how they got their hands on that piece of shit Tyler Harmon."

Dudley shattered the brandy snifter when he mentioned Harmon's name, and he stared dumbly at the mess, not quite understanding how it had happened. I imagined another glass, and poured Dudley another glass of cognac.

"How'd you find Ruby Jane?" I asked.

Dudley made a sour face. "I had flown up to New York, and I was with the Jersey people after they got Harmon. He broke easily and sold out his girlfriend. From what he told us, they had a falling out with Harmon taking the money. We had him call her with some bullshit story about how he didn't want to leave the country without her. He arranged to meet her at a nightclub in the Bronx." His lips clamped shut, his jowls quivering. When he could talk again, he said, "Harmon claimed the kidnapping was all his girlfriend's idea, and he also tried selling us that she was the one who murdered my boy. I'm convinced he was lying out of his ass, but she was still responsible and she had to pay."

"She was dragged into the men's room and shot in the chest?"

"I'm not sure of the details since I didn't want to know them, but she was killed inside of the nightclub."

We both grew silent after that. I had the whole picture then, and I knew Dudley had told me the truth. He turned out to be one of

DAVE ZELTSERMAN

the few people in hell who wasn't a pathological liar. I couldn't blame him for ordering Ruby's murder. I might've done the same in his shoes. I noticed his cigar had burnt down to mostly ash and I asked him if he wanted another one. He shook his head.

"It's possible the shelves in this room might one day be filled with books," I said. "I've seen stranger things happen."

"It won't ever happen," he said. "If I had only ordered that scum Harmon killed, then maybe that might be true, but once I had that girl killed I damned myself to an eternity of sitting here in isolation without even a book to keep me company." He gave me an imploring look, and said, "I've been tortured over the years by the thought that that girl was as much under Harmon's thumb as poor Bruce ended up being."

Again, we both fell silent. I broke it by telling him that if it was any comfort his son wasn't in hell.

"I knew he wouldn't be." Dudley's face aged several decades as he stared at his empty glass. "Bruce was too kind and generous a soul to ever end up here. I know no one else in my family is here. This is my burden alone to suffer for giving in to my hatred and need for revenge."

I had nothing else to say to him. I thanked him for his honesty and I left him.

Chapter 30

I might've had Ruby's murder figured out, but I wasn't done. I still had Lewis Jane to visit, and it was no surprise that he was suffering in a particularly nasty private hell. Several demons had him bent over and abused with red hot pokers in ways that would cause unimaginable agony. It wouldn't begin to make up for what he did to a young Ruby Jane, but at least it was something. As much as I hated to interrupt the demons, I needed to get the name of Ruby's mother from him, so I chased them away. Fortunately he still had his tongue even though it was badly burnt, and with little effort I was able to trick him into croaking the name out to me. While I wasn't surprised by what he told me, a piece of me died when I heard her name.

I didn't need anything else from him, and I didn't want to keep the demons from their task, so I left quickly after that.

When I returned back to my New York, Bob must've sensed something was wrong with how quiet he got and the way he hung back as he trailed along after me. It was all pointless, but I spent the next week at the Gotham Lounge pouring shots of whiskey down my throat. As I've said before, denial's a killer here in hell, and none of that whiskey was going to do a damn thing in changing what I knew, especially since I couldn't even get blissfully drunk from it. I was going to have to visit Ruby Jane's mom eventually, but I guess I needed to spend that week debasing myself sitting among those other degenerate alkies. When I finally pushed myself off the bar stool, I headed back to my office building to find the directory listing for Ruby Jane's mom. I knew I'd find it since there wasn't going to be any other place for her than hell.

.Even with how ruined her flesh was and all the damage the demons had done to her, I had little trouble recognizing Suzanne. Within seconds of stepping into her private hell, I imagined holding a razor-sharp sword, and I used that to kill all the demons there. I then conjured up a key so that I could unchain her from her shackles. It wasn't going to do her any good. Once I left, more demons would come and they would chain her back to the wall and torment her for the rest of eternity. There was nothing I could do to change that.

I was twenty-four when I got involved with her, and she was only nineteen. She was so young and beautiful then, with the same thick red hair Ruby has, and while she was thin and slender there was nothing to indicate that her flesh would become as wasted and ravaged as it was now. How old could she have been when she died? When I did the math I realized she couldn't have been much older than her forties, but she looked so much more ancient than that.

As I laid her down on a bed that I had conjured up, I forced myself to look into her eyes and all I saw was insanity. Back when I was with her, I'd catch glimpses of that madness, but nothing like what was raging in them right then. My throat tightened up as I remembered how beautiful she had once been, but also how crazy neurotic. I knew early on that things weren't going to lead anywhere with us, but she was so wild and exciting in the sack that I stayed with her for nearly six months and let her believe what she wanted to about us. While I never lied directly to her about my plans, I never corrected her about her assumptions. No matter how much I wanted to sugarcoat it, the truth was I used her, and when I was done with her I disappeared completely. I didn't say goodbye or leave her a phone number or address. I just packed up what I needed and moved out in the middle of the afternoon while she was working a shift as a cashier at a hair salon. I was a coward. I didn't want to deal with her histrionics, and so I did the most cowardly thing I ever did, and I never looked back, at least not until now.

I was thinking she was too far gone to get anything out of

her when she whispered my name. It stunned me, both because I thought that she was beyond being able to recognize anything and how disembodied her voice sounded. At first I thought I was hearing things even though I had seen her lips moving, although only barely, and then in that same disembodied voice she said, "Mike? Is that really you? Have you come to save me?"

"It's me, Suzanne, and I'll do whatever I can," I said, my voice sounding badly strangled to my ears.

"Can I have some water?"

"Of course."

I conjured up a glass of water. I held her up in an inclined position, and after first using my index finger to wet her lips, I slowly tilted the glass back so she could drink from it. It was a slow process, but she eventually emptied the glass.

"I must look like hell," she said, her lips forming a sad smile.

The insanity had dimmed in her eyes. It was still there, but there was less of it. "Not at all," I told her, which was only one of many lies I was going to tell her. I tried forcing my own smile, and asked, "Is Ruby my daughter?"

I already knew the answer, but I had to ask her. She bit down on her bottom lip as if she were trying to keep from crying, although I was sure all her tears had already been cried out long ago. She nodded so slightly that I would've missed it if I had blinked.

I had all these other questions for her, mostly settled around how she ever let someone like Lewis Jane near Ruby, and how our daughter ended up in foster care, but it all seemed so pointless. As I knelt by her too tongue-tied to ask her what I wanted to, she asked if I could take her out of her dungeon cell.

"I'll figure out a way," I said, knowing full well there was nothing I could do. The only way for her to leave this type of private hell would be to sink into a far worse hell. Once you were where Suzanne was now, you were truly damned.

"You won't leave me?"

"Just for a little while," I said, adding one more lie on top of the others.

"Will more of those demons come here while you're gone?"

"No. You'll be safe."

From the way her whole face seemed to crumble, this time she knew I was lying.

DAVE ZELTSERMAN

I left her then. I couldn't help myself. It would've been hell staying with her for even a second longer.

Suzanne's portal was located in Flatbush, and I had walked to it in a futile attempt to put off seeing her, even if I was only buying myself an extra hour and a half. When we were together I never had any idea that she was pregnant with my daughter. If I had I would have stayed with her even as crazy as she was, and I would've made sure Ruby was safe. It wasn't a coincidence that Ruby had sought me out here in hell. There are never any coincidences like that here. However things are orchestrated in hell by whoever is pulling the strings, Ruby was meant to find me. This was so I would discover my culpability. It didn't matter that I didn't know I had a daughter, I now had to carry the burden that because I wasn't there for her, I was ultimately responsible for all the misery Ruby suffered. As Olivia once said to me after I commented about hell not seeming so bad for us: 'just give it time.' What she could've said instead was that no matter how bad things are, give it time and it will only get worse.

When I stepped through the portal back into my own world Bob was nowhere in sight. That was okay. I needed to be alone then. Even a demon Rottweiler would've been too much company.

I was walking along Flatbush Avenue with these thoughts about Ruby and Suzanne and my failures in life buzzing like a swarm of angry horseflies through my head when I noticed the sky had shifted from my more subdued grayish-white to a deep and violent purple. I was too dense and too caught up in my thoughts to understand its significance, even when jagged bolts of lightning crackled in the sky. It was only when I turned around and saw off in the distance that my New York was melting away and being replaced by a barren, desolate landscape that I started to get a sickish feeling in my gut that something was very wrong. But still, it wasn't until thunder exploded in the air that I was fully knocked out of my stupor and began to accept what I was seeing, including the lone rider off in the distance coming my way. A rider so massive that he made his demon stallion look like a pony.

As I said, give it time, and things will always get worse.

Chapter 31

At the time I knew I was only lying to myself that it didn't matter about the mortuary man asking about Al Zaoud. But that's what we do here, right? We lie to ourselves and to others over and over again. We can't help it. I had my chance to sic Bob after the mortuary man so he could tear that living ghoul into pieces, but I had to lie to myself, and now I had a vengeful Al Zaoud chasing after me.

If the cab was nearby I might've had a chance of outracing that barbarian, but my situation was hopeless. I considered heading back to Suzanne's private hell, but if I did that I'd be trapped inside of that dungeon cell since the portal to return me to my world would disappear once Al Zaoud fully absorbed my reality. It would reappear again if Al Zaoud moved on and my world popped back into existence, but if that took too long to happen, I'd end up sinking into a worse hell than even Suzanne's. I didn't think there was anything Al Zaoud could do to me that could be worse than that.

At first I stood resigned to my fate, but then a full-blown panic hit me and I started running. It was a pathetically senseless thing to do, but I couldn't help myself. Even though I was blind to where I was going, I kept running and I didn't stop until I felt something sharp and piercing enter the base of my neck. Up until then I hadn't been able to hear the pounding of the demon stallion's hoof beats over my own heart, but all at once I could, as well as feel the hot sulfuric steam that the demon stallion was snorting into my face. I looked down to see the tip of a spear push through my stomach.

A sense of vertigo hit me as I was lifted and flipped over. By this time I had my eyes squeezed shut. Al Zaoud in his ancient, dead language growled at me that if I didn't open my eyes he'd rip the lids off. I opened them, and found myself looking directly into Al Zaoud's upside down face. He had to be even larger than eight feet now, and he had me skewered on a spear like a piece of shish kabob, and was holding the spear so that our faces were less than a foot apart. It was all very disorienting being held like that as his demon stallion raced along, and I was too terrified to even notice the pain caused by the spear lancing through my body.

Al Zaoud's expression was surprisingly inscrutable as he stared at me. I expected him to be angrily snorting out steam every bit as much as his horse. After what seemed like an interminable amount of time but was probably only a minute, his eyes narrowed and he said, "Where is the wizard Beelzebub?"

"I'll show you the way to him."

A harsh grin twisted his lips. "You think I'm a fool? I know you lied to me!"

"That's not true."

"No? Then explain this."

He swung me around on the spear so that I could see his new collection of severed heads. There were already dozens of them attached to his horse's mane. I had little doubt over time that number would grow substantially, and the odds were I was going to be his latest addition. I was also sure he'd be building up a new horde, but that would wait until after he had his revenge on me.

There was one severed head in particular that he wanted me to see. Nicolaus Bratianu's. As I looked at Bratianu with his sucked in cheeks and eyes darting wildly, I saw something in the White Devil that I never thought I'd see. Fear.

"I made a deal with him because you left me no choice!" I shouted so I could be heard over the hoof beats and exploding thunder.

"How did I not give you any choice about betraying me!"

"Three full moons wasn't enough time for me to deal with the Wizard Beelzebub. But he's real. And he knows how to escape hell. I can take you to him. You might be powerful enough to handle him."

He grunted at that, and said, "You are a liar."

There was a hint of doubt in his voice, and that was all I could hope for. I wasn't proud of what I was planning, which was to trick him into Olivia's reality and hope that her awareness was still greater than his. If it wasn't, then I'd be dooming her as well. But it was the only chance I had to keep my head from being torn off my body and added to the rest of his collection.

"What's the harm in having me show you the way to him? If I'm lying then you do to me what you want—"

"I will be doing to you what I wish whether or not you are lying to me!"

"True, but at least you will know where the Wizard Beelzebub resides, and you can later decide if you're brave enough to challenge him. If you're weaker than he is he will rip your heart from your chest before you realize it, but if you're stronger, you will be able to force him to tell you the way out of hell."

"And how long a trip is to this wizard?" he said in a forced scoffing-like voice, which showed that he was actually buying my story.

"Less than a day's ride."

The next minute while I waited for Al Zaoud to speak was probably the longest of my existence. Then he readjusted the way he was holding the spear so that I was facing front, and he ordered me to direct him to the wizard. I had to bite my tongue to keep from crying out in relief. I was still a long way from surviving this, but at least now I had a chance.

My New York was completely gone, and I had no landmarks to guide me. But when Al Zaoud was chasing me down, he was coming directly from the south, and I had the sense that we'd been heading north the whole time. Which meant we'd be somewhere in my Manhattan. I needed to turn him around back toward Brooklyn, but a canyon with sheer cliffs that must've been a half mile straight down had opened up to the left of us and stretched to what probably would've been the Bronx in my reality. That was okay. I'd lead him there before cutting over and heading back.

We rode for only another few miles when the sky quickly changed from violent purple to the blackest black and a small sliver of a moon showed in the sky. So it turned out Al Zaoud not only had night in his hell, but the moon. He brought his horse to a stop and he flung the spear skewering me into the ground, the tip going in deep enough to leave me suspended vertically.

Al Zaoud got off his stallion. There were enough flashes of lightning so I could see him glaring at me. I was right about him being larger. He had to be at least ten feet tall now with the same body proportions as before. He moved over to me and crouched so he sat on his heels, which put us face to face. Lightning crackling in the sky lit up his face enough for me to see the violence and madness raging in his dark eyes.

"Tell me the path to this wizard," he demanded, his breath like decaying bodies as he exhaled in my face.

"It would be better if I showed you tomorrow."

"No. You will tell me now, or I will rip your head from your neck and feed your body to my horse."

He wasn't making an idle threat. I could tell from what I saw in his eyes that he was itching to do just that. I had to guess somewhat, but I gave him the directions that I believed would take him to Olivia's reality. And then I braced myself expecting him to do what he so badly wanted to. He surprised me by backing away from me.

"Tomorrow I will see whether this wizard exists or if you are lying to me as I suspect," he said. As he stared at me, a sneer twisted his lips. "First I will honor a bargain that I made and will deliver you to a sorcerer in another land. This sorcerer will cut you open and remove your heart, liver and kidneys which I will eat in front of you. He will then drain you of all your blood and will replace it with a poisonous, burning liquid which will leave you in agony. The remaining husk of your body will then be placed into a metal box and stacked among thousands of others. That is what you have waiting for you for the rest of eternity."

Al Zaoud's sorcerer and my mortuary man had to be one and the same. So Vera and I were both right. The guy *was* a mortician, and for whatever reason he wanted to add my body to his collection.

What happened next happened so fast that it was barely a blur, and if a flash of lightning hadn't captured it I would've missed it except for the sound that was made. What the lightning framed was Bob airborne, his fangs glistening as he prepared to rip into the back of Al Zaoud's neck. But that damn stallion reared back his hind legs and kicked the demon dog squarely in the side. The impact was a sickening thud that must've sent Bob's flying a good thirty yards away because a few seconds later another flash of lightning showed his body lying still on the ground. The blow had to have injured him enough to where he wasn't going to move from that spot again. Al Zaoud leered in the direction of where the demon Rottweiler lay, but didn't bother to go over to him.

"Tomorrow," Al Zaoud threatened, and then he disappeared into the blackness of the night.

As I hung in the air like a pinned insect and the shock of what had happened and what was going to happen faded, I found myself sinking into a despair every bit as dark as the night. It wasn't over the fate that Al Zaoud and the mortuary man had planned for me, but how badly I had failed Ruby. I had failed her in life and I was failing her in death, because now I wasn't going to be able to tell her the truth about herself and that was the only chance she had of breaking through all of her denial and possibly surviving a less hellish existence.

As I thought about her trapped inside of that nightclub thinking that I abandoned her, I started sobbing. I could help myself. While I couldn't see Al Zaoud's face, I could hear the sneer in his voice as he grunted out that I was a coward. That just made me sob more. Because he was right. I knew the moment Lewis Jane gave me Suzanne's name that Ruby was my daughter, but instead of visiting her so I could help her, I spent a week holed up in that dive bar so I could put off seeing her. And now it was too late.

The thing with us souls in hell is that we can lie to ourselves for all eternity, but as I hung in the air pinned by that spear, the lies I'd been telling myself cracked open. Because as much as I'd been trying to convince myself otherwise, the truth was I knew that Suzanne was pregnant, and that's why I fled. She never told me, but I knew, and I knew with all of her insecurities and narcissism that she would be a miserable mother. So what I told myself was that I was dodging a bullet, and without me in the picture, she'd realize how unsuited she was for motherhood and end the pregnancy. But even that turned out to be a lie because seven months later a friend told me he saw a very pregnant Suzanne walking into the hair salon where she worked. What lies did I tell myself then? That she'd be giving up the baby for adoption? That she got pregnant with some other

DAVE ZELTSERMAN

dude after I left so none of it was my responsibility? That I owed the baby nothing? Whatever lies they were, I made sure to stay out of Suzanne's neighborhood, and soon I was able to pretend that I was a decent guy who wasn't going to hell.

The reason I gave Olivia for my ending up here was all bullshit. I might have believed it at the time, but it was still bullshit. I knew full well the damage Suzanne could inflict on a child, and I let it happen to my own daughter. And all the misery and pain that followed with Lewis Jane, the McClechans, Dickie Rascine and Tyler Harmon was all on me. Ruby never had a chance. Even if she was the one to slit Bruce Dudley's throat, it could have just as well been my hand, because how else was she going to turn out without anyone ever looking out for her, especially her own father?

My total abandonment of Ruby is what sentenced me to hell. And it's what I deserve.

And so I sobbed as I accepted my responsibility for what Ruby has had to go through both in life and in death. At no single moment, though, was it because of self-pity, but only over the pain that I knew my daughter has suffered throughout her existence, and knowing how it could've been so different for her. As I did this a thought so startling hit me that it sucked my breath away. For several minutes all I could do was wonder in amazement at this thought and feel it build inside of me. I started imagining it as an intensely bright light filling up my whole body until the light began shooting out of my eyes and nostrils and ears and other parts of me. And then I started laughing.

"I know how to escape hell," I yelled out to Al Zaoud while laughing like a crazy person. "Not the lie I've been telling you about an imaginary wizard, but how to really do it!"

"You think this latest ploy will save you?" he tried growling at me, and I say tried because there was a fear in his voice that cracked his growl into the same sort of high-pitched tone that might've escaped from a prepubescent boy. Something about the way I was laughing made him suspect that I was telling the truth this time, and I was. I could see it all with such clarity. All of us create our own hells because it's all we feel we deserve. But we could just as well be creating our own heavens. It could be that easy. If we could just believe that we deserve it.

Everything changed then. All at once the blackness was gone, replaced by the white sky I was so used to from my hell. At the same time a dizzying whirl of motion sent us over a thousand feet into the air, and when the whirl stopped, I was no longer being skewered by a spear, nor did I have any wounds or injuries left over from it. Instead my New York was back, and I was on top of the Empire Statement building. Actually, not quite on top of it, or on the observation deck, but what must've been a landing on the eighty-fifth floor.

I heard a demonic braying noise, and turned to see that the demon stallion had been brought into my hell and was hanging off the edge of the building by its front legs, and was slipping quickly. It let out one last desperate bray, and then it was gone.

Al Zaoud was also on the landing with me. He was no longer a giant, and none of his weapons made it into my world, but he was still a large man. After the shock wore off over what happened— namely that my awareness had grown stronger than his own—an animalistic snarl twisted his face and he let out a noise that was somewhere between an ancient war cry and a bellow. And then he came charging at me.

Maybe he thought I'd be too intimidated to fight back, but I'd be damned if I was going to lose my chance to save Ruby. When he got within tackling distance, I threw myself shoulder first at his knees. The bigger they are the harder they fall, right? The impact of the hit flipped him over and he hit the landing like two hundred and fifty pounds of bricks. He was a bit dazed when he tried standing up, and I bull rushed him, hitting him like a tackling sled, and before he realized what was happening I had him falling off the edge of the building. I watched as he fell those eighty-five floors and disappeared into a spray of red on impact. I was never going to have to worry about Al Zaoud again. He had been obliterated to where he'd be sinking into a private hell. Good. Let the demons have him.

I had a lot of stairs to climb down, but it gave me time to think about what I was going to do for Ruby. It wasn't going to be easy convincing her that she deserved to be in a heaven of her making, but whatever it took I was going to see that she got there. This time I wasn't going to fail her.

When I stepped out onto Fifth Avenue, I found Bob waiting for me. He was limping, but otherwise seemed no worse for wear. He pulled up alongside me and kept pace as I made my way to see my daughter.

DAVE ZELTSERMAN

CPSIA information can be obtained
at www.ICGtesting.com
Printed in the USA
LVHW110729160919
631184LV00001B/23/P